Love takes a special kind of courage...

Captain Sterling Garlington has faced down enemy fire without losing his nerve. But after a life-altering injury derails his military career, the former US marine is suddenly taking his marching orders from a sexy, edgy beauty at the Elk Heights Ranch. Even more amazing, equine therapist Harper Matthews makes him want to not only embrace life again—but give in to the attraction simmering between them.

Her love of horses is Harper's magic bullet—her way of healing the painful past. And in the wounded soldier she recognizes a kindred spirit. Part of her wants to bolt, yet at the same time Sterling is drawing her closer. Maybe it's his courage. Or his mega-watt smile. Or both. Either way, she'll make a cowboy out of the wary war hero yet. It's like getting back on a horse. They'll just have to learn to trust each other—and be willing to open their hearts...

The Cowgirl Meets Her Match

Kristin Vayden

LYRICAL PRESS
Kensington Publishing Corp.
www.kensingtonbooks.com

CHAPTER 1

Captain Sterling Garlington.

He read the top of the envelope, a thousand realities hitting him like the shrapnel that had almost destroyed his leg earlier that year. It was crazy how much of his identity was attached to his name, his rank—his history.

A wave of regret hit him. History. That's exactly what the envelope held. *His* history, meaning he had an utterly different future than he had planned, or expected. But that couldn't be helped.

How could he be only twenty-eight and feel like an eighty-two-year-old? He walked over to the couch in the living room of his sister's ranch house, his leg still aching from the injury so many months ago, but it was part of him.

Like his history.

Like his rank.

And somehow, he was supposed to make that into a bright new future that he knew jack shit about.

As he tossed the now-empty envelope to the coffee table, he unfolded the letter, his eyes zeroing in on the two most important words.

Honorably Discharged.

Meaning everything that had solidified his identity was now in the past. It wasn't as if he hadn't asked for this; rather, he had been given the chance to go back to the Marine Corps, but to do what? He couldn't fight anymore; he couldn't run away from enemy fire. He could plan, sit at a desk, and while that was undoubtedly an important job, it wasn't for him.

He couldn't be there and not participate with his own two hands, his own gun.

So, he wrote the letter, signed his name, and walked away from it all. But asking was different than receiving, and the finality of the missive weighed heavily upon his broad shoulders.

"Hey! Sterling?"

He tensed immediately at the sound of her voice. "In here," he called out reluctantly.

The sound of her boots preceded her entrance into the living room, and just as he'd anticipated, her green eyes flashed with irritation as she set a hand on her hip and ducked her chin.

He'd had drill sergeants who were more compassionate.

He'd faced enemy fire with less hostility.

"Today, if it pleases your highness." Harper Matthews arched a dark brow in contrast to her platinum-and-purple highlighted hair. "And I swear, you're worse than my brother when it comes to answering your damn phone."

"Are you done yet?" Sterling asked, taking a deep, calming breath.

"Nope, not even close. Get your ass in gear. Let's go." She turned on her heel, and Sterling purposefully looked away, not wanting to be tempted to study the detail on her blinged-out jeans that settled tightly around her perfect ass.

But he glanced back anyway.

Because some things deserved to be appreciated, and some risks were worth taking.

Harper Matthews's ass deserved appreciation, but checking it out constituted a risk, because if she knew, he wouldn't put it past her to vice-grip his balls.

Or cut them off in his sleep.

The day just kept getting better and better.

"Today, sunshine!"

Sterling reluctantly tossed the letter onto the oak coffee table and cautiously shifted his weight to his good leg. As he started to follow Harper, the pain sliced through him with each step as his weight shifted to the mangled area of his calf. He limped slightly, hating the way it made him feel.

Weak.

Washed up.

Worthless.

His sister would hamstring him if she knew he felt that way, but Laken had always seen the good, the silver lining.

Sterling had seen too much destruction, too much greed, enduring too much pain to see past the blood-stained dirt. Even if he loved his military career, that didn't mean it was perfect, or easy.

Truth was, he loved it because it was damn hard. But each day, he'd made a difference.

And that was gone.

"Watch your step." Harper's voice cut through his depression, and he gave her an irritated glance.

"Hey, just trying to help. You don't want to fall on your face. Or maybe you do." She shrugged. "Suit yourself."

Sterling made a show of stepping down the three stairs to the front porch carefully.

"Aw, good work, grandpa," Harper teased.

"One day, Harper. One day you'll pay for each little insult—"

"And that day is clearly not today. So, if you wouldn't mind...?" She gestured to the round pen just beside the barn where Margaret, his brother-in-law's horse, waited.

"Slave driver," Sterling grumbled.

"Yup." Harper closed the distance to the round pen quickly, her pink boots getting dusty as she strode across the gravel drive.

Sterling glanced away and focused on the scenery as a way to ignore the pain. Russian olive trees dotted the landscape along with sagebrush and rabbit bush. Blue sky stretched across from horizon to horizon with only a few cirrus clouds separating the blue. Manastash Ridge cut along the south with Elk Heights Ridge, which shared a name with his sister and Cyler's ranch.

"You ready?"

Sterling rested an arm on the iron gate and watched as Harper untied Margaret's lead.

"As I'll ever be." Sterling sighed.

"I was talking to Margaret." Harper gave him a cheeky grin.

Sterling swallowed a retort and kept his peace. Some smartass remark now would just result in Harper taking it out on him during therapy.

That woman was nothing but a pain in his ass.

"Aw, look who's learning to play nice." Harper goaded him on as she tugged Margaret's lead away from the gate and toward the middle of the pen. "Just like we practiced."

Sterling unlatched the gate, the iron squeaking as he swung it open and then closed it behind him. Little clouds of dust puffed around his boots as he walked to where Margaret and Harper waited. Hands damp with sweat, he rubbed them absently on his jeans and then fisted them.

Margaret nickered, her brown eyes watching him as if confused as to why he was so nervous. Harper said horses could sense your emotions.

He was pretty sure Margaret had his number, but thankfully, she wouldn't use it against him.

Or so he hoped.

"Foot here." Harper held out the stirrup and adjusted it slightly as his foot rested in the *U* shape. "Good. Hands on the horn and back of the saddle," she coached.

Sterling knew the drill, but that didn't make it any less disconcerting. He gripped the saddle horn, his sweaty palm sliding just a little before gripping hard. His other hand held the back of the saddle, and he took a deep breath then swung onto Margaret's back.

"See, gets easier every time," Harper commented, patting his leg.

Damn, he wished she wouldn't touch him. It created this strange mix of irritation, arousal, and longing. "Sure, sure," he replied, ignoring the sensations her touch left with him.

"Okay, we'll start at a walk, get your bearings and balance, then I'll hand you the reins, and we'll post a bit. All good?"

"Whatever you say, boss." Sterling grinned through his teeth, trying to be at ease. The horse was simply walking! He could freaking do this. He could drive a Humvee through wicked terrain in gunfire; he could certainly ride a horse at a walk. But truth was, the Humvee didn't scare Sterling, and horses still freaked the shit out of him. You could put the brakes on the Humvee, but you could not exactly put the brakes on a horse if it wanted to bolt.

It wasn't exactly a rational fear, but since when did rationality have anything to do with being afraid?

"You're doing better than last time. How does your leg feel?" Harper asked, her green eyes darting to his leg and back up to his gaze.

He'd learned the first time that it would only be hell if he didn't tell her the truth. She'd simply push his injury past where he was comfortable. Even if it was safe, it didn't *feel* safe to have that much pain. "It's not as bad today."

"Good. We'll take any improvement," she answered. "You about ready to try posting? We'll try at a walk first."

Sterling groaned. This was where it started to really suck. "Fine."

"Start slow, keep your heels down, and as the horse moves forward, rise ever so slightly and use those calf muscles to lift your body. Don't overwork them. Just feel the tension."

Sterling took a deep breath and made sure his heels were lower in the stirrups, then slowly rose, his calf muscle in his right leg aching with each slight movement.

"That's it, up a little more."

Sterling pushed slightly higher, his calf no longer aching but screaming as he posted while the horse walked.

"Ass down. You're not a jockey. Try not to lean so far forward. Balance yourself above your ankles, use your knees. Yeah, that's better."

Sterling listened to her voice, modifying his position as she directed, and found his center of gravity a little easier as he continued to lift then lower himself back down as he posted.

"Much better. Do you feel how much smoother you're transitioning?"

"Yeah, actually. It doesn't feel as choppy."

"Exactly. It's more of a circular motion rather than a jack-in-the-box."

Sterling chuckled. "Yeah, I can imagine that."

"Margaret appreciates it too. It's easier on her. She's not a young filly anymore, and your heavy carcass isn't exactly a picnic," Harper replied.

Sterling watched as a grin teased her lips, showing off her white teeth and one-sided dimple. Her coloring was quite similar to her brother's, Jasper. Light eyes, light hair, and tan skin, she would look like the girl next door if it weren't for the bright purple tips in her hair that hinted at a wilder nature.

Jasper was opposite in personality. Where Harper was sarcastic, sassy, and reckless, Jasper was more direct, honest, forthright, and as solid as granite. Which was why he was perfect for Kessed. Just thinking her name sent a different kind of pain through him, aiming at his heart. It wasn't so long ago that he'd made a play for her, but he was man enough to admit that Jasper was a better fit for Kessed. It was a difficult truth to swallow, and it didn't diminish the sting of rejection, but it was the truth nonetheless.

Sterling knew he wasn't in a healthy enough place to care for someone's heart. Yet it still sucked to see Jasper and Kessed together. But he'd forced himself to at least tolerate it. After all, Kessed was his sister's best friend, and Jasper was good friends with Cyler. They were all one big, dysfunctional family—whether he liked it or not.

"Hey, you. Did you hear what I asked?" Harper smacked his good leg.

Sterling shook his head and narrowed his gaze. "What's up?"

"I think those pain meds are messing with your brain. Focus, cowboy." She pointed two fingers at her eyes and then directed them to him.

"Not a cowboy." Sterling rolled his eyes then grinned. "I'm a badass in every other way though."

"Yeah, sure you are." She pulled up Margaret's lead and handed the reins over to Sterling. "Go around the pen once by yourself, moderate the pressure on your leg, post, and then bring her to a slow trot and increase your posting speed. Got it?"

"Sure." Sterling gripped the leather straps, his palms growing damp again. Damn, it felt like his body was constantly betraying him. First, his leg that just wouldn't heal fast enough; then, he was a pathetic mess whenever he rode the stupid horse, his hands constantly breaking out into a sweat. For once, he just wanted to feel in control.

As if he had power over his own destiny, his own future.

Hell, he'd take power over the next five minutes.

"Go ahead." Harper stepped back from the horse and waited.

And he couldn't exactly just sit there and stare, so he gently kicked Margaret in the flank, his calf muscle protesting as he did the small kick. The horse lazily moved forward, kicking up dust as she circled the round pen. Sterling focused on his motion, keeping the movements smooth as he posted in rhythm with Margaret's cadence.

"Good work. Try the slow trot." Harper called from the fence where she perched, sitting on the top rail. Her cowboy hat shielded her eyes from the afternoon sun.

Sterling gritted his teeth and encouraged Margaret with a click of his tongue. Margaret responded by increasing her pace, and Sterling felt his ass bounce in the saddle.

"Post!" Harper called out.

Sterling leaned forward, rocking his weight onto the balls of his feet as he lifted himself from the saddle just a bit then eased down as he posted carefully along with Margaret's gait.

"Hump the saddle. That's right. Better."

Sterling had nearly choked on his tongue the first time she said that, but now he was used to the phrase. And oddly enough, the strange wording made sense and always helped him correct his posture.

"Heels down," Harper reminded him.

Damn, just when he figured out one part, he screwed up another. "Demanding much?" he called out to her.

"Always. You shouldn't be surprised anymore by it," Harper replied, a smile in her tone.

"Pain in the ass."

"Takes one to know one!"

Sterling focused on Margaret's neck as it mimicked her trot's gait, and he found the rhythm, sticking with it.

"Okay, slow down, make her stop now... Good." Harper jumped from the fence and walked over to him. "That was a huge improvement from last week. How does your leg feel? How much fatigue are you experiencing?"

Sterling took his boot from the stirrup and flexed his leg. He frowned as his leg ached but actually didn't give him the throbbing pain he had experienced when they first started therapy. "It's still painful, but it's not the bone-deep pain that it was before."

"Have you heard back from your physical therapist in Seattle?" Harper asked, petting Margaret's neck softly.

Sterling nodded. "Yeah, he said that the notes you sent in were helpful. He agreed that the posting and balancing was pretty vital to my therapy. When I go back he's going to test me again for a mile marker."

"Great. I'm glad we're on the right track. You feel up to taking her around again?" Harper asked.

Her green eyes challenged him, dared him to say no.

"Sure, I've got one more round in me."

"Right answer."

He put his boot back in the stirrup, adjusted his position on the saddle, and encouraged Margaret back into a walk, then a trot. Harper watched from the fence rail. He could almost feel her gaze scrutinizing his every move. In a lot of ways, she reminded him of a drill sergeant at boot camp.

"Push harder."

"Don't give up."

"One more time."

"Do it again."

But she was a hell of a lot better to look at than any of the officers he'd ever served under.

Even if she was a hardass.

"One more time!" she yelled as Sterling circled the pen.

As he finished up the round, she called out again. "You can do another."

He'd heard that before, and he was damn well certain that she'd shout out the same thing for the next ten times.

But odd thing was, it made it easier. It wasn't ten more; it was just one more.

One more time.

One more round.

And somehow, it had translated to his life.

One more morning.

One more try.

One more day.

One more was always more manageable than a million more.

Even when a million was probably closer to the accurate number.

As he rounded the pen again, he reminded himself. *Just one more.*

He could do it.

He could do *one*.

And someday, he'd find out that *one* had turned into a million.

And that million times had made him stronger.

Better.

Whole.

He had to hope.

CHAPTER 2

Harper watched as Sterling wiped the sweat from his forehead and leaned forward again in the saddle. "Back! Lean back. Slouch a little. It won't kill you."

"Unfortunately," he shot back, though the morbid answer was softened with a smile.

Damn, that smile was lethal.

And scared the shit out of her.

But she wasn't going to retreat or turn her back on him just because he was too hot for his own good. Sterling Garlington was even more damaged than her, and two damaged people didn't make a whole. They just made a mess.

And she had enough of a mess to deal with on her own, thank you very much.

But that didn't prevent her from enjoying the view.

"If you clench your jaw any harder, you'll crack your teeth. Relax!" she shouted too loudly, just to irritate him.

He shot her a glare and unlocked his jaw a little. Harper could only imagine how much it hurt him to go through the simple therapy. His injury wasn't small, and he had a long road ahead of him before he'd be in the same shape he was before the shrapnel hit him. But he would recover, someday, and sooner rather than later, if she had anything to do with it.

She knew all too well the helpless feeling.

It hadn't been more than two years ago she had been in a similar condition.

Bruised.

Broken.

Bitter.

It had been a long road, too, and she was still on it, the end not in sight yet. But the people who'd refused to give up on her, when she was more than willing to give up on herself, had saved her from the darkness that threatened to swallow her.

She was a survivor.

She was stronger now, and each day she felt a little more alive, a little less worthless.

Abuse was more than what you learned in high school psychology class. It systematically disabled you, piece by piece.

It wasn't one black eye. It wasn't one mean comment—though those were certainly aspects.

It was the shift to believing your abuser was speaking the truth about you. That you deserved each hit.

Each word.

Everything.

That you really were as worthless as they said.

Because you could only fight back for so long before you started to wonder—*what if?*

What if they are right? And that small sliver of doubt would grow. It didn't happen overnight, but it did happen. It was the reason why people stayed in abusive relationships.

Why would anyone else want me if I'm this worthless? He might hit me but...

Till it's too late, and you find yourself being pushed down the stairs.

Waking up in a hospital room, your heart monitor beeping—with only one heartbeat.

When yesterday there had been two.

Harper took a deep breath, focusing back on Sterling, pushing the pain away, shoving it down inside.

Some wounds never healed. And she was pretty sure that losing her baby was that type of wound.

She blinked against the warm tears that threatened whenever she went back to that place and forced herself to focus on the skyline.

The sound of the horse's hooves on the dirt.

The call of a red-tailed hawk.

"Head in the game, Harper!" Sterling called out, slicing through her attempt to find a Zen moment.

She swallowed her emotions and strained a dry grin. "Giving you some privacy. You're cute, but I'd rather not stare at you all day."

His gray eyes slid to her, his face crinkling into a sly grin. "You think I'm cute? Not sure if that's a compliment or insult."

"I'll let you decide." She shrugged, watching as he rolled his eyes.

"I'm going to go with insult, based on what I know about you."

The comment raised her hackles, yet she refused to let it show. "Good guess."

He circled the pen once more, his form sorely lacking, probably from fatigue and more than a little pain.

"Last time."

"Sweeter words I've never heard." Sterling sighed, his face pinching into a frown as he rose on the stirrup to post.

"Be a man about it, finish strong," Harper instructed as she jumped down from the iron fence.

Sterling cast her a glare but clenched his jaw and corrected his form. Damn, it had to hurt, but she also knew that going easy on him wouldn't actually help.

It would only enable him.

And rather than heal, he'd stay right where he was.

Plus, if there was one thing she was absolutely certain about, it was that Sterling didn't want her pity, he didn't want her to go easy on him, and he sure as hell didn't want to show weakness.

And the part about being weak was that you have to fight to become strong.

And Sterling was a fighter.

In more ways than one.

He just had to remember that. Harper was certain his struggle was more against himself than his body. His battlefield was in his mind.

She knew, because that was the same place hers was as well.

She recognized that same expression in his eyes, that determination, that steely resolve, that need.

To conquer, to fight, to win.

And the person you're fighting is yourself.

"That's all." Harper strode out to Margaret.

Cyler's horse was as sweet as they came and perfect for what Sterling needed. Poor guy was scared shitless of horses, even if he'd never actually admitted it out loud. Margaret was too wise to bolt and too old to try even if she wanted to. As Harper took the reins from Sterling, she patted down Margaret's neck and caressed her jawline to her velvet muzzle. The horse leaned into her hand, breathing deeply. Margaret needed to feel Harper's calm in contrast to Sterling's tension. As Harper stroked her nose, the mare relaxed.

As did Harper.

It was *her* therapy.

Horses.

"Why don't you stay up there till we get to the barn, and you can help me take off her saddle. It will train you to balance awkward weight," Harper suggested, glancing up to Sterling.

As if he'd say no.

Sometimes it was fun to work with a person who didn't back down from a challenge.

"Sure," he replied casually. But the tic in his jaw gave away his tension.

"Easy there, you've already worked Margaret into a lather with your stressed-out self."

"Sure, worry about the damn horse."

Harper led her from the round pen. "I like her better."

Sterling snorted. "Surprising."

"Not really." Harper couldn't resist.

As she led Margaret into the barn, the scent of old leather, tractor oil, and hay flooded her senses. It was a comforting smell, one that reminded her of home and her own barn where Spartan, her barrel-racing gelding, waited.

As she tied the lead to the stall rail, she backed away. "Go ahead and get down."

Sterling shifted his weight to his foot, his gaze focused as he balanced his body over his good leg, but the difficult part came when he had to step onto the ground, his weight completely on his bad leg.

Harper edged around to his back, just in case.

The first time they tried this, he'd fallen into a heap, swearing a blue streak the entire way.

She had spotted him ever since, even if he had never needed her help after that.

It sucked to fall.

After all, don't we all wish someone was there to catch us?

"Easy now."

Sterling didn't reply but slowly rested his boot on the floor of the barn, his breath hissing out as he shifted his weight to the leg. Swiftly he took his other boot from the stirrup and evened out the heaviness.

"Someday, I'm going to jump off this damn horse like the Easter bunny, and it won't hurt." Sterling gave her a slight grin that didn't reach his eyes; they were too clouded with pain.

Soon it dissipated though, and Harper simply nodded. "Someday you will."

"Okay, so how do I take this thing off?" Sterling asked, turning toward Margaret.

Harper came to stand beside him on the left side of the mare. The scent of sweat, man, and old leather assaulted her senses. His body radiated heat that called to her to inch closer. Doing her best to ignore her instincts, she put a hand on the saddle horn. "It's easy, but your therapist had mentioned that balance is important right now, and this saddle isn't heavy, but it is kind of awkward if your balance isn't up to snuff."

"Which mine isn't."

"Yup. So here, loosen the cinch." She tugged the leather strap under the stirrup and then stepped back, watching as Sterling followed her instructions. Soon they had unstrapped the saddle, and it rested untethered on Margaret's back.

"Slide the saddle off on the left side, always the left side," Harper coached. "You're bigger than me, so you'll probably want to carry it in front of you. I balance it on my hip."

Sterling cast her a wary glance then zeroed in on the saddle. His strong hands gripped the leather, causing it to squeal slightly as he planted his good leg in the dirt of the barn floor. With a slight wince, he slid it from the mare and took a step back as the full weight settled in his arms.

His biceps strained his T-shirt, drawing Harper's attention to the soaring eagle tattoo hiding just beneath his shirt sleeve. Her focus shifted to his eyes, watching as his brow furrowed. He shrugged the saddle into a more comfortable position.

He paused then started walking toward the tack room. As he turned, she lost sight of his face, but a sharp intake of breath alerted her that it wasn't an easy process for him. She followed, keeping enough distance to protect his pride, but close enough she could help if he needed it.

It was a thin line.

Pride.

Protection.

Harper wondered, not for the first time, if Sterling had ever been on the receiving end of the protecting, or if he'd always been the protector.

She assumed the answer was no.

"Where do I put this damn thing?" Sterling asked with only a slight tension to his tone.

"On the rack, the vacant spot in the middle." Harper pointed to the location and watched as Sterling planted his good foot then set the saddle on the correct place.

He turned to her and shrugged. "Cake."

"Sure it was." Harper rolled her eyes. "But it was good for you, and last week you couldn't have done that. We're making progress." She slugged him on the shoulder.

"Sometimes I wonder if you're actually encouraging me or patronizing me." He arched a sarcastic grin then limped from the tack room and toward the barn door.

"Eh, probably a little of both. Don't want you thinking I'm going soft on you," Harper replied, earning a low chuckle as Sterling walked into the sunlight.

"Yeah, you don't need to worry about that. I have no misconceptions for how much you love to cause me pain."

"Hey! It's working!" Harper jogged to catch up with him. "You move fast for an old man."

Sterling glared at her. "I'm what, maybe five years older than you? Not enough to be called old man. Besides, age is a state of mind."

Harper bit back a laugh. "Giving yourself license to be immature your whole life?"

"Damn, I walked into that one." Sterling shot her an irritated glare that melted into an amused smile. "Fine. You win. All I want is to watch the rest of the preseason Seahawks game and not move for at least an hour."

"Wear you out?" Harper asked as they walked toward the house.

"Dealing with you is mentally exhausting."

Harper snickered, thinking of several smartass replies, but her attention was arrested by the sound of a truck coming up the drive.

Cyler's pickup pulled into its usual spot, and soon he and Laken were striding toward the house.

"How did it go?" Laken asked, her gaze raking over her older brother as if answering the question before he could.

"Fine, fine. I'm improving and missing the first quarter right now. Cyler? You in?" Sterling jerked his chin toward his brother-in-law.

"I've been dreaming of the couch, a cold beer, and that game all day."

"Whew, way to dream big," Laken teased, bumping her husband with her hip.

"Hey, I did. I got you." He kissed the top of her head and then turned toward the house.

"Still not used to that." Sterling gave a wry grin to his little sister.

Harper held back a laugh as Laken scrunched up her face. "Deal with it."

Sterling raised his hands in defeat.

Laken turned to Harper. "Do you want to stay too?"

Harper shook her head. "Thanks, but I gotta head home. I have a race this Saturday, and I need to get Spartan out of that barn and get him exercised."

Laken nodded. "Got it. Well, it was nice to see you. Say hi to your brother and Kessed. Because you see her more than I do these days." Laken rolled her eyes.

Harper glanced to Sterling, watching as his gaze flickered to the ground; then without a word, he started toward the house.

Talking about Kessed still had to sting.

"Fine, I didn't want to say goodbye to you either!" she hollered, knowing that irritation toward one person was a preferable feeling over remembering the sting of rejection from another.

Sterling turned and waved, giving an annoyed grimace. "Bye, Harper."

"That's better. I'll see you Friday."

"Can't wait," he replied dryly.

As he disappeared into the house, Harper turned to Laken. "Someday we'll be able to talk about them and not have him freak out... But today is not that day apparently."

Laken rubbed her lips together, her brow pinched in concern. "Yeah, I shouldn't have opened my big mouth. I swear, I'm usually more aware of things, but it's like my brain is on vacation half the time. Gah. So frustrating. I'll talk with him."

Harper held up a hand. "Let it go. I wouldn't want to talk about it. I'd want to forget about it. I'm assuming Sterling feels the same."

Laken nodded. "Since he's inside, how's the progress?"

Harper shrugged. "He's improving, but it's not as quick as he'd like. He's determined though, and I can't ask for more than that."

"Thank you. I—we—really appreciate you coming out here to help him. I've done some research on this type of therapy, and I think it's going to help him improve between Seattle visits."

Harper shook her head. "It's not a big deal. I'm happy to do it. Jasper doesn't need me as much now that he has Kessed doing the appointments and the paperwork part of the veterinary business. I've got the time, at least right now. After Jasper and Kessed's wedding I'm going to look for a job, but I figure I'll wait till they're back from their honeymoon. That way I can take care of things at the clinic while they're gone."

Laken nodded. "I'll keep my ears open if I hear of someone hiring."

"Thanks." Harper lifted her hand in a wave and started to her old white Chevy pickup. The door squeaked as she opened it wide; then it crashed shut in the way only old trucks could.

As she drove toward home, she turned up the country station and sang along, drowning out her own thoughts.

She'd learned that you couldn't always trust them.

And she'd traveled down memory lane enough for one day.

All she needed to do was make it home.

Then she could saddle Spartan and run.

Leaving everything behind.

At least for a few hours.

And that would be enough.

It had to be.

CHAPTER 3

Sterling stepped out from the shower, the steam filling the room in billowy clouds as he dried himself off. As he slid the soft towel down his leg, he studied the scars. Red, shiny, and twisted, they curled around his calf muscle, giving it a strange shape. The pain wasn't as severe as it had been, but it ached—and never stopped. Always pain, always hurting, always on the edge of his mind and never fully able to be ignored. Unless he took the meds, which he almost never did since he'd been discharged from the hospital.

Damn it all to hell.

He didn't know what was worse. The fear of getting addicted, or the constant pain that drove him crazy.

He shifted his weight slightly and walked with as little limp as he could manage till he reached the mirror. Sliding a hand down the condensation, he studied his reflection.

How can you look the same, yet feel like a different person?

Just then his calf muscle seized up, and he groaned, leaning his weight against the sink as he lifted his bad leg and stretched it.

To hell with it.

As the muscle relaxed, he opened the mirror cabinet and pulled out his prescription. After removing two pills, he swallowed them before he could reconsider his choice.

Wincing with each step from the cramp's lingering pain, he strode to his adjoining room and dressed. Today, he had things to do, mountains to climb.

Even if they were just the figurative kind.

They felt massive. And he used to think life deployed was hard.

Ha.

He still had several weeks before the doctor would clear him to find work, so he'd done his best to help Cyler and Laken out on the ranch.

Which would be comical if it wasn't so damn depressing.

It's amazing how much you can't do when your leg won't work right.

But Cyler had never mentioned it, never brought attention to what Sterling couldn't do, rather kept him focused on what he could accomplish.

In that, Cyler reminded him of Laken.

"You ready?" Laken tapped on the door.

"Almost." He rolled his eyes.

"Just because you're gimpy doesn't mean you can take three years to put your pants on."

"Okay, Mom."

He heard Laken's giggle.

Soon he was walking to the door, his sister giving him a strange expression. "What?"

Laken shook her head. "You're not limping."

Sterling paused then tested his weight on both feet. No pain.

No. Freaking. Pain.

"Huh, I guess those meds really do work."

Laken frowned. "You're just now taking them? What have you been doing this whole time?" she asked, blinking in confusion.

"Avoiding them like Satan himself," Sterling answered, striding to the door and savoring the feeling of walking like a man again.

"Why? No wonder you've been a bear. That had to be unbearable—"

"Pun intended?" Sterling interrupted as she followed him out the door.

"No, happy coincidence. Still..."

"Laken"—Sterling paused and turned toward his little sister, studying her green eyes—"you have no idea how many guys come home injured and get addicted to those damn pills. I don't want to be one of them. I'm already a statistic just being injured. I don't want to be another kind too."

Laken nodded. "Good. I don't want that for you either. Do...do you want me to take them away so that you have to ask me to get your dose?"

Sterling considered her offer. "It's not a bad idea, but I think I'm good for now. Just watch me, question me. Okay?"

Laken nodded once. "You've got it. I'm proud of you." She reached out and grasped his forearm. "You're going to be stronger from all this, you know that, right?"

Sterling gave her a half smile. "I sure hope so."

After a pat to her hand, he turned and walked to the door, finding his way toward the barn.

Margaret nickered as he went in, the sunlight streaming across the dusty boarded floor.

"Hey, old girl," Sterling greeted, going straight to the back of the barn. He found a few tools and carried them out into the sunlight. After tossing them into the back of the old Ford F-150, he used his good foot to get into the cab. The twenty-year-old diesel engine roared to life, and Sterling put the truck into gear, thankful yet again that the old thing wasn't a manual transmission. He pulled forward and followed the dirt road that went parallel with the west pasture of the ranch. Cyler had mentioned that several of the cows were getting close to delivering, so each day Sterling went out to do the rounds, checking for new calves and making sure no complications had occurred overnight. As ranch cattle, the cows were wilder than dairy cows and required less attention. Sure enough, as he crested a small hill, he noted two little calves nestled in the dry grass beside their mothers.

After putting the truck into park, he left the engine on and moved toward the barbed-wire fence. Since the bull was in the east pasture, Sterling could walk into this area safely and check on the gender of the calves. His leg protested, but only slightly, as he ducked through the fence and strode, focusing on the fact that he still felt no real pain, toward the bedded-down calves. The momma cows lowed softly but didn't startle as he approached slowly. Carefully, he walked in a wide circle, the baby calves ducking down, then their curiosity getting the best of them as they stood to get a better look at Sterling.

He retraced his steps to arc around to get a view of their backsides. Heifers.

Cyler would be pleased. It was always better to have females born when you were building up your herd.

Or so Cyler had said.

As Sterling headed back toward the fence, a lowing caught his attention. It wasn't the low-toned "moo" that he had grown used to hearing. It was a strained sound, almost shrill. He walked along the barbed wire toward the sound. As he passed several Russian olive trees, he spied a cow bedded down in a small clearing between the trees. She kept arching her neck toward her belly, lowing and stretching out a moment later. As he stepped closer, he noted the telltale bloody tissue behind her that said she was in labor.

But Cyler had said that cows gave birth standing.

This cow was lying down.

Concern caused him to furrow his brow as he slowly stepped away and pulled out his phone.

Cyler answered on the second ring.

"What's up, Sterling?"

Sterling quickly gave the rundown. "Is that something that we need to be concerned about?"

Cyler paused. "Call Jasper. Do you have his number? It sounds like she's struggling, and the calf might be breach."

Sterling shook his head then answered. "I don't have it."

"I'll send you the contact. Call him right away, okay? If the calf is breach, I could lose the cow if we don't help her."

"Got it." Sterling ended the call then waited a few seconds before the text came through with Jasper's phone number.

He tapped the blue numbers and paused as it rang. He refused to think about anything other than business.

It wasn't personal.

And he actually liked Jasper; he was good guy.

But that didn't make it easier to deal with rejection.

"Matthews Vet Clinic."

Sterling smiled at the familiar tone. "Hey, Kess. Your boy toy there? I need help with a cow." He paused.

"Sterling? Hey, you! Cyler have you doing his dirty work?" she asked, her sassy streak going strong.

It had always been of his favorite quirks of Kessed's personality.

"Pretty much."

"Well, keeps you out of trouble. I'll get Jasper. He just came in. Wait up." The hold music played for a few seconds before it abruptly cut off.

"Hey, Sterling. What's up?"

Sterling took a breath. "I'm out doing rounds for Cyler, and I saw a cow lying down. It looks like she's in labor, and she's making this weird mooing sound, if that makes any sense." He was pretty sure *mooing sound* wasn't exactly a technical term, but the hell with it. He wasn't a rancher. He was a soldier.

Or had been.

"Is she bleeding behind her?" Jasper asked, his tone direct yet kind.

"Yeah." Sterling rubbed the back of his neck as the cow let out another shrill moo.

"I heard that one. Yeah...it sounds like she's struggling. Which pasture are you in?"

"East."

"Okay, I'll be out there in about fifteen minutes. See you."

"Thanks." Sterling ended the call.

Fifteen minutes wasn't technically long, but each minute stretched on as he listened to the cow struggle, feeling helpless to do anything to assist the poor animal.

Soon a cloud of dust rose in the distance, and Sterling watched as a truck with *Matthews Veterinary* on the side pulled up beside his pickup.

Sterling groaned as a pair of sexy legs appeared from the opening door, drawing his eye up to the vivacious grin of Kessed soon-to-be-Matthews.

Jasper walked around the pickup, holding his hand out to her. She gripped it, casting him an expression that could only be interpreted as deep love as they walked hand in hand to the back of the pickup.

Well, this was about to be all kinds of awkward.

It seemed as if he'd traded one pain for another.

His leg wasn't hurting. But he had a feeling those painkillers wouldn't work on the ache in his heart.

He forced a smile as the happy couple walked toward him. Kessed's brown eyes apparently saw right through him by the way she narrowed her gaze slightly. But to her credit, she didn't say anything.

And if Jasper held a grudge against him for making a play for Kessed's heart, he never mentioned it.

At least not yet.

Just as Sterling was about to say hello, the cow let out another, shriller moo.

"Over there?" Jasper nodded his chin toward the trees.

"Yup." Sterling said, tucking his hands into his jean pockets.

"Sounds painful." Kessed scrunched up her nose, frowning.

"Let's take care of that." Jasper lifted the barbed wire for her, and she stepped through, with Jasper following behind her. Soon they were nearing the cow.

"Cyler would have put a squeeze in the pasture with these pregnant cows. Do you know where it is?" Jasper's inquiring gaze cut to Sterling.

"Squeeze?"

"Don't worry, Sterling, I had no idea what it was a month ago." Kessed came to his rescue.

"It's to keep the cow from killing me when I examine her. These free-range animals are dangerous to work with. A squeeze is a metal cage of sorts that allows me to keep the cow upright and restrained all at once. It doesn't hurt her at all, it just protects whoever is working on her," Jasper explained.

Sterling cursed Cyler inwardly for not informing him about the tool, but he had seen something blue and metal toward the opening of the pasture gate, thankfully not too far away.

"Follow me."

Jasper set a few items down and followed after Sterling as they passed through the copse of Russian olive trees. Sterling gestured to the metal structure. "This what you're looking for?"

"Yup." Jasper nodded once. "Kess, we're going to need to chase her in. Sterling, I need you to help me round her up, and honey, you put the squeeze on when she gets in the chute."

"Aye, aye." Kessed gave a playful salute, earning an amused grin from Jasper.

Sterling shook his head. Some people changed as they grew older. Kessed simply grew into herself; it was part of the allure and charm.

He forced his thoughts into line and followed Jasper as they approached the cow.

"She's going to be a stubborn bitch, but if we don't rush her too much, it shouldn't be too hard. Keep her to the fence line. That way we can duck through if she gets too cranky and charges us."

"Wait." Sterling paused, watching Jasper. "Cows will charge? I thought it was only bulls."

Jasper shook his head, a sober expression in his eyes. "Bulls will impale you, but cows will break every bone in your body if you don't get out of their way. Did you know that the most deaths by an animal are done by cows?"

Sterling narrowed his eyes. "Sure."

"No, seriously. They're pretty laid back, but you don't want to see a momma cow in a pissy fit." Jasper held up a hand.

"Point taken."

"So, let's stay to the fence line, and we'll get this girl taken care of."

Sterling followed Jasper's lead as he encouraged the cow to stand. All the while Sterling watched warily in case the bovine decided to be a pain in the ass and turn on them. Slowly, the momma rose and groaned.

Jasper gestured to him, and they cautiously walked behind the cow. She reluctantly trotted then walked toward the squeeze.

Kessed waited, watching them carefully as the cow approached. As the animal neared the opening, she darted left, and Kessed waved a hand to startle her straight. The cow went too far right, and Jasper jogged ahead, yelling "Ha!" just loud enough to be surprising, and the cow jerked straight, entering the squeeze.

Kessed pulled the lever, tightening the bars around the cow and holding her in place. The poor animal let out a low moan but lowered her head as if the whole ordeal had her exhausted.

"That's better. I'll be right back, I'm going to grab my gear." Jasper jogged back to the copse to retrieve his things.

"Cyler's going to make you a rancher yet," Kessed teased.

Sterling gave her a wry expression. "Sure he is."

Her laughter echoed in the pasture. "I take it this is not your idea of fun?"

"No." Sterling shook his head but smiled. "I'd rather be doing a lot of things other than watch a cow be violated when Jasper gets back with that long latex glove."

Kessed burst into a fit of giggles. "Yeah, that's not usually the highlight of the day for Jasper either."

Sterling regarded her. Everything about her expression was open, secure, loved. It looked good on her, belonging to someone.

He only wished it was him.

But it wasn't. And it sucked that he was realizing that Jasper was better for her.

"You doing okay, really?" Kessed asked, her amused expression shifting to one of concern.

Concern was better than pity. Damn, he hated pity.

"Yeah. Dealing," he answered honestly but kept it short. He didn't exactly like to elaborate on all the reasons his life sucked at the moment.

"Harper going easy on you?" Kessed asked, a slight twinkle to her eye.

What the hell is that about? "No, she's a pain in the ass, but I kinda need that right now, but if you tell her, I'll rat on you to Jasper about the time you fell ass first into the mud puddle after stalking your business prof."

Kessed's gaze narrowed. "You wouldn't."

"I would."

"You would what?" Jasper asked, making long strides toward the squeeze.

"He threatened to be a jerk, his natural state of being, so I'm not too concerned." Kessed smiled.

"Really? Here I thought he was going to tell me the story about Doctor Samerson."

Sterling turned to Jasper, shock lancing through him. That was probably the worst dirt he had on Kessed, so he was surprised that Kessed had disclosed that particular story.

"No secrets." She winked.

"Damn it all, here I thought I had something to hold over your head." Sterling rubbed the back of his neck, narrowing his eyes at her.

"I was going to let you think you did, you know, just to be kind."

"And here I thought being in love would soften you up, make you less of a pain in the ass," Sterling spoke jokingly, the action of teasing her about loving Jasper oddly not hurting much, for once.

Jasper started to chuckle.

Kessed shot him an irritated glare that melted into a grin.

Maybe things worked out for the best. As odd as it was, it kind of helped seeing them together, working and interacting. Made the focus less on rejection, and more on the fact that for them, it just worked.

And if he were being honest, it never really had for him and Kessed.

She'd tried.

He'd ignored.

And when he'd finally pulled his head from his ass, it had been too late.

Maybe that was what fate had intended.

And maybe fate knew what he or she was doing.

Maybe.

Jasper set down his case and opened it; he pulled out a long latex glove.

Kessed bent down and set out several tubes and then stood and helped Jasper shrug out of his long-sleeve flannel shirt.

The latex glove snapped into place, and Jasper approached the cow impatiently waiting in the squeeze. Another shrill moo came from her as he slowly inserted his hand into her backside.

Sterling glanced away.

"I feel only one, but it's head is stuck. I gotta move it around," Jasper muttered.

"Need anything?" Kessed asked.

Sterling glanced to her, watching as she kept her attention on Jasper and the cow.

"Not yet, hold up."

Sterling winced as Jasper reached his other hand inside the cow, his brows furrowing as an expression of deep concentration flickered across his face. As if seeing with his fingers, his eyes remained on the distant horizon, then he leaned back, pulling two stick-like legs with him.

"Do you think it's alive, or are we too late?" Kessed asked, walking around the back of the squeeze toward Jasper.

"We'll find out," Jasper replied in a strained tone as he reached into the backside again.

"He's making sure the head's in the right place." Kessed filled Sterling in.

"Got it," Sterling replied, not needing any more details.

"Here we go," Jasper replied, the cow interrupting him with a loud moo as if bearing down.

A lanky calf slid out halfway, dangling in a manner that made Sterling question if the poor animal was alive. Jasper took a step back, and the cow finished delivering the calf. A moment later, Jasper picked up a piece of dry grass and tickled the calf's nose with it, earning a sneeze.

"He made it!" Kessed clapped, her expression one of joy.

Sterling grinned in response, thankful as well that the little one had gotten a shot at life.

"Actually, it's a *she*." Jasper grinned at Kessed.

Sterling watched as Jasper collected his things and stood back from the squeeze. "Let's back up so momma can do her job and take care of her baby. Kess, can you loosen the squeeze?"

"You bet." Kessed pulled the lever, and the bars loosened. It only took a moment for the cow to realize it was free, and she exited the squeeze and went to her waiting calf. Sniffing the little baby cautiously, the momma started to lick it clean, her long pink tongue making gentle strokes across her fur.

"Well, let's leave them to it." Jasper walked away toward the pickup, and Kessed jogged to catch up, her hand wrapping around his waist even as his arm circled her shoulders.

Sterling shook his head. If snuggling up to a man that just had his gloved hand up the business end of a cow didn't deter her, then that was a special kind of love.

Sterling watched as she continued on, his thoughts jumbled. He'd never loved that way. And he realized that his standards for love weren't as high as they should be.

And they needed to be.

Damn it all, if this injury wasn't making him re-evaluate everything in life.

Everything.

CHAPTER 4

Harper galloped around the course once more. Spartan's heavy breathing was the only sound in her world. As they approached the first barrel, she leaned left, squeezing with her legs as her horse made the lightning fast turn and sped off to the next barrel. Surging forward, she tugged the reins to guide him around the second barrel, kicking him swiftly to encourage him to move faster as they raced to the third and final barrel. His black mane flowed over Harper's hands as she tugged the reins to the left, completing the turn around the final barrel. "Ha!" She kicked his flanks again, racing to the finish.

As soon as she crossed the finish line, she clicked the stopwatch. Pulling it from around her neck, she took a deep breath and then looked at the time.

16.999

It wasn't perfect. But it wasn't too bad either.

She took a deep breath as she rode Spartan around the ring at a fast-paced walk to cool him down. They could do better.

Deep down, she knew Spartan was a champion.

But something kept holding him back.

Or maybe it was her.

She fell into the rhythm of Spartan's steps, the familiarity a welcome and soothing security in a world that didn't seem safe anymore. She wanted to try again, run the course over and over. But sometimes more practice didn't make you better; it just made you more frustrated. It was better to end on a high note. So, after several more laps of cooldown with Spartan, she decided to put the barrels away.

"Whoa, mister," she crooned to the gelding. The dust settled around Spartan's hooves as she swung her leg from one side of the saddle and jumped down. Setting his reins on his neck, she didn't even bother to tie him up.

She trusted him.

He trusted her.

Some things were just simpler with animals.

As she walked to the first barrel, she tipped it to the side and rolled it outside the pen. The familiar muted thud of Spartan's hooves followed close behind as she walked to the second barrel. Only this time, he bumped her butt with his nose, almost knocking her off balance.

"You think that's funny, don't you?" She glanced behind her, narrowing her eyes.

The gelding tried to rub his head on her back, making her lurch forward and almost trip over the tipped barrel. "No, you know better." She turned and pushed his big head away, making eye contact. "Good manners. You don't get to be all up in my business. Alpha." She pointed to herself. Then to him. "Not alpha."

He lowered his head.

"That's right." She stroked his white star in the middle of his forehead. "But I love you," she whispered softly.

Spartan leaned in to her as she started to scratch his forehead. When she stopped, he shook his head and blew out a deep breath.

Harper shook her head then began rolling the final barrel outside the pen. As she straightened, she turned back to Spartan, who was waiting where the barrel had been. Whistling, she nodded toward the barn.

The horse trotted to her then slowed, lagging behind her as she walked toward the small barn on her family's old homestead. The giant sycamore trees that framed the old farmhouse were turning a muted brown as the evening temperatures continued to fall. The sun was setting, reminding Harper that autumn was here, closing the book on another summer.

Spartan waited as she rolled the sliding door open. With a quick glance, she made sure he waited for her to enter the barn first. Horses were like dogs, they needed the pack organized and needed to understand that they were not the alpha.

In this case, she was.

One bad habit led to others, and it wasn't fun or safe to have a thirteen-hundred-pound animal with bad manners.

Spartan sighed, as if annoyed that she even questioned his understanding of who was in charge, and followed her into the barn. The scent of horse, dirt, and hay filled her lungs, making her smile. It was a familiar scent.

A safe scent.

Reminding her that she was okay.

He couldn't hurt her anymore.

Spartan nickered, pulling her thoughts back to the present, away from the past.

Away from the pain.

She petted his nose tenderly. "Let's get you cleaned up."

Soon she was walking out the barn door, the sound of Spartan rummaging through his hay following her into the evening light.

Jasper's pickup started up the drive, and she waved when he got closer. Kessed was with him, as was the usual. Harper waited as they killed the diesel engine and swung open the truck doors.

"Hey, you." Jasper waved, absently reaching out and grabbing Kessed's hand.

It was both sickeningly sweet and utterly adorable to see her big brother completely in love. He obviously worshiped the ground Kessed walked on, and Kessed's smile conveyed that she returned the adoration. At times, it was uncomfortable, but for the most part, Harper was thrilled to have an almost sister-in-law.

Just a few weeks.

The wedding was quickly approaching, and honestly, it couldn't get here fast enough. Already she'd been helping Kessed with the final plans, and in the midst of it, Harper had come to the conclusion that she didn't like planning. Or weddings.

Or flowers.

She also didn't really care about what the invitations looked like.

But she did care about Kessed. So, she'd helped with everything she could to make it easier on her friend.

As depressing as it sounded, she was glad she'd never have to go through all that again.

Once was enough, thank you.

One nightmare had translated into a worse one.

"Harper? Did you hear me?" Jasper tilted his head in that annoying big brother, arrogant way.

"No. Ignoring you," Harper teased, covering for her lack of attention.

Jasper rolled his eyes. "I just asked if you had dinner yet. I'm thinking of ordering pizza."

Harper shook her head. "Nope, but you know that no one delivers way out here..."

Jasper grinned.

She narrowed her eyes. "You want me to go and pick it up, don't you?"

"Please?"

Kessed giggled as she smacked Jasper's arm. "Getting your little sister to do your dirty work? Shameful."

"What she said." Harper pointed to Kessed.

"I'll pay," Jasper added.

"You're paying regardless." Harper folded her arms. "Fine. I'll do it. But not for you, for her. And me. We deserve pizza." Harper unfolded her arms and followed them into the house to grab her purse.

"And why do you deserve pizza? Not," Jasper added quickly, "that I'm questioning it, just curious if we're celebrating something?"

"I ran under a seventeen on the barrels." Harper shrugged.

Jasper gave a quick clap. "Awesome. You entering the Naches race?"

"Fall Frenzy? Yeah. I registered last week." Harper pushed the door open, the squeak growing higher in pitch the wider it opened.

"You going to win?" Jasper asked.

As usual.

"Maybe." Harper shrugged then grabbed her purse from the chair. "You going to come watch me?"

"Hopefully," Kessed answered for him.

"I have one fan." Harper raised her hand and high-fived Kessed.

Jasper pointed to himself. "Biggest fan." He tugged her arm and pulled her into a suffocating hug.

"Gah, why?" Harper groaned then inhaled a deep breath as Jasper released her. She met his green gaze, so much like her own. "Thanks for the chiropractic readjustment."

"Anytime. I'm calling in the pizza now, so it should be ready by the time you get there."

"Fine, fine. Domino's?"

"Yup."

"Deviate once in a while."

"They are the only ones that don't use caraway seeds. You know that." Jasper nudged her as she walked back out the door.

"One day I might forget," Harper threatened.

"Mean!" Jasper called out to her as she walked to her pickup.

Harper grinned and swung open her door and slid into the truck. Her brother had a pretty epic allergic reaction to caraway seeds, one that had doped him up on Benadryl more than once.

One of those times happened because Kessed had brought him dinner. And hadn't known he was allergic.

The idiot had known the seeds were in the sauce and ate it anyway.

Love was not just blind, but in some cases, deaf, dumb, stupid, and a hazard to your health.

Kessed, from that point on, had been paranoid about the little seeds being in sauces, or really anything. And Domino's Pizza was the only place in town that didn't have the little allergy triggers.

It wasn't Harper's favorite place, but it was worth it to keep Jasper from swelling up like a balloon.

She flicked on her lights as she drove toward town and turned up the music to drown out her thoughts.

It sucked to not be able to trust yourself.

"In the morning, I'm leaving, making my way back to Cleveland..." She sang the Kenny Chesney song loudly and probably off tune. She couldn't tell. As she passed the Elk Heights Ranch's drive, she glanced over to the hillside and did a double take.

Smoke.

It wasn't much, almost a wisp, but that didn't mean jack shit.

Each year, the hills caught fire, at least in one place or another. And brush fires were no joke. She pulled off to the side and spun the truck around and sped down the driveway. After pulling out her cell phone, she dialed the fire department, letting them know about the location. As she got closer, she could see the smoke growing from a wisp to a cloud. She ended the call when they had the information and tossed the phone to the passenger side. When she pulled in beside the barn, she left her truck on then ran to the ranch door.

Knocking loudly, she bounced on her heels as she waited.

"Harper?" Sterling answered the door, his gray eyes confused as he glanced from her running pickup to her. "What's up?"

"Cyler—Is Cyler here?"

"Yeah, what's wrong?" Sterling lowered his chin, leveling her with a commanding stare.

"Fire."

"Shit." Sterling darted back into the house. "Cyler!"

Soon Cyler was rushing out the door with Sterling close behind as Harper pointed to the hill just above the ranch's property.

"Aw hell," Cyler whispered.

Harper watched as the orange flames became visible against the charcoal smoke.

"Has anyone called the fire department?" Laken asked, coming to stand beside Harper.

"I did." She turned to Cyler. "Did you make a firebreak this year?"

"Yeah." Cyler nodded. "But it doesn't always hold. Let's go check it out." Cyler ran back into the house, leaving Sterling, Laken, and Harper watching the flames grow.

"Where's the tractor? Is it in the south pasture?" Harper asked, turning to Sterling.

"I—I'm not sure. It should be there unless Cyler moved it."

"Good. Do you know if there's any cattle in that pasture?"

Sterling nodded. "Sure is."

"This is what we're going to do." Cyler came charging out of the house as sirens sounded from the direction of town. "You guys, take the two quads and move the cattle into the north pasture. Get them as far away from the hill as you can. I'm going to take that damn tractor and clean up the firebreak. We don't need that bastard of a fire jumping across and making hell of my ranch."

Sterling nodded.

"What do you need me to do?" Laken wrapped her arms around her body, clearly concerned.

"Man the phones. Harper, is yours in the car? Grab it. We need to keep in contact. And stay the hell away from the fire, you hear me? All of you. It moves faster than the devil."

"Laken, can you call Jasper and Kessed? I was on my way to pick up pizza, and they don't know I'm here. My brother will get freaked if he doesn't hear from me." Harper ran to her pickup and killed the engine. Grabbing her phone, she sprinted to the side of the barn where the quads were stored.

Sterling met her there. His eyes were intense, focused in some sort of soldier mode.

"Let's evacuate some cattle." Harper put a knee on the seat and turned the key. "Ready?" she yelled over the sound of the second engine starting.

"I'll follow you." He made a circular motion with his hand, and she nodded.

She backed the quad out and then took off toward the hill. The sun was starting to set, narrowing their window of daylight. She glanced behind her, making sure Sterling was following.

The scent of smoke filled the air. Keeping the quad on, she jumped off and swung open the gate. Sterling drove past her, and she followed. As soon as she was through, she jumped back off the quad and closed the gate behind them. The smoke was growing thicker, making the sunset a bloody red on the horizon.

"Where do we start?" Sterling asked over the growl of the quad engine.

Harper loaded back up on her quad. "Let's open the pasture gates first, then we'll start to round up the cattle."

"Would it be better to tag team?" Sterling asked over the sound of the engines.

"The cattle will be down by the water, but they'll keep away from the fire—instinct. Let's just get those gates open so once we start moving them we don't have to stop. I'll get the first, you ride through and get the second, and so on. There should be three or four to the most northern section."

"Got it." Sterling nodded and took off, sending a cloud of dust behind him that swirled around Harper as she followed. As they approached the first entry, she swung off and opened the gate quickly, watching as Sterling sped through.

When she approached the second gate, Sterling was already waiting with it wide open for her. And she did the same for him at the third one. Without delay, Harper spun her quad around and headed back toward the fire. The sound of sirens pierced through the air as the flashing lights made their way toward the curling smoke. As she drove to the water where the cattle would be lingering for the evening, she kept her eye on the rye grass. Still.

No wind.

Praise God.

As she rounded the corner to the water, she slowed down. The goal was to herd the cattle, not spook them. Instinctively, they were keeping away from the edge of the pasture closest to the hill. As she gave them a wide berth and circled behind them, she saw Sterling approach. His quad's light helped illuminate the growing dark as he followed her lead and met her behind the herd.

"You ever done this before?" Sterling asked, his face dusty from the dry dirt the quads kicked up.

Harper shrugged. "More or less. Basically, we need to go slow enough to not freak them out, but be bossy enough to not let them be stubborn about staying. Yell a little, rev the engine, and keep the stragglers with the herd. Make sense?"

"More or less." Sterling glanced to the cattle.

Harper looked at his leg, curious as to how he was holding up. At least they were riding the quads, not horses.

"Let's go."

Sterling nodded, and she took off at a steady pace. The cattle watched her warily as she approached.

"Ha! Get!" she shouted, slowing down and curving toward the back of the herd.

A few trotted away from the group, but Sterling went around her, cutting off their escape, and soon the herd started moving toward the open gate.

They worked together, Harper keeping the majority of them moving forward, while Sterling kept the stragglers in line, revving his quad's engine when they got a little bold.

Against her better judgment, her gaze kept flickering to him. This wasn't his area of expertise; he was anything but a cowboy, yet it was like as soon as you gave him a purpose, he made it his own. A unique trait, and she kind of admired that.

As they passed through the third gate, she stopped the quad and hopped off so that she could swing it shut. Sterling met her gaze and nodded, taking up her previous position and moving the herd along to the final gate. Harper jumped back on the quad and caught up, and together they ushered the final steer into the north pasture. She killed the engine and swung the gate shut.

Sterling turned off his quad as well, and as the dust settled, they turned to the hill.

Glowing.

"Shit," Harper swore.

"What do we do now?" Sterling asked, and Harper studied him.

"I—I don't know. We pray the wind doesn't come up. We pray for rain." Harper watched as he turned back to the flames. And it struck her, oddly enough, Sterling hadn't found it difficult to ask for direction.

As a guy, she'd expected him to be pushy, demanding, arrogant. After all, he probably had a good reason to be, used to giving orders and having them obeyed.

But also used to being under authority and following direction.

Which was hard.

Damn, it was hard.

Sometimes he stunned the hell out of her.

"Harper?" he asked, his tone questioning.

"Yeah, sorry. Let's ask Cyler." Harper got back on her quad and started the engine, heading toward the south pasture. After they passed through the gates, they swung them shut, and soon the heat from the fire was warming the air as they approached where Cyler was disking the pasture.

The flames were bright red and orange, flickering with an angry edge as the black smoke hurled through the air. Several fire trucks were shooting out a layer of water along the ranch's property line, while others were doing their best to contain the flames.

"What's over there?"

Harper hadn't heard Sterling's approach, and she turned to him, watching the orange light flicker across his face.

"Nothing but more grass to burn. For miles." Harper took a deep breath of heated air.

"In other words, nothing to stop it." Sterling met her gaze.

"Basically."

Sterling frowned. "What if they started a control fire?"

"That's probably the next step. But there's always the chance that the wind will kick up and blow the control fire out of control as well. Right now, it's a miracle that it's calm out. It won't last forever."

"I see. I'm out of ideas then." Sterling shook his head. "So we just...wait?"

Harper shrugged. "For now."

And waiting was always the hardest part.

CHAPTER 5

Apparently, feeling helpless was his thing.

As the flames consumed all the dead grass covering the hill, he racked his brain for ways to help.

Anything was better than doing nothing.

Harper's arms were wrapped around her waist as if hugging herself. It was a mannerism he'd seen her do often, and it spoke volumes.

I'm holding myself together.

He didn't know her full story, but he'd heard enough to know that, for Harper, survival was a victory in and of itself.

Movement caught his eye, and he turned his gaze ahead and saw Cyler approaching. Nodding, he waited for his brother-in-law to get close enough to talk over the sound of the water hoses and fire crackling.

"Good work, guys." Cyler slapped Sterling on the shoulder and gave a nod to Harper. "I disked the firebreak, and the marshal thinks the fire will burn south rather than north—which is good news and bad news. Good news, because it will keep the hell away from my ranch. Bad news, because it can go unhindered for miles. They are calling in the helicopters, and Yakima County Fire Department is laying out a firebreak farther down in the canyon. Hopefully, it will be enough."

Sterling nodded, meeting Cyler's direct gaze. "Seems like that's all they can do."

"Yup. Unfortunately, this is one of the hazards of living out here. A few years ago, the Hanford fire burned about one hundred thousand acres. It was massive. We haven't had a fire in this part for a while, which only means there's more than enough fuel for a hot one."

"I'll stay out here, just in case the wind comes up or if the fire changes its mind about the direction." Sterling watched the flames lick the sagebrush.

"I'm already planning on it. You can—"

"Cyler, go home to Laken so she doesn't have a heart attack. She was already white as a sheet when you left. Later, you can come back out and take a shift, okay?" Sterling placed a hand on his brother-in-law's shoulder.

Cyler frowned, but his gaze darted behind Sterling toward the house.

"Go," Sterling encouraged.

"I'll be back"—Cyler checked his phone—"around midnight. That way, you can get a break. But first, I'll bring water and a few other things."

"I'll just follow you in and pick it up so you can stay with Laken," Harper chimed in. "She's not used to this like we are, Cyler." Harper headed back to the quad, swinging her long leg over the back.

Those legs.

It seemed like every time he saw her she was wrapping them around something.

A saddle.

A quad.

It was too easy to imagine them wrapped around him.

Damn, he needed to stop that line of thought before the fire wasn't the only thing burning.

"Sterling, you cool with that?" Cyler asked, and Sterling nodded, not sure if he was agreeing to something new or just what they had said earlier.

And not really caring.

At least he was outside, doing something, contributing something.

"See you in a few." Cyler took the quad Sterling had used, and soon he and Harper were headed toward the ranch house.

Sterling walked toward the fence line farthest away from the flames and leaned against it, taking some of the weight off his leg.

He hadn't taken any more pain medication, and he was starting to regret that act of stupidity.

Or valor.

It was a toss-up.

Damn, he was going to pay for this tomorrow. His leg was going to kill.

The darkness was illuminated by the orange glow. Ash swirled in the air, and Sterling lifted his shirt to wipe the sweat and grime from his face. The fire was a little too warm, even from such a distance, and he pushed off from the fence line and walked down the row. Sparks flew and landed on nearby brush, igniting new fires.

It was one huge nightmare for the firefighters. They ran line after line of hose, sending the water into the air, but it was plain to see it wasn't enough. The sound of a diesel engine approached, and Sterling watched as a semitruck pulled up with a huge backhoe on the trailer. *Probably to create another firebreak.*

They were doing everything they could, and just as Sterling leaned against another fence post, he felt a cool breeze.

He inhaled deeply then froze.

Wind. The grass beside him stirred. Well, the evening was about to get more interesting.

The firefighters took the backhoe off the trailer and started it up. The implement began to take a small path up the hill and lowered its blade like a snow plow. Soon it was clearing a road behind it, churning up the dirt and making a break.

The sound of a quad approaching distracted Sterling from watching the heavy machinery, and he glanced behind him to see Harper approach. She killed the motor, and he averted his eyes away before he could watch her swing her leg over.

If he didn't get his reactions under control, he was going to do something stupid.

He heard the crunch of dry grass under Harper's boots as she approached, and he turned.

"Hey, you. Thirsty?" She tossed a bottle of water to him, and Sterling reached out and caught it, placing his other hand on the post to make sure he didn't lose his balance.

Damn leg.

The bottle was icy cold, making him thirsty just thinking about it. He unscrewed the cap and downed the whole bottle.

"I'll take that as a yes. Cyler said you ate, but I always feel weird if I eat, and the people around me don't, so..." She set down a cooler beside them and slid the top open. "...sandwich?"

Sterling shook his head, grinning at her hopeful expression. "What? You don't want me to be creepy and just stare at you while you feed your face?" He took the sandwich, and Harper glared.

"Who says you have to stare to be creepy," she shot back.

"Aw, you get *hangry*, don't you?" Sterling teased.

Harper rolled her eyes and opened the plastic around her own sandwich. "It's a real thing."

"Apparently," Sterling replied before taking a bite.

"Ass," she replied, but it was muffled around her huge bite of sandwich.

"Classy," he said after he swallowed.

Harper saluted him with her middle finger.

Sterling chuckled, shaking his head as she made a big show of taking another huge bite.

"Backing off. What big teeth you have," he flirted.

Wait. *What the hell.*

He turned back to the fire. No, he wasn't. Was he?

He squinted back to Harper, who was fishing around in the cooler for something else, and then he turned back to the fire.

He couldn't flirt with Harper; she was a pain the ass, demanding as hell, and...

Fun.

And probably even more broken than he.

Yup, sounds like a great life choice. Ruin your life and someone else's heart in the process.

He shook his head and took another bite, trying to distract himself.

"What I wouldn't give for some ice cream." Harper sighed, and Sterling turned to her.

"Pretty sure it would melt in this heat."

"Ice cream melts regardless. Not a deal breaker. It just means you have to eat it faster." She arched a brow, as if proving her point.

"Observant."

"Coffee is my favorite. What's yours?"

"Flavor?" Sterling asked.

"No, color. Yes, *flavor.*" Her purple-tipped hair appeared dark against the light blond that reflected the orange glow.

"Coffee." Sterling's lips curled into a half grin. "Or vanilla."

"You would pick vanilla," she teased.

"What's wrong with vanilla?" He turned to face her.

"Boring," Harper singsonged.

Sterling shook his head. "Vanilla is like a blank canvas. You can put it with dark chocolate or caramel. You can put strawberries with it, or make it into apple pie a la mode. Vanilla isn't boring. Vanilla is versatile."

She blinked. "That was beautiful."

Sterling tilted his head. "Say what?"

"Nothing. I think I might like vanilla too." She lowered her gaze, a small grin on her full lips.

"I knew you'd see it my way," he teased, a sense of fulfillment flooding him when he earned a cheeky grin in response.

"And there's the ass I know." She winked and lifted a bottle of water as if toasting him.

"So why did you come back out?" Sterling asked as he finished his sandwich.

Harper shrugged. "Honestly, it sucks being alone, and I kinda wanted to watch the fire. Laken called Jas and Kessed for me so they know what's up."

"Jasper pretty protective?" Sterling asked, though he was certain he knew the answer.

"Yeah. To say the least. But it's actually not as annoying as you'd think. It's...nice. I like it." She shrugged, but her tone wasn't as blasé. "It makes me feel safe, you know? That's not a bad thing."

"No, no it's not," Sterling replied, nodding once and studying Harper. Her shoulders rolled in slightly as if she were curling into herself. Her whole body conveyed a message that she usually opposed with that snarky mouth of hers.

It was a reality that Sterling echoed all too easily. *Stay on guard, protect yourself, and don't let them see your weakness.*

And sometimes that meant that you hid it from yourself as well.

Part of him wondered if she even realized the mixed signals she expressed. Probably not.

And truth of it was, he probably did the same thing.

He turned away, not wanting her to read his expression.

A dull ache throbbed in his leg, stealing his attention.

"You're quiet," Harper commented.

Lying about the pain was always easier than facing it.

"Just watching the fire." The words tasted bitter on his tongue, and he opened his mouth to be a little more honest, but she spoke first.

"It is pretty epic."

Sterling watched the flames crest the hill.

"Scary as hell but beautiful at the same time. It's kinda like life."

Sterling met her gaze, curious as to how she would continue.

"Really though, sometimes the scary shit is that way because it's the most powerful, and not in the least in control." Harper wouldn't make eye contact but tucked her wrapper into the cooler and then turned her gaze to the fire.

Sterling studied her. "And that's good?"

She lifted a shoulder. "Sometimes yes, sometimes no."

He readjusted his weight to try to alleviate the pain then gave up when it didn't help and lowered himself to sit on the dirt. Well, he wanted to be more honest, and honesty usually meant admitting when you were weak.

Or wrong.

"Good idea." Harper took a seat beside him, her presence taking away some of the sting of acknowledging his weakness. In that moment, he was simply thankful.

Sterling turned his gaze to the fire, studying the way the flames grew and faded then grew again, trying to ignore how his body was fully aware that Harper was less than a foot away from him. It was a constant push and pull with her, much like the flames. It would grow, then fade, and then hit him with a fresh wave just when he thought he had it under control.

She leaned back against the post beside him, her shoulder brushing his, and he swore he could hear her sharp intake of breath.

Smoke tinged the air, yet he could still smell her exotic scent.

Heat swirled around him, yet it wasn't from the flames.

"Why does life always find ways to make us give up control?" Harper asked, her tone making it sound as if she wasn't looking for an answer, just voicing the question.

Sterling wondered the same thing.

Because right then, it was like he had no control either.

Of his life.

His leg.

The fire outside.

The fire that somehow was starting inside.

"I'm not sure," he answered anyway, the question too close to his own thoughts to remain unspoken. "But it sure seems that way, doesn't it?"

He felt her take a deep breath. "Yeah. Yet, I don't know if I could actually trust myself if I was actually in control, you know?"

Sterling met her gaze. "I used to think I'd be good at it."

"Now?" she asked, her gaze piercing through him.

"Now, I'm just as screwed up as the next guy." He blew out a deep breath.

"Nah, you're not," Harper answered with conviction, causing him to frown slightly.

"You sound pretty sure about that."

She twisted her lips, drawing his attention to their perfect shape. "I am."

"How?" Sterling turned back to the flames, his body tense as he waited for her answer, knowing it would carry more weight than someone else's opinion.

"Because you don't give up. When it hurts, you push through. You don't let pain own or define you, even if you think it does. But your biggest problem is that you're impatient."

Sterling met her gaze with a narrowed one. "Impatient?"

"Yeah, really impatient."

"And how do you know that?" he asked, his lips pulling into a grin.

"Because I'm the same way." Harper lowered her gaze and took a breath. "It's easier to see things in others than yourself, but the strange part is that when you recognize things, deep down, you know that the same problem, same issue, same fear is in you." She slowly lifted her gaze to meet his then flickered it away to the bright flames.

Sterling paused before asking the question. "And what do you see in yourself?"

Harper blew out a breath. "Fear. And I absolutely hate it."

Sterling waited for her to meet his gaze, but she stared steadfastly at the flames.

He reached out and touched her chin, directing her gaze back to his. "Harper, you terrify me," Sterling replied, grinning when her lips bent into a surprised smile.

"What?"

Sterling should have released her chin, he knew it, but couldn't bring himself to let go, to pull away from the beautiful smile that lit up her face. "Seriously."

"Why?" Harper's expression opened further, the tension and fear from earlier melting completely away.

He could have said a thousand things about her strength, her determination, her penchant for yelling at him...but instead he took a deep breath and leaned forward, slowly at first, watching her expression.

Her gaze went wide, then her eyes fluttered shut as he closed the distance, his fingers tilting her chin ever so slightly as he met her lips. The sound of the fire crackling punctuated the moment, and Sterling instinctively leaned into the kiss, savoring the smooth texture of her lips. He fought against himself, wanting more, wanting to run away, thinking this was either stupidity of epic proportions...

Or his saving grace.

And he was stuck in purgatory waiting for the verdict as he leaned back and met her gaze.

Confusion, desire, and indecision all flickered across her green eyes as she bit her lower lip.

His fingers slipped from her chin, and he held his breath, watching... waiting...

Letting her lead.

With the slightest lift of her chin, she leaned forward, her lips parting just enough to capture his lower lip, setting his body on fire, yet her kiss wasn't deep, wasn't pressing, and he didn't force it.

Rather, he locked down his instinct to move closer, to feel her body against his, and waited as she ended the kiss.

Because Harper had tilted her head so slightly, a length of hair slipped from her shoulder and framed her face, the firelight illuminating the complexity of her expression as she opened her mouth to speak, then closed it. A smile crept across her face while her gaze flickered downward. Tucking her wayward tresses behind her ear, she glanced up. "So, you don't seem too afraid of me."

Sterling released the breath he was holding and grinned, her comment breaking any ice that had frozen over the moment while he waited for her response. "I said I was afraid of you, not that I wasn't brave, or stupid enough to overcome it."

She broke into a giggle at his words, her smile softening her features in a way that set his blood on fire.

And he caught a glimpse of the girl that she once had been.

Before whatever tried to break her had happened.

More than anything, he wanted to bring that back.

"Don't be a girl." Harper smacked his shoulder, breaking through his thoughts.

"Huh?"

"Yeah, you. Stop analyzing this. We're cool. You kissed me. I kissed you back. We can be adults about it, right?"

Sterling nodded, immediately on alert. Her words didn't ring true.

Leaning forward, he tested his theory. "And there it is."

Harper frowned. "What?"

"Fear. What if I like kissing you? What if I wasn't overanalyzing it, was simply enjoying the fact that you're here with me. Would that be so bad to actually put a personal investment in the whole kissing thing? For it to mean something? Rather than nothing?"

Harper blinked then lowered her gaze. "I need to go." Quickly, she hopped up and ran to the quad.

Sterling lifted himself and stood, gripping the fence post as his leg screamed in pain at the sudden movement. Even if he wanted to chase her, he wouldn't get more than a few steps.

She flickered a quick peek at him then started the engine. Soon a cloud of dust trailed behind her as she headed toward the ranch house.

"That went well." Sterling lowered himself to the ground once more, wincing in pain as he stretched out his leg.

But her actions had spoken louder than her words.

Harper Matthews was a runner.

And if there was one thing Sterling knew how to do, it was chase. Bum leg or not.

CHAPTER 6

Harper woke up to the familiar scent of coffee coming from the kitchen. Kessed had been a Starbucks barista before she started to work with Jasper, so coffee was a staple at the Matthews house.

Which was perfectly fine with Harper.

This morning, she needed more than just caffeine. She needed a fresh serving of dignity, too.

Damn it all. She'd been such an idiot last night. And as luck would have it, she had to see Sterling today.

She could be a woman about it, apologize and level with him, but honestly, she just didn't want to. It was so much easier to pretend, to beat around the bush—she was used to playing the game. And for Sterling to be so blatantly honest...it freaked the hell out of her.

Because that meant that it was real.

The kiss, it wasn't just a spur of the moment act of insanity.

It was thought out, intended.

Enjoyed.

And that meant that he wanted more...and more wasn't something she was prepared to give.

Maybe ever.

Harper rolled over in bed, putting the pillow over her head as she sighed deeply. *Well, nowhere to go but through it.* She took another slow breath then tossed the pillow aside and stood up from the bed, running her fingers through her snarled hair and tucking it behind her ear. As she looked to the tips, she noted their fading color and mentally made a note to call and get a hair appointment. With the race coming up, she wanted to be all fresh and ready.

In control.

Even if it was just of her hair color.

It was the little things, and eventually the little things added up. She may have a lapse of judgment here or there...

Like running away from Sterling.

She closed her eyes and relived the moment again.

Shit.

Twisting her lips, she pushed her thoughts aside and got dressed. After wrapping her hair into a quick messy bun, she followed her nose into the kitchen, her gaze zeroing in on the coffeepot.

"Morning," Jasper's raspy tone called to her as she poured herself a large mug of coffee.

"Morning," she grumbled, her voice thick with sleep.

"You sound awake," he teased, and she glanced over to him and glared.

"Are your eyes even open? I can't tell." Jasper narrowed his eyes and leaned forward.

Harper flipped him off.

"Ah, yup, she's awake." He chuckled.

"Hey, morning." Kessed walked into the room in her cut-off shorts and one of Jasper's flannel shirts.

As she walked by him, he smacked her ass playfully.

"And we're done. None of that before I've had my coffee. I can't deal with you two normally, let alone before I've had at least this entire pot of coffee." Harper lifted her mug and took a seat at the kitchen table.

"Leave your sister alone," Kessed teased Jasper, leaning down and giving him a quick kiss on the lips. Turning to Harper, she raised an eyebrow. "PG enough for you?"

Harper nodded once. "Thank you."

"What won't be PG is when—"

Kessed smacked the back of Jasper's head as she walked behind him to grab a coffee mug from the cabinet.

Harper snickered.

"Don't encourage her." Jasper folded his beefy arms across his chest.

"We gotta stick together," Harper replied, and as Kessed passed her, she lifted her hand, and they high-fived.

"It's a conspiracy." Jasper sighed.

"Basically." Kessed shrugged, pouring herself a cup of coffee.

Harper grinned and lifted the saltshaker. "Hey, Jasper..." She waited till she had her brother's attention.

He narrowed his eyes as she sprinkled some salt in her hand. "...I a-salt you."

"Lame." Jasper brushed the salt from his sleeve that Harper had just tossed in his direction.

"Best joke ever." Kessed took a seat beside Jasper.

"If you didn't grow up with it happening all the time. I swear, I've swept more salt off this floor."

"Whatever, like you've never done it to me." Harper teased.

"Regardless...I'm the one sweeping it up."

"You're a good maid." Harper chuckled.

Jasper shook his head. "Anyway, so Kessed and I have a full day of making the rounds. What are you up to?"

Harper leaned back in her chair. It was the usual start to the morning. Jasper was a planner, and being the overprotective brother that he was, he always let Harper know where he was...and in return wanted to know where she'd be as well.

"I'm helping Sterling later this morning, then I'm working on your paperwork for the vet calls you did yesterday. Spartan and I have to practice again, so I'll spend the rest of the afternoon riding. It's not supposed to be too warm, so I think he'll be good to go."

Jasper nodded. "Sounds productive. I charged my phone—"

"Miracles happen," Harper commented.

"Are you done?" Her brother gave her a beleaguered expression.

Harper grinned and took a sip of coffee as her answer.

"So, if you need me, you can actually call my phone, rather than Kessed's."

"Cool." Harper stood and walked to the cabinet and pulled down a bowl. "Well, you guys have a good day, and let me know if you need any supplies from storage. I can run it out to you if you get in a bind."

"Thanks, Harper," Kessed answered for Jasper, who was mid-sip of coffee.

"Anytime."

Jasper and Kessed left soon after, and Harper was chasing her last Cheerio in her bowl when her phone buzzed. The number wasn't familiar, so she let it go to voicemail.

She placed her bowl in the sink as her phone buzzed with a voicemail.

Frowning, she unlocked it and tapped on the voicemail icon. As she waited for the transcript to process, she sat back down.

Her eyes widened as she read the short message, her heart pounding quickly as her eyes zeroed in on the name.

Mr. Linden.

The office of the prosecuting attorney who had convicted her husband. Ex-husband.

The paralegal wanted her to call back.

Harper locked her phone and tossed it onto the table, her hand shaking. This couldn't be good. Could it?

She peeked at the phone then bit her lip. Her heart pounding an erratic rhythm, she felt adrenaline course through her system.

Damn it all, she hated the way he made her afraid, even when she knew he wasn't anywhere close.

It was stupid to have that kind of a reaction. It was over, he was in jail, and she was safe.

Safe.

Safe.

Yet *knowing* she was safe wasn't the same as *feeling* safe.

She bit her nail and looked to the phone once more.

With a shaky finger, she dialed the number and held her breath when it rang.

"Hello, Tacoma office of Livingston, Linden, and Owen. How may I direct your call?"

Harper gave her name and was quickly directed to Mr. Linden's paralegal.

"Ms. Matthews?" the paralegal asked, her tone detached as if robotic.

"Yes." Harper took in a slow breath, one arm wrapping itself around her in a hug as she waited.

"Thank you for returning my call. We will be mailing out the official papers, but we wanted you to be aware that your ex-husband is up for parole."

Harper closed her eyes, the words vibrating through her like a bullet in a steel box.

"Ms. Matthews?" the paralegal asked, her tone inquiring.

"Yes. Thank you for letting me know."

"Of course. The parole isn't approved yet, and if so, we will be issuing a restraining order, just so you're aware."

"Thank you," Harper managed, her hand shaking as it held up the phone.

"Do you have any questions?" the woman asked.

Only about a million. Like why is that bastard up for parole? "No."

"You have a good day, Ms. Matthews."

"You too." Harper ended the call and set the phone down in the middle of the table. Rubbing her hands together, she tried to warm them up from the chill that had overtaken her body.

Her mind flashed back to the stairs, the way her body had instinctively folded around her unborn baby...the scent of cigarette smoke and then of hospital cleaner...the sound of the heart monitor in the hospital room.

One heartbeat.

One.

Tears landed on her lap before she even realized she was crying.

Mourning.

Would it ever end?

She swiped the tears away angrily.

She was stronger than this! It was the past; it was history.

It was part of her. But it would not define her.

Not if she could help it.

Yet, that didn't make the fear any less real, or her body's reaction any less violent. But it did help her to see through it, to make the conscious effort to move forward in spite of it.

Grabbing her phone, she marched to the bathroom. She set it to the side and splashed her face with cold water, meeting her own gaze in the mirror.

She took three deep breaths then opened the medicine cabinet behind the mirror to grab her toothpaste. As she reached for it, her eyes caught the orange bottle with a white cap.

She glanced to the toothbrush then back to the bottle.

Her name was printed across the label, the dosage and name of the medication all too familiar.

All too easy.

Her hand shook as she took the bottle from its place on the shelf. She paused before she put the bottle away and all but slammed the cabinet shut, the mirror vibrating with the force of the swing.

"No." She spoke out loud.

Brushing her teeth, she gripped the toothbrush with a tenacity that wasn't required, but one that reminded her to hold on.

To not let go.

Don't give in.

She spat and didn't put away the toothpaste or brush, not wanting to face the temptation again.

And as she walked from the bathroom, she looked to the mirror and back.

She really should throw them away.

She took a small step back then paused.

What if...

What if she needed them someday?

The prescription couldn't be refilled, and she only had a few pills left....
What harm could it cause?

There wasn't enough to do any real damage.

Keeping them was safer. Making her feel like she had options. An escape.
Even if she never planned on taking them.

After turning the light off, she walked down the hall, her focus on the
upcoming events of the day.

Forcing herself to not think about the past.

Or what might happen in the future.

But just the next breath.

Breathe. Just breathe.

She could do this.

One breath at time.

CHAPTER 7

Sterling knew something wasn't right as soon as he saw her. First of all, she was late.

Harper was *never* late.

Second, she was hugging herself again. Gone was the giggling, carefree girl from the night before.

And third, he had the sinking suspicion it had to do with him.

Damn it all to hell.

This was going to suck.

Harper kicked a rock across the gravel drive as she approached the arena. As she met Sterling's gaze, a tint of pink colored her cheeks.

Sterling released the smile he was trying to restrain, ducking his head slightly to keep from grinning too wildly.

Who knew a blush could be so damn sexy?

When he could control his grin, he met her gaze once more, this time slightly more hopeful that he hadn't completely ruined their tentative friendship by kissing her last night.

But his memory was quick to remind him that she had kissed him back.

That kiss had *not* been one sided.

But that didn't mean a whole lot.

But maybe, just maybe, it meant *something*.

"You're entirely too cheerful for this early in the morning." Harper arched a brow, jerking her chin toward the barn.

Sterling fell into step beside her. "I haven't said a word."

"You're smiling."

"And that's a crime?" he asked, sliding the barn door open for her.

"Not a crime, just annoying to those of us who aren't morning people."

Sterling chuckled. "Fine, no smiling. I'll act like I have stick up my ass. Better?"

Harper cast him an annoyed glare. "Grab me the saddle."

He felt her eyes on him as he strode to the tack room. He'd swallowed his pride and taken the pain medication so he was able to walk with an almost regular stride.

The odd things that you take for granted till they are taken away.

Walking without a limp.

Swaggering.

It felt so damn good to not wear the pain of his injury on his sleeve.

To have it erased, even if it was only temporary.

He'd take it.

"You're walking better," Harper commented, her tone curious.

Sterling lifted the saddle from the rack and walked back, concentrating on the way he stepped with his injured leg. Just because it didn't hurt as much didn't mean it was strong. "I caved and took the meds my doctor prescribed. They help a hell of a lot more than I was expecting."

Something flickered across Harper's expression before she glanced away. "That's good. You deserve a break from the pain."

Sterling didn't press her but filed away the reaction to evaluate later. "Yeah, we'll see if it helps me with riding."

"Yeah, doubtful. That's skill, which you don't fully have yet."

"Ah, look who's all encouraging this morning." Sterling lifted the saddle onto Margaret's back just over the folded blanket that Harper had placed.

"Encouraging, honest—take your pick," Harper teased, her green eyes flickering to his before she walked around to Margaret's head and stroked her nose. "Can you peacock over there and get me the bridle?" Harper bit back a grin.

Sterling frowned as he looked at her. "Peacock?"

Harper grinned as she returned his gaze. "You so totally peacocked just now. It's a real thing."

"What the hell is it?" Sterling leaned back on his good leg, regarding her.

Harper shrugged then stroked down Margaret's face. "It's when you strut around like you know someone's watching you. Showing off."

Sterling peeked to the dirty floor, pinching his lips together to keep from smiling too wide. "Ouch."

"So peacock. I'll watch and give you an audience." Harper was giggling now, her body practically shaking with amusement.

"Damn it all." Sterling shook his head and rubbed the back of his neck. "Go. We don't have all day."

He started toward the tack room.

"I'm...too sexy for my boots, too sexy for my boots," Harper sang under her breath.

"Not wearing boots," Sterling shot back, his face breaking into a grin. He tested his leg's strength and paused, giving his ass a shake.

"Wow, look at that!" Harper gave a little woot as he did it again.

Sterling shimmied his shoulders, earning a burst of laughter from her as he made a show of lifting the bridle from the eye-level hook.

"Work it!" Harper yelled between her laughter.

"Yeah, work it."

Sterling froze and looked over his shoulder to the barn door, his face heating with a blush as Cyler gave a slow clap.

"Best part of my day." Harper was leaning her head against Margaret's, laughter shaking her entire body.

And even if he had made a total idiot of himself, it was worth it to see her let go of whatever dark shadows had followed her this morning.

"Is dancing part of your therapy? I've heard stranger things." Cyler strode into the barn, a crooked grin on his face as she shook his head.

"Pretty soon, he's going to be dropping it like it's hot. You just wait." Harper had calmed down enough to speak clearly, and she gave a wide grin to Cyler.

"Let me know when that takes place so I won't be around. No offense, dude." Cyler lifted a hand as he glanced to Sterling.

"None taken." Sterling walked back to Margaret, handing the bridle over to Harper and giving her a sidelong glare. "Did you know he was there?"

"Nope. I swear," Harper replied, giggling. She took the bridle and started to place it over Margaret's head.

Sterling turned to Cyler. "You heading to the burn site?"

"Yeah. I just called in, and they have the blaze at least halfway contained."

"And that's good or bad?" Sterling asked, regarding his brother-in-law.

"Actually, that's pretty damn good for it just starting last night. It could be much worse. We'll take what we can get. I wish I had irrigation lines in the south pasture, but it is what it is. I don't think it will come back this way. It burned farther south like we hoped. They were able to keep it from jumping the firebreaks they put down yesterday, so by tonight, I bet it's even closer to being put out."

"Do they know what started it?"

Cyler shook his head. "No, but it could be any number of things. It doesn't take much when it's that dry out. They'll keep me updated if they find anything suspicious."

"Sounds good. What do you need me to do to help?" Sterling shifted out of habit, not because his leg hurt. As he noticed his tendency to favor the leg, he made a conscious effort to evenly distribute his weight.

"After Harper's done with...whatever it is ya'll have planned today..." He winked at Harper. "...why don't you ride out around the perimeter and make sure there's no hot spots?"

"Will do, boss." Sterling saluted Cyler.

Cyler paused, regarding Sterling. "It's really good to have you here, man. I know you don't feel up to snuff with your leg and all, but you help out more than you realize." He walked over and slapped Sterling's back then walked out of the barn.

"You ready, cowboy?"

"Making fun of me again?" Sterling asked as he walked over to the left side of Margaret.

"Yup. Always. Climb up, and I want you to walk her to the arena. I'm not going to lead you around. You fine with that?"

Sterling swallowed his trepidation and placed his good foot in the stirrup. Thankfully, it was his right leg that was injured, so he was able to use his good leg to push up onto the saddle. Swinging his leg over took some coordination, and he tucked his left shoe into the stirrup and reached out to take the leather reins from Harper.

"Go on, I'll follow." She took a step back, and Sterling clicked his tongue and gently squeezed Margaret's flanks, encouraging her to walk.

The horse tossed her head, making the bridle jingle slightly as she started forward. Sterling's muscles locked down initially at the horse's movement, but he forced himself to loosen up, relax.

"Slouch." Harper called out from behind.

Sterling sighed. It went against everything within him to slouch. Now, standing at attention? That he could understand. Slouching, it just felt wrong.

"Relax into the saddle, let it be part of you. An extension," she coached.

He reoriented himself in the saddle, following her suggestion and finding it much easier to achieve. "Like this?" He glanced behind him as they walked out into the sunlight.

"Yeah, better," Harper affirmed.

As Sterling guided Margaret to the arena, Harper ran up ahead and swung open the gate.

"Go for it. You know the drill," she instructed as she closed the gate. Soon she was climbing up onto the rail, watching.

Sterling focused on Margaret's cadence, her rhythm, as he tried to make his body follow her lead.

It wasn't natural for him, which was frustrating. But he persevered.

Soon Harper was encouraging him to trot, correcting his posting technique.

The hour passed quickly, the lack of pain making the whole experience far less tiring.

"You feeling good still?" Harper asked from her perch on the fence.

"Yeah, more than before. Of course, that's the meds, but I'll take what I can get."

"What are you noticing, since you're not focusing on the pain? Are you weaker? Out of balance?"

Sterling frowned slightly as he thought, evaluating his leg. He posted higher to experiment, and his leg gave out, causing him to smack the saddle with his ass a little harder than was comfortable.

"Weaker for sure." He winced, meeting Harper's gaze.

"What about coordination? Usually strength and agility go hand in hand."

Sterling slowed Margaret's pace and then pulled her to a halt. "Yeah, I wouldn't want to be doing the NFL combine right now, but it's getting easier to do most things without my leg failing me."

"Good. I noticed that you're not squeezing with your legs as tightly as you could be when Margaret increases her speed." Harper jumped from the fence and walked over to where he and Margaret waited.

"When you tell her to trot, use your quads to hold on, think of them as anchoring you." She reached up and grabbed his thigh, squeezing it. "Right here. This should tighten up along with your calf." She slid her hand down his leg.

Dear Lord. Did she have any idea what that did to him? Her touch echoed through his entire body, making him hyperaware of each sensation she created. His body reacted with enthusiasm, the memory of their kiss all too fresh in his mind, adding fuel to the fire she was unknowingly creating. As her hand rested on his good calf, she squeezed slightly again, and he bit back a groan of pleasure.

"Here. Squeeze," she coached.

Sterling obeyed, trying to focus on her words so that he didn't make a fool of himself.

"Good. Keep it tight." She smacked his leg and stepped back.

As if his world hadn't just caught fire like the hill behind them.

"Try it again." She turned around and walked back to the fence.

His gaze dropped to her ass before he closed his eyes to try to calm his state of arousal.

"Waiting, sunshine," she teased, and Sterling gave her an irritated grimace as he encouraged Margaret into a walk.

"Practice at a slower pace. Squeeze. Good. Like that."

Sterling kept the tension in his leg, his bad leg already starting to tremble with the exertion.

"Try it faster."

Damn, he was pretty sure that anything she was going to say would be twisted in his head to turn him on more.

Great.

Taking a deep breath, he clicked his tongue, and Margaret trotted. He squeezed his legs tighter, trying to post as well, and finding the whole combination anything but coordinated.

"Slow it back down!" Harper called out, and he quickly obeyed.

His bad leg was trembling harder, and he relaxed the muscle, giving it a break.

"What did you notice?" she asked.

Sterling looked to his right leg. "I'm needing to build up more strength. That was hard," he admitted, cursing his weakness.

"Only the strong can admit when they are weak. Don't let it get you down. Last week, that would have been impossible. Right? Good work."

Harper jumped down from the fence and opened the arena gate.

Sterling guided Margaret out of the arena and toward the barn, Harper following behind.

Sterling watched as she ran up ahead and opened the barn door. Internally, he debated whether to talk to her about the kiss last night or to let it go.

After a moment, he decided to let it go.

"So, about last night..." Harper started.

Or maybe not...

Sterling took a deep breath and waited, curious as to what she'd say. He pulled up Margaret beside her stall and carefully got down from the saddle, all the while focusing on Harper, waiting for her to speak.

When she didn't continue, he turned to her and asked, "Yes?"

Her purple hair was twisted into a messy bun, the colored tips spiking out from her head in a mass of tangled loose curls. Her green eyes darted to his then back to the dusty floor of the barn. Her expression gave nothing away, and Sterling swallowed his impatient nature.

"I..." Her nose scrunched up, and she met his gaze with a rueful one of her own. "Can we forget I even said anything just now?"

Sterling's tension broke, and he gave a small chuckle. "And let you off the hook? Nope. What gives?" He walked over to a post and leaned against it, giving her some space.

Harper sighed deeply then turned to Margaret, sliding her hand down the mare's long nose and tracing her muzzle. "I was stupid and scared and ran, and I'm sorry because there I was talking about hating how afraid I was...and then I acted all afraid." The words gushed out. She continued to pet Margaret's face, not meeting Sterling's gaze.

Sterling thought over his words before he spoke them. "Sometimes it's all right to be afraid. Not all fear is bad. Sometimes it protects us. And last night...you might have needed to protect yourself." Sterling waited, watching her carefully to see how she'd take his words.

Harper's eyes cut to him. "But I wasn't in any danger. It was stupid to run."

Sterling pushed from the post but didn't move closer. "Nonetheless, I'm sorry that you felt the need to run, regardless of the reason."

Harper regarded him, her green eyes piercing through him as if weighing and measuring his words. "Thanks," she answered after a moment. "That... uh...actually was really...sweet." She frowned a bit at the words, as if confused by them.

"And that's a good or bad thing?" Sterling couldn't resist asking, given her adorably confused expression.

"Good?" Harper asked.

"Are you asking me?" Sterling teased, moving toward Margaret and starting to loosen the cinch on her saddle like Harper had taught him.

"Good. It's just not something I'm used to...unless it's from my brother. But that's different."

"Let's hope so." Sterling winked and gave her a sidelong glance.

"Ass." Harper rolled her eyes and came to stand beside him, helping to get Margaret's saddle off.

"So, was that what had you all in knots when you got here this morning?" Sterling asked as he lifted the saddle from Margaret's back and balanced his weight. He started walking to the tack room when she replied.

"Not exactly. I learned that my ex-husband is up for parole."

Sterling tripped, swore under his breath as he righted himself with his good leg, and continued to the tack room. When he hung up the saddle, he met Harper's watchful gaze. "So, I bet that ruined your day."

"To say the least." She turned back to Margaret, unlatched the bridle, and swept it off her face. "It's been a hard morning."

Sterling walked back to her, watching as her hand had a slight tremor to it as she lifted the bridle to him.

"So...if you don't mind me asking, what did the son of a bitch do?" he asked, his jaw clenching after he spoke the words. But he hid his protective instincts, knowing they could be easily misinterpreted for aggression, and his gut told him that Harper would be sensitive to those kinds of reactions.

"It's a long story." She turned to Margaret, sweeping a brush across her flanks as Sterling sighed, turning back to the tack room.

"I've got time!" he called over his shoulder and waited for her response.

The moment dragged on, and Sterling hung up the bridle. As he walked back toward Harper and Margaret, he waited, not pushing her.

Letting her decide.

Letting her lead.

"How much time?" She gave him a tentative glance then focused back on the horse.

A flash of insight struck him. While he used horses to help his leg, Harper used horses to help her heart.

It was an odd twist, yet he understood it, giving him a window into how Harper worked.

And giving him an idea.

She has a horse, right? Spartan...

"I'll tell you what. I need to check on the pasture, and you're more than welcome to come with me. After that, how about I invite myself over to your house, and you can introduce me to Spartan and tell me your long story. You'll...be more comfortable there. Am I right?" He watched and waited.

Harper's gaze shot to his, her expression shifting from suspicion to indecision then relaxing into peace. "Am I that transparent?" She scrunched up her nose again, and Sterling noted the way it highlighted the few freckles smattered across her face.

"You and horses." He shrugged.

"Yeah, well..." She hitched a shoulder in response.

"So...good idea, bad idea?" he asked.

"Good idea." She led Margaret into the stall then met his gaze with a challenging one of her own.

"Race you to the pasture." She ran from the barn toward the quads.

Sterling shook his head, walking behind her.

It was nice to have someone to chase. Even if he couldn't run.

Sometimes, slow and steady won the race. And he was most assuredly slow. Maybe a little unsteady.

But for once, he thought that maybe that was exactly what he needed to be. For Harper.

Maybe even for himself.

CHAPTER 8

Harper seriously hadn't thought this through.

Like, at all.

She didn't regret her decision, but that didn't mean it was easy.

Part of her wondered if this was exactly what needed to happen, to see if she could scare him off.

The other part of her was terrified because if her story didn't send him for the hills...nothing would.

And that was almost scarier than her past.

Almost.

After they'd checked the hills for hot spots, she and Sterling had parked the quads and headed to the house.

He'd grabbed his phone.

She'd fought for something intelligent to say, but failed miserably, and with that sexy as hell grin of his, he had walked to her pickup.

And here they sat as she took the winding road up to her and Jasper's home, her thoughts as tangled as knotted fishing line.

But if Sterling noticed, he didn't comment.

Smart guy.

"You like country?" Harper finally broke the thick silence.

"I don't know much of it, but I like what I know. Thanks for driving me, by the way. It kinda kills me that I still can't drive anywhere but the ranch." Sterling sighed as he turned his gray gaze out the window.

"You'll probably get cleared when you go back to Seattle for your check up. As long as you don't drive a stick shift."

"I'll put that on my list of what not to buy when I go to purchase a car." Harper looked to him. "You don't have a car?"

"Nope." Sterling shrugged. "I liked being deployed. There wasn't much use for one when you were overseas most of the time."

Harper nodded once. "I see. Do you even know how to drive a stick?"

Sterling gave her an irritated grimace. "I can drive anything with more than one wheel. Over any terrain, thank you very much."

"Touchy." Harper grinned, relaxing since she was able to tease him a bit.

"I may be crippled for the moment, but don't take away my skills."

Harper lifted a hand in defense. "No skill shaming here."

"Good. So, tell me about your horse," Sterling said.

Harper relaxed further, even as she could feel his gaze like a caress. She pushed the awareness of it to the back of her mind as she focused on the question.

"Spartan is a barrel racer. He's a gelding, about sixteen hands, so he's a big boy."

She saw Sterling nod from the corner of her eye as she took the driveway to the barn.

"He's persnickety and basically a huge lap dog. But he races like hell is on his heels and has my back." Harper smiled as she thought of the big black monster. Damn, she loved that horse.

"How long have you had him?"

Harper felt her smile fade. "Only a few months, but it feels like a long time. The horse I had before him died. It about broke my heart." She gave a mournful look to Sterling as she put the truck in park. "But she died giving me Rake. He's at the trainers right now, but he's pretty amazing. He'll be a good barrel racer like his momma was. He's just got to grow up a little bit. Well...a lot." Harper grinned, opening her pickup door.

Sterling slid from the seat and shut the door, his gaze scanning his surroundings. It was different than how most people scanned their surroundings. Sterling's gaze seemed to catalog each detail, as if evaluating the exits, entrances, and places for cover. Oddly, it didn't make her feel on edge; rather, it made her feel safe.

"You done?" Harper asked, leaning against her truck as a slow smile spread across her face.

Sterling's gaze cut to her as his brows furrowed. "What do you mean?"

"You're evaluating our position, soldier." She winked and pushed off the truck, turning to the barn, but catching the chagrined smile that teased his lips.

"Caught that, did you?"

"Yup."

"Good times," he replied from behind her.

Harper could hear the crunch of gravel under his shoes as they approached her barn. As she slid the door open, Spartan let out a welcoming nicker.

"Hey, handsome." She strode over to him, kissing his muzzle and tracing his cheek with her fingertips. "Miss me?"

"You two need a moment?" Sterling asked from behind.

And Harper turned to glare. He was slowly making his way into the barn, the sunlight silhouetting his form, accentuating the broad expanse of his shoulders and the trim V of his waist. She forgot her irritation and turned back to Spartan to distract herself.

"Nope. Jealous?" Harper teased when she regained her senses.

"That would be weird," he answered with a teasing tone as he approached the horse slowly.

Spartan straightened his neck; his ears perked forward as he blew out a breath and sniffed the air around Sterling. Pawing the ground impatiently, he nickered lowly and shook his head.

"Is he trying to tell me something?" he asked, tucking his hands in his jean pockets.

"He's telling you to back off." Harper bit her lip, grinning.

"Backing off." Sterling took a step back.

Spartan kept his dark gaze on Sterling as if deciding whether he was friend or foe.

"He's fine, you big dork."

Harper tickled Spartan's nose, and the horse relaxed, turning his gaze back to her.

"Come here." She waved Sterling over, and Spartan froze, waiting.

Carefully, Harper took Sterling's hand, its warmth seeping into hers. Gently, she placed it below Spartan's muzzle, letting him get a good whiff.

She released his hand. "Let him get used to your scent. Then, when he relaxes, slowly move your hand so he can figure out what you're doing, and pet his nose softly."

Sterling gave a meaningful nod and waited.

Spartan took a few breaths, and then his ears relaxed, twisting to listen to other sounds rather than focusing on the man in front of him. Then, just as Harper instructed, Sterling moved his hand purposefully and stroked a long line down Spartan's nose. The horse stilled and then pushed into his hand.

"Aw, he likes you." Harper grinned then broke into a fit of giggles when Spartan started scratching against Sterling's hand.

"Whoa." Sterling balanced himself as he cast Harper a confused and amused expression.

Harper rescued him. "Hey, none of that. He's not your scratching post." She shoved off the horse's massive head and met Sterling's grin. "He's a wily one. Likes to get away with that stuff."

Harper stepped away from Spartan, wondering when Sterling would break the ice and ask about the phone call earlier.

Or was he simply waiting for her to be ready?

As if that would ever happen.

Like a Band-Aid, rip it off.

"So, you ready for this?" Harper asked, bracing herself for the story.

Sterling's gray gaze was resolute, strong, determined. "Only if you are."

Harper gave a humorless laugh. "Not at all. You could Google it if you wanted, public record and all, but I'd rather you hear it from me."

"Google. Teller of secrets," Sterling joked, and Harper relaxed slightly.

She reached out and stroked Spartan's nose again, taking a calming breath. The familiar scents reminded her that she was safe.

It was safe to talk.

Safe to release her demons.

They had no power over her here.

"I met Brock when I was a freshman in high school," she started, focusing on the way Spartan's breathing was an even, rhythmical cadence. Closing her eyes, her memory flooded her with images. Brock's smile...the way his dark hair waved over his eyes...the strength in his hands when he squeezed her hand tightly—too tightly—reminding her that she was weaker.

That he was stronger.

"We got married the summer after we graduated high school. We were the same age, literally." She cast a furtive glance to Sterling. "We were born a week apart."

Sterling nodded, regarding her with a cool gaze that gave nothing away.

She continued. "I didn't... No. That's not true. I did know. But I didn't understand. That's probably a better way to say it." Her brow pinched as she considered how to continue. "Brock was abusive. It started small, in ways that I couldn't quite pinpoint, and in ways that were easy to excuse— normal to excuse. Or so I thought." Harper took a deep breath, inhaled the sweet smell of hay and horse, then continued. "It got progressively worse after we moved to Seattle to go to college. I hid the bruises, but what was more dangerous was that I believed him. Everything he said—at first I fought it—which led to the bruises—" She took a shaking breath. "But that's the hardest part of abuse. You believe the lies. And I did." She met Sterling's gaze.

His full lips were drawn into a firm line, his Adam's apple bobbing as he forcibly swallowed, nodding once for her to continue.

Harper exhaled a tense breath. "When I found out I was pregnant..." She paused, blowing out a breath, trying to keep her emotions together. "...I thought, surely this will make things better. I mean, a baby." She hitched a shoulder as a warm tear slid down her face and dangled from her jawline. "How could you not love a baby, your own little miracle?" She shook her head, and the tear fell from her jaw, landing in the dust.

She turned back to Spartan and stroked his soft nose. "When I told Brock, he seemed happy. And I had hope, you know? Real hope. Things got better for a month or so, at least I wasn't as scared. Looking back, I can see just how depressing it was to think things were better, it was just *that* bad that only verbal assault was a huge improvement in my life, rather than verbal and physical." She shook her head. "I got a few texts from my ob-gyn, and I didn't add the name of the clinic as a contact. Brock found my phone and accused me of cheating on him. He didn't even read the messages, just saw the random number and jumped to that asinine conclusion." Harper wiped a hand across her face, smearing the tears from her cheeks as she stared at the ground, not able to make eye contact.

"I was putting away a few things I had purchased for the baby. The spare room was at the top of the stairs, and I remember shivering as Brock yelled, his shoes pounding up the stairs. The sound was so loud—I don't know why, but that sound...it's like I knew, you know?" She wiped her nose and hazarded a glance at Sterling, watching as his nostrils flared, but his eyes were gentle, not full of anger like she'd expected.

It gave her courage to continue. "He yelled, accused me—I won't go into detail—but I tried to run away, and that just pissed him off more. As I made it to the stairs, he pushed me from behind..." She breathed in through her nose, closing her eyes and focusing on what she could feel, what she could smell—home.

"I woke up in the hospital, and the first thing I remember was the heart monitor. I was far enough along that I'd already heard the baby's heartbeat once. And even in my foggy state, I knew that I only heard one heartbeat—one heart monitor." Warm tears streamed down her face, and she hiccupped a breath. "There should have been two." She shrugged.

She collected herself, taking a few deep breaths before she wiped away her tears almost furiously. "I was lucky to be alive. The stairs were oddly steep and hardwood. When I landed, I broke my collarbone in two places, broke six ribs, and one punctured my lung—to name a few things. I was busted up to say the least." She sighed. "But what I found out later was that I'd already miscarried. So, my fall didn't kill the baby, which is the only reason why Brock isn't behind bars for a long time, and why he's able to apply for parole." She released the tense breath she was holding and met Sterling's gaze. "The divorce was finalized before I even got out of the hospital, but that doesn't mean he doesn't scare the shit out of me. So, I moved home, and I'm really good about telling Jasper where I am at all times, and I have a really big horse that makes me feel safe." She shrugged, glancing to Sterling.

Waiting for the verdict.

His gaze was kind, but not pitying. His jaw was tight, gritted, but Harper wasn't afraid of his silent fury. She knew it wasn't directed at her.

His hands clenched, then relaxed, then clenched again as he seemed to work through all her words before opening his mouth then closing it. Tilting his head, he exhaled a deep sigh, glanced to the ground, then nodded once, making eye contact again. "I'm sorry I kissed you."

Harper's heart froze then picked up double-time. *Well, you wondered if you'd scare him off...*

Seemed like she had her answer, and she realized just how disappointed she was, and that told her how much she had wanted the opposite.

Which was terrifying.

She took a breath to say something—anything—but Sterling lifted a hand for her to wait.

"If I had known, I wouldn't have put you on the spot like that. It probably freaked the hell out of you, given your history." He shifted his weight and frowned as he met her gaze.

"That's not why I told you—" Harper shook her head. "You deserve to know that my issue isn't with you. It's with my past trying to haunt me. And if there's one thing I hate, it's lying. So, I'll be honest, too honest—every time. So, this is my laying it out. Take it, leave it, do what you want, but there it is." She lifted a shoulder.

"That took a lot of balls, Harper."

Harper burst into a laugh. "Wow. Thanks?"

Sterling rubbed the back of his neck. "Seriously. It's a compliment."

"Good to know. Anyway, that's all." She blew out a breath and glanced up at Sterling, feeling all sorts of awkward. How did someone move forward after giving the rundown of a sordid past?

"You hungry?" Sterling asked, tilting his head just enough to make his gaze slightly sideways.

Harper blinked but nodded. "Sure?"

"You don't sound sure." Sterling grinned.

"I'm hungry." Harper rolled her eyes. "But I can't go anywhere. I gotta finish up some paperwork." She remembered the filing and documentation she promised to do for Jasper. Biting her lip, she quickly thought of a way to keep Sterling around and get her work done.

She ignored the concept that she wasn't ready to say goodbye.

That didn't necessarily mean anything.

Right?

"I didn't mean to keep you." Sterling took a tentative step back and winced.

"Actually, I was going to offer to make you lunch here."

"Oh. Well, since I just realized you're my ride back"—he cocked an eyebrow—"that sounds like a plan."

"Didn't realize I'd keep you captive, huh?" Harper teased as she walked out of the barn and into the sunshine. The warm air relaxed her from the tense atmosphere of the barn.

"If I'm willing to stay, I'm hardly held captive!" Sterling called out as he exited the barn.

"You saying I haven't scared you off yet?" Harper asked, turning around and walking backward so that she could see his face.

"Believe it or not, you're not the scariest thing I've seen," he shot back.

"Really?" she replied in a disbelieving tone, joking with him.

"Not even close," he replied. "Don't get me wrong. You can be plenty demanding and a hardass when you want to be, but not that scary."

"Good, as long as we know where we stand." Harper chuckled and turned back around, thankful she hadn't tripped on the stairs that she'd almost run into.

"Smooth!" Sterling called out.

Harper lifted her middle finger and saluted as she swung open the metal screen door.

Sterling's chuckle followed her into the kitchen. As she scanned the small but homey room, she opened the closet door that led to the pantry shelves.

"So, you can ride horses and cook? I'm almost impressed." Sterling's voice preceded his footsteps into the room.

"More than you can say," Harper replied without giving a backward glance. She pulled out two cans of tomato sauce and a loaf of bread.

"I can make some mean French toast," Sterling defended.

"Mad skills." Harper shook her head and tossed the bread on the counter. It felt good to be able to joke, to have the air clear, to not feel like she had to pretend. It was a constant struggle. To try to act normal when your life wasn't, but to feel like you needed to behave that way so that people didn't suspect, but it was a vicious cycle, and it simply moved in circles that never ended.

There was a freedom in not keeping secrets. But it also wasn't information she divulged to just anyone.

But Sterling was safe, instinctively she knew that.

"Do you like grilled cheese?" Harper asked as she moved to open the fridge door.

"Sounds great."

"Good, there wasn't a Plan B." Harper took the cheddar cheese from the sliding compartment of the fridge and set it on the counter. "Can you start slicing this?"

She opened a drawer and pulled out a knife and set it to the side of the cheese then pulled out the cutting board.

"Trusting me with sharp objects? I feel honored." Sterling ambled over and lifted the knife, tilting it slightly to study the edge.

"Meet with your approval?" Harper asked as she opened a nearby drawer and grabbed the handheld can opener.

"It will get the job done. How do you want me to cut this?"

"Like I said. Sliced." Harper gave him a sarcastic grin.

"Yeah, caught that. Are you a thin-slice girl or a thick-slice girl? Trust me, there's a difference." He pointed at her with the knife then set it down on the counter, and slid the cheese from the plastic bag.

"I want to taste the cheese on my sandwich. If you give me some skinny-ass piece of cheese—"

"A thick girl. I like it," Sterling flirted.

Harper glared. "Don't mess with my food."

"Point taken."

Harper bit back a grin as she went to make the tomato soup. She dumped the contents of the two cans into the pot and added several things, tasting in between each addition to make sure it was up to standard.

"You ready?" Sterling called to her, and she set the spoon down.

"About time. Now, answer this very carefully. Because there will be judgment if you answer wrong."

Sterling chuckled, glancing to the floor and shaking his head. "All right, noted. What's the burning question?"

"Mayo or butter on your grilled cheese." Harper arched a brow and cocked a hip, waiting.

Sterling narrowed his eyes, tilted his head and took a step toward her. "Both."

"No." Harper rolled her eyes.

"Yup. Both. Haven't you ever seen *Diners, Drive-ins and Dives?* It's like the secret sauce for grilled cheese."

"It is not."

"Totally is. Google it."

"Google." Harper scoffed.

"Seriously. Try it." He rubbed his hands together. "Let me educate you."

Harper narrowed her gaze, studying him. "If I hate it, I'm blaming you. And you get to deal with my hangry self till I deem it enough punishment and take you back to the ranch."

"Deal. And when you love it, you owe me." Sterling didn't wait for a reply and turned to the loaf of bread on the counter. "Where's a bowl?"

Harper reluctantly pulled one down from the shelf beside her and handed it to Sterling.

"Mayo and soft or melted butter, if you've got it in the cabinet."

"Always."

"Soft butter, soft heart."

"Don't get carried away," Harper shot back.

After she offered him the dish of room-temperature butter, she moved to the fridge and took out the mayo. As she handed it over, she caught his stare, and her face heated with a blush.

It was strangely intimate, cooking in the small kitchen with Sterling. She hadn't anticipated the cozy atmosphere they had created, and it was doing peculiar things to her nerves.

Making them far more sensitive than they needed to be.

It was just the kitchen.

It was just lunch.

It didn't mean anything.

Yet, she was reminded that she kept saying that over and over.

It didn't mean anything.

And she was pretty sure it was just a lie she was telling herself.

Because the truth was, it *was* something.

Odd, how she was so damn determined to be honest with everyone.

But herself.

CHAPTER 9

Sterling couldn't wipe the self-satisfied smile from his face as he handed a stack of notes to Harper.

"Stop grinning like that, or I'm going to make you pay for it next time you have therapy," she told him.

He coughed to cover up his laughter.

"I heard that."

Sterling gave up and chuckled. "Really I'm just replaying your facial expression when you ate your grilled cheese. I'm pretty sure your mouth had an orgasm."

"I already said you won. I gave credit where credit is due. What else do you want from me?" Harper set down the pen and glared at him.

"Nothing, just enjoying my fifteen minutes of victory."

"It's been more than fifteen minutes." She picked up the pen. Her phone buzzed on the table, and she eyed it warily.

Sterling studied the phone. Immediately, his thoughts targeted on the phone call she had received this morning, the one that had led to their later conversation about her past. He locked down his expression, even as his body reacted with a fierce drive to protect her. He'd known enough of her story to assume she'd had a rough go of it, but he hadn't a clue to the severity. As she had unfolded her history, it had taken everything within him to contain his fury toward her ex. It wouldn't help her to see him all bent out of shape and pissed, but it tore at him, ate him alive to think that she'd endured so much, so unnecessarily.

It was a hard transition. In combat you could shoot at the bad guys and rescue the people needing to be saved. In civilian life, the bad guys were just as bad, but you couldn't exactly run after them with your gun.

As much as I want to.

Yet Sterling knew that if he allowed that more violent nature to bleed through his expression, Harper might misinterpret it. And it was more important to protect her than to unleash his aggression, however deserved it might be.

"Hello?" she answered the phone, her body relaxing as she listened.

As the tension left her shoulders, he assumed that it wasn't a call like the one she received this morning, and he found that he calmed as well.

"Sure, what dairy?" She nodded once, her gaze flickering to the table as she listened. "Anything else?"

Sterling listened to see if he could determine who was on the other end. His money was on her brother, Jasper.

"I'll be right there." She ended the call and met his gaze.

Sterling raised his brows, curious.

"Jasper needs extra calcium. Dairy cow has milk fever. Let's go."

He watched as she rose from the wooden chair at the table and stacked the files into a neat pile. "So...cows."

"Yup. Lots of them around here." Harper gave him a sassy little smirk.

"Smartass. So, I'm tagging along?" Sterling asked as he followed her out the front door.

"Unless you want to keep Spartan company." She nodded toward the barn as they walked by. "Hold up." She ran into the barn and came back out with a small box and motioned her chin toward her pickup.

"Trying to pawn me off on your horse?"

"Yup."

"Cows or horses, those are my options. Damn, I miss bullets and guns."

Harper snorted, grinning in disbelief as she opened her pickup door. "Really? You'd rather be shot at?"

"Don't knock it. I loved my job," Sterling remarked as he got into the passenger side of the truck. He covered his feelings as he spoke, but his chest pinched at the honesty of his words. He really did miss it.

Harper started the engine then backed out, heading down the drive, her green gaze shifting to him then back to the road. A tiny furrow in her brow had him anticipating that some sort of question was forthcoming.

He was proven right as she glanced to him again. "What did you love the most? Or do you not want to talk about it?"

Sterling shifted his gaze to the sagebrush dotting the landscape as they pulled onto the main road. "I don't mind talking about it. At least, I don't mind much." He gave her a sidelong glance then turned back to the passing terrain. "I miss having everything cut and dry. I miss knowing that I was

making a difference, and doing it with my own two hands, my two feet."
He shrugged, taking a deep breath. "I miss that I knew my future, and
the certainty it held."

Harper sighed, and he turned to watch her. "I get that. Did you always
want to be a marine?"

Sterling nodded once. "Pretty much. You can ask Laken, but I don't
ever remember a Christmas going by where I didn't ask for some sort of
military toy, and when I got older, I asked for gear."

"So, getting injured..." She let the words linger in the air.

"Sucked balls," Sterling emphasized, earning a slight chuckle from
Harper.

"Sorry, I shouldn't laugh." She bit her lip, and he tore his gaze from
the temptation it presented.

"It's okay, I was trying to lighten things up," he admitted. "But yeah,
it sucked. It still sucks."

"You couldn't go back, even after you healed up?" Harper looked at
his leg then back to his eyes before returning her attention to the road.

Sterling shrugged. "That was one of the first decisions I had to make
even before I left the hospital." He glanced down to his jean-clad legs.
Through the denim they looked the same, but he could feel the definite
difference in their strength, their power. And they sure as hell wouldn't look
the same if he were wearing shorts. "I asked the doctor and the therapist
if I'd regain full strength. And neither of them could give me any positive
news. In my gut, I had already known that, but it about killed me to hear
them say it out loud. And in the field, you gotta run. You gotta move, be
agile, and if I can't do that, then I'm a threat to myself and my team out
there. I can't do that." He met her gaze with a forthright one of his own.

"But, what about other...what do you call it...departments? Couldn't you
have done a different type of job rather than be out in the middle of it all?"

Sterling lifted a shoulder. "Yeah, I could have, but...I just couldn't do
it. It would slowly kill me to see but not be able to participate. You know?
I realize my limits, and that's just something that I didn't think I could
do, at least well. And I'm not going to do something where people's lives
might depend on me when I can only give a half-ass effort. I'm not made
that way."

"So...you resigned," Harper stated. It was common knowledge, so it
didn't surprise him that it wasn't a question.

"Yeah."

"And do you regret that?" she asked.

"Some days." He rubbed his hands down his jeans and turned to glance out the window.

"Some days are better than others," Harper said simply, yet the words had such a deep meaning.

"Some are."

The sound of the engine was the only noise in the cab as she turned off the main highway and down a dusty dirt road. Metal fencing lined the drive as Holstein cows plodded in their pasture, barely casting the truck a glance.

As she pulled up beside Jasper's pickup, she killed the engine. "You coming?"

Harper's brows were arched above her face in a challenging expression, and Sterling couldn't resist. "Lead the way."

She jumped from the cab and started toward the metal barn, and Sterling tucked his hands in his pockets, slightly uneasy at the prospect of Harper's brother questioning just why Sterling was with his sister.

This could be interesting.

"Hey!" She lifted the box in her hands as she approached Jasper and Kessed.

Jasper waved in welcome, then as he caught sight of Sterling, his eyes narrowed into a wary confusion before he smoothed over his expression.

"Hey." Sterling nodded, keeping his hands in his pockets and wishing he'd stayed in the pickup.

"Hi, Sterling. What brings you out here? I told you, cows kinda grow on ya." Kessed winked and shoved Jasper with her shoulder, further shaking him from his study of Sterling.

"Yeah, you never said that, and nope, I'm actually being held captive so..." Sterling teased, thankful for how Kessed had broken the ice.

"He's my bitch for the day." Harper shrugged as she handed over the box to Jasper.

Sterling laughed then turned it into a cough when Harper glared at him. "Sure, sure," he teased.

"Thanks for dropping this off. I swear I put enough in the truck this morning—"

"This was on the shelf beside the door. I think you probably took it out but somehow missed it."

"Yeah, probably. Something..." Jasper turned to Kessed, arching a brow. "...must have distracted me."

"Innocent." Kessed lifted her hands.

"La, la, la." Harper covered her ears. "Don't want to know. And I'm sure that Sterling doesn't either. You two, have fun." She lifted her hands and turned around, heading back toward the pickup and disappearing out the door.

Sterling grinned, feeling a new kinship with Harper. He wasn't exactly comfortable with this line of conversation either. But thankfully, it didn't sting like he would have expected.

Which was both good and bad.

Good, because it meant he was moving on from Kessed.

Bad, because it meant he might be directing his attention elsewhere. And he was pretty sure Harper was the target of his own personal distraction.

"Hey, Sterling." Jasper nodded to him then cast a glance to Kessed. He stepped toward Sterling as he returned his gaze.

Kessed bit her lip, her expression amused as Jasper approached Sterling.

"Yeah?" Sterling focused on Jasper, guessing what was coming.

"Take a little walk with me." Jasper placed his hand on Sterling's back, smacking it once as they fell into step together.

"Busted!" Kessed called out.

Sterling wanted to one-finger salute her but restrained himself. No need to add fuel to the fire.

"What's up?" Sterling asked, waiting for Jasper to speak his mind.

Jasper slowed his steps and then stopped, facing Sterling. His gaze evaluated Sterling. "Quite honestly, I don't know what to think of you, man. You toyed with Kessed's heart for years before you finally pulled your head out of your ass, and I'm damn lucky you waited so long to grow the hell up. Because while you were growing up, I found her, and she's everything to me. *Everything.* And now, I see you with my little sister..." Jasper worked his jaw slightly, his gaze narrowing. "Harper might come off a hardass and strong, but she's not as tough as you think. And I swear that if you lead her on, hurt her, or if you do anything to make her life less than the safe place that we've fought to make it, things will not go well for you. Understand?" Having spoken his mind, he simply waited.

Sterling nodded once. What more could he say? Was he certain he was long-term interested in Harper? Was he at a place in life where he should even think about it? No. Jasper was doing what he should do.

And Sterling hated that he was everything that Jasper had said.

His head had been stuck up his ass for too long.

And he wasn't totally convinced he had remedied the issue.

Didn't Harper deserve more than that?

"Do you have anything to say?" Jasper asked, his stance relaxing slightly.

Sterling tilted his head, regarding his confronter. "You're a good man, Jasper. And I'm...I'm really glad that Kess has you. I'm not going to lie.

It sucked hard when I realized I was too little and too late, but it was for the best."

Jasper nodded once, waiting for Sterling to continue.

"As for Harper, I don't know what to tell you. I'd kick my own ass if I hurt her. She's been through hell. She deserves that safe place to heal. All I can say is that I want that for her too. And I know you're thinking I'm chasing her skirt, but as tempting as it is, I know I'm not ready...and maybe she isn't either."

Sterling's chest constricted as he spoke the words, knowing the truth of them was a letdown. Because if he were honest with himself, he had wanted more from Harper than she was able to give.

And maybe more than he was able to give back.

Jasper reached out and placed a hand on Sterling's shoulder. "Good to hear. I'm assuming that she's opened up a bit about her past?" Jasper removed his hand.

Sterling nodded. "We talked earlier. Turns out we both have shit we're dealing with." He gave a humorless laugh.

Jasper blew out a breath. "Well, I'm glad she's talking to someone. It's easy for her to wrap herself up in her racing, in her thoughts, and just run away."

Sterling shifted his weight, his leg starting to ache as the pain medication began to wear off.

Thankfully, it was still easy enough to ignore.

"Well, good talk." Jasper turned and walked toward the barn, and Sterling followed.

Kessed was waiting, her hands in her pockets as her gaze flickered between Sterling and Jasper. "No blood?"

"No blood," Jasper replied, his tone beleaguered.

"Disappointed?" Sterling teased.

"Eh, no. He could take you." Kessed winked at Jasper as she directed the statement to Sterling.

"We'll call it even." Jasper chuckled, pulling Kessed in and kissing the top of her head. "Let's take care of this cow."

"Sweet nothings in my ear," Kessed teased then turned to Sterling. "See ya."

Sterling waved as he went to Harper waiting in the pickup, her focus on her phone. Sterling was half tempted to smack the window and scare her, but he thought better of it. No reason to freak her out; woman was already frightened enough for one lifetime.

As he opened the passenger door, he smiled.

She narrowed her eyes in response. "What did I miss?"

Sterling shrugged then decided to take a different route. Knowing Harper, she'd just get pissed at her brother for doing his job in protecting her. So rather, he just asked, "Do you think Jasper could take me in a fight?"

Harper blinked, a slow grin working across her face as she started the truck.

"Right now?" she asked, her hair spilling over her shoulder as she turned to back out.

"Yeah." Sterling nodded, thankful she had taken the bait.

"Between the two of us..." she started.

"Yeah?"

"My money's on you. But don't tell Jasper."

Sterling grinned. Even if it was hypothetical, it felt good to have someone bet on him.

Especially when he wasn't sure he would bet on himself.

CHAPTER 10

Harper was just taking the store-bought lasagna out of the oven when she heard Jasper's diesel engine pull up the drive. As he got out, she noted that Kessed wasn't with him—one of the rare occasions when she'd stayed at her apartment.

While she loved Kessed deeply, she was happy to have a little time to spend with just her brother. Ever since her mom ran out on them, she had clung to Jasper and their dad like a life jacket. When their dad died...it only made her bond with Jasper tighter. So, while she was happy for him to have Kessed, she sometimes missed the time with her brother. He was one of the few people that made her feel safe, truly safe.

"Smells amazing." Jasper came through the door, setting his wallet and keys on the table beside the door after he'd shut it behind him.

"I slaved all day," Harper teased as she tossed the cardboard box into the garbage.

Jasper rolled his eyes. "I can see that."

"I'm assuming you're hungry?" Harper proceeded to cut through the thick layers of cheese and noodles.

"Famished. Let me wash my hands, and I'll join you."

Jasper strode to the kitchen sink, and Harper served herself a portion of the lasagna and then dished up a much more generous portion for her brother. "Here." She handed him the plate as he passed by and then picked up her own. When she joined him at the table, he handed her a fork and she smiled her thanks. "Where's Kessed tonight?"

Jasper blew across the food on his fork. "She and Laken are having a girls' night. Plus, she said that you and I needed some time together." Jasper gave her a sidelong glance.

"I love Kessed. She gets me."

"So, she's right? Why do you want your overbearingly protective older brother around?" he teased, but Harper sensed an underlying meaning. Her thoughts flickered back to earlier when she'd been waiting forever in the truck for Sterling to show up. To his credit, Sterling hadn't mentioned anything...but that didn't mean she wasn't suspicious.

She knew her brother too well.

"Overbearing, overprotective...sounds like you're confessing." She tested the waters.

Jasper studied her for a moment before taking a bite. "Maybe."

"Which means yes. Okay, spill. What did you do and how mad am I going to be?" Harper asked, pointing at him with her fork.

"Just had a man-to-man talk with Sterling." Jasper shrugged, clearly trying to downplay whatever had happened.

"Ah, that was a long-winded talk. I waited in the pickup for quite a while. What did you say?" She blew across her food then took a bite. Her stomach rumbled in appreciation.

Jasper twisted his lips slightly. "I found out that you and he have had some pretty honest conversations. That told me what I needed to know."

Harper frowned. That didn't exactly answer her question, but it most certainly did create new ones. "What do you mean by that?"

"It means you feel safe with him. And while I'm not sold on your judgment skills—" He gave her a wary glance as if concerned he had offended her.

"No offense taken." Harper raised her fork slightly.

"It's just that—"

"No, I get it. And I agree. I can, uh...pick 'em. The bad ones. I don't trust my judgment either. But you are right. I don't feel scared around Sterling. I see a lot of the issues I'm dealing with on my own reflected in him, but nothing that makes me frightened. He's more of the protector type."

"Yeah, I got that vibe too. I already have some marks against him in my book."

"Because of Kessed," Harper finished.

"Yeah."

"Rightfully so. But I think he's past that." Harper's mind flashed back to their kiss.

Maybe it's okay for it to actually mean something. She thought back over his words after she'd all but freaked.

They had stuck with her ever since.

"I agree. He seems fine with how things turned out, but...I want you to be careful, too. Okay? Just, I don't know if you like him more than just a buddy but—"

"You did not just call him a *buddy.* Seriously? Like first grade. The buddy system." Harper rolled her eyes.

"You know what I mean," Jasper replied in an exasperated tone.

"I do, but that literally was the world's worst way to say it."

"Fine! I'm not nearly as cool as you."

"You never were," Harper told him, laughing.

Jasper gave her an irritated glare. "Can I finish?"

She waved her fork.

"I don't know where you guys stand, if you are interested in him, but I want you to be careful. Okay? Rant over. Done. Just—"

"Guard my carnal treasure?" Harper barely spoke the words before she broke into a fit of the giggles.

"I will hate that movie forever because of that one line." Jasper closed his eyes, a pained expression on his face.

"I still love that movie; it speaks deep to my soul." Harper sighed then giggled again when Jasper opened his eyes to glare.

"You and Kessed can watch it sometime."

"*Win a Date with Tad Hamilton!* Classic."

"Sure. Right up there with *Gone with the Wind*," Jasper replied sarcastically. "But yes, I was thinking more of your heart. Guard your heart. Done. End of conversation. How about them Seahawks?" He took a drink of water and washed down the lasagna.

"Fine, I'll let you off the hook." She let out an amused chuckle as Jasper gave her a grateful expression and took another bite.

"For now."

He rolled his eyes.

Harper turned back to her plate. She was thankful for her brother's protective nature; it was comforting. But she had the sinking suspicion that its effect on Sterling was more sobering.

She thought back to when they'd left the dairy. Sterling had smiled and engaged in conversation, but something had been off. She hadn't been able to quite pin exactly what it was. When she offered to take him back to the ranch, he'd agreed quickly. Almost too quickly, and as much as she hated it, she was slightly hurt. It was stupid, but that hadn't stopped her from having the feeling. When they'd arrived at the ranch, he'd thanked her, teased her about the mayo and butter sauce, then headed into the house.

With a limp.

Harper rewound the memory in her mind. His pain medication must have been wearing off. Just how much pain did Sterling deal with on a daily basis? The whole concept brought her to a darker place. Her own pain was like a phantom injury that sent a shiver of awareness through her body; pain like that haunted you. It was real. And in the middle of it, you couldn't even imagine what it would be like to live without it.

It was too strong.

Lifting her glass of water, she tried to focus on something else, anything else.

With her, she knew the pain was not only physical, but it also had a deeply rooted association with the mental torture she had experienced. Because of her abuse, it was impossible to separate the two kinds of injury.

She'd gone to therapy for several months after her injury, both the physical kind and the kind that made you dive deep into your heart.

Both sucked.

Both hurt like hell.

But both helped.

And what she'd learned was that it was a fight.

One she'd have to combat every day.

She set the glass down and pushed her plate away, no longer hungry.

"You're too quiet. What's up?"

A slight grin teased the corner of her mouth. "This coming from the man of few words...."

"I'm apparently feeling talkative today." Jasper arched a brow. "You want to talk about something?"

"No," Harper answered, picking up her plate and walking to the kitchen sink.

"Is there a reason?" he asked, prodding gently.

"Because sometimes talking about it doesn't help. It just makes the memory stronger. And right now, I kinda just want to forget," she answered with as much honesty as she could muster.

"I can respect that," her brother replied after a moment.

"Thanks." Harper leaned against the kitchen sink with her back. "I'm going to go and check on Spartan." She pushed from the counter and walked to the door.

"Sometimes I think you love that horse more than you love me!" Jasper called out as she turned the door handle.

Harper paused and glanced over her shoulder. "I don't, but that's only because you bought him for me. You understand." She walked out into the evening light.

"I'll take what I can get!" Jasper called to her just before the door shut.

The night air was crisp and cool. Eastern Washington was technically a desert famous for its temperature inversion. While it was great for growing wine grapes, it was also fantastic as a reprieve from the oppressive Indian summer heat. A few lonely crickets sang as she walked to the barn, and a coyote howled in the distance. It was a haunting and beautiful sound.

As she slid the barn door open, she flicked on the overhead lights. Spartan nickered softly, nodding his head as he watched her approach from his stall.

"Hey, handsome," she murmured, placing her head against his, inhaling his equine scent.

They had run through the barrels that afternoon after she'd dropped off Sterling. Her head hadn't been in the game, and she had given up timing their circuit after the first three rounds and had just ridden for pleasure rather than practice. It had been exhilarating and freeing. Though she knew they both needed the practice, she also just needed to breathe.

Spartan sighed gently, leaning into her just enough to push her off balance. She stepped back and gave him a mock glare. "How about a short little ride?"

Spartan blew out a low nicker and stomped his foot.

Harper opened the stall and stepped inside. She unhooked the bit-less bridle from the nail beside the horse's hay manger, slipped it over his head, and latched it below his cheek.

She opened the gate and led him out, stopping beside one of the open stalls. She stepped on top of a bale of hay, and hoisted herself onto Spartan's bare back. After a soft pat to his neck, she clicked her tongue and led them out into the twilight.

The path around the hill was well worn from her constant use of it, and she opted to meander around their property rather than just circle the arena. Spartan's head bobbed as he wound among the sagebrush and followed the trail that circled the old homestead. The crickets silenced as they passed by. Harper kept her eyes open for wandering rattlers, but chances were they wouldn't see any this late in the evening. Even if they did, they were old enough to have rattles and sound a warning.

It was the spring when the snakes were a problem. Baby rattlers didn't have rattles on their tails; they couldn't warn, and they were mean as hell and didn't let go when they bit.

Spartan heaved a sigh as they wound around a basalt boulder, and Harper started to relax further. Her mind drifted back to when she was younger. Her parents had always had horses. And she had always thought friends with four legs were better than those with two. After all, they couldn't make fun of you, avoid you, or push you around—well, not in the same way. So many times, while Jasper would be away with his friends, Harper would be off riding in the sagebrush, bareback, leaning back all the way and watching the sparse clouds dance across the sky while the horse meandered and grazed.

It had been a beautiful childhood.

And all too short.

She had never been close with her mom, and in hindsight she wondered if maybe that was because she somehow knew that her mom had never been in it for the long haul.

Maybe she'd been protecting herself even when she was little.

But that didn't mean it hadn't destroyed part of her heart when she woke up one morning with her mother no longer at home.

Gone.

She still didn't understand it.

As someone who'd lost a child, even before it had been born, she couldn't imagine not loving that little life....

Parents' love should always be unconditional.

Love in general should be....

If there are conditions on it, doesn't that mean it isn't actually love?

She twisted her lips as she pondered the deep things in her soul.

Her father had done his best, but he had been heartbroken too, dealing with his own pain and rejection.

And probably some guilt.

Soon, Harper had lost him too.

Which was probably why she'd latched on to Brock so fiercely.

Letting go of him was so terrifying.

It might hurt if he gets angry, but at least I'm not alone.

She remembered thinking those thoughts, and how twisted and sick they were.

But not any less true.

The past was in the past, and like her therapist had said, "It happened, but it isn't where you are now. Grow where you are."

And she was determined to do that.

But days like today, when her past seemed so close to the surface, made it very hard.

Like treading water in quicksand, but it was one breath at a time.

Breathe.

Just. Breathe.

Spartan nickered, jolting her from her thoughts, and she glanced around to see what he'd noticed. "Whoa, boy." She pulled up on the reins and narrowed her eyes.

She didn't see anything...but that didn't mean something wasn't out there. Mountain lions, coyotes, deer—it could be anything. Turning Spartan around, she headed back home. It was still light enough that she felt comfortable encouraging her mount into a lope. His black mane flowed over her hands as she leaned forward, and her grip on the woven reins relaxed. A smile stretched across her face as she felt the wind tease her hair.

Freedom.

She slowed Spartan to a trot, then a walk as they approached the barn. The sunlight was fading over the Manastash Ridge in streaks of pale orange. She slid from the horse and led him back into the barn. Her jeans were itchy from his coarse hair, but it wasn't anything the washer wouldn't take care of. After she put Spartan back in his stall, she took off his bridle and hung it back on the nail. She walked to the tack room and filled a small bucket with molasses oats and shook it around a little, grinning when his ears perked up at the sound.

"You like that, don't you?" she said, walking toward him.

He stretched his neck out, trying to get closer to the bucket.

"Greedy," she scolded jokingly.

She took some out of the bucket with her hand and offered it to Spartan. He lipped it up hungrily and then sniffed her hand for more.

"Here you go." Harper dumped the remaining contents into the hay manger and hung the bucket back up. "Night, old man," she called out as she switched off the main lights.

She closed the barn door and sighed, soaking up the peaceful evening air.

Night was falling, and she was thankful.

She was more than ready for this day to be finished.

Tomorrow would have its own issues. But it was a beautiful thing to have a fresh start.

And each day she was given that gift.

Something new.

Hope.

Because each day really was better than the last.

And that was what healing was all about.

CHAPTER 11

Sterling couldn't sleep.

The damn leg was killing him, and it was crazy, but when the pain was constant, he could almost get his mind around it.

But when it was gone and then came back when the medication wore off, it drove him insane.

He couldn't think around it.

He couldn't think beyond it.

It was just there, gnawing at him, burning on the edges of his mind.

Never.

Stopping.

Ever.

He threw the sheets over and stood up, his leg protesting at the movement, and he bit back a low curse.

After limping to the bathroom, he opened the medicine cabinet and took out his prescription and swallowed two pills, closing his eyes and reminding himself that the pain would be gone.

Soon.

He leaned down and turned on the faucet, taking a drink and wiping his mouth. Tomorrow was going to be a long day, and he really needed to get some freaking rest.

But his mind was as restless as his body.

Tomorrow, Laken would be taking him to Seattle to see the therapy specialist. It was just a benchmark appointment, but that didn't stop him from having concerns.

What if he wasn't healing as fast as he should?

What if his leg wasn't progressing in muscle development?

What if he never would get away from the pain?

He leaned over the sink, bracing himself with his arms as he took a deep breath.

No. He would. His body would heal; this wasn't permanent.

But it sure as hell felt like it was.

He pushed from the sink and hobbled back to bed, hissing through his teeth when he almost tripped on a discarded shoe.

Lying back on the cool sheet, he closed his eyes—but his mind wasn't willing to relax.

He thought back over the day, replaying certain aspects, his emotions in high gear as he remembered Harper's words.

Her story.

Her pain.

And he'd be lying to himself if he didn't consider that maybe Jasper was onto something.

That maybe he was a real threat to Harper's heart.

Was he willing to risk that?

To hurt her?

He wasn't. At all. And that really sucked.

Because with her, it was different.

Better.

And he didn't want to give that up.

But at what cost?

He'd kissed her, implied that he wanted more.

And he'd had no right. Because he couldn't offer her what she needed.

Stability.

He was off balance in the worst way, and not just because of his damn leg.

Sterling needed to get his shit together before he even thought about another person. He sighed heavily. Why did everything always look so miserable at night? He stared at the ceiling through the darkness of his room, focusing on his breathing, forcing a calm, just like he'd taught himself when he was in a war zone. Mortars and guns sounding in the distance, yet you had to catch some sleep when possible.

He gave a humorless laugh. Certainly, if he could sleep through *that*, he could get through this.

Yet sometimes, the thoughts inside were louder than bombs exploding outside.

And he wondered if maybe he had traded one battlefield for another.

One war for another.

He wasn't dodging bullets.

But he was fighting a real enemy.

And it scared him shitless to think that the person he was fighting was himself.

Because how did you win?

Was it even possible?

He'd expected to experience some PTSD, but what he hadn't expected was for it to take the form of learning how to deal with everyday life.

It was a special kind of messed up that he could deal with life and death, but couldn't deal with the normal.

Sighing, he closed his eyes and focused on something good, anything good.

And the first thing that came to mind was Harper.

Her smile, her sassy-ass streak that both frustrated him and made him so damn aroused that sometimes he couldn't think straight around her.

Her bravery, and the fact that she just wouldn't give up.

On herself.

Or him.

He wouldn't see her for a few days, and the thought struck a chord. He'd kind of grown used to seeing her regularly. But maybe this was good, healthy even.

Distance.

Then maybe he wouldn't do anything stupid.

Like kiss her again.

And have the kiss only be the beginning.

Damn, now he was *aroused* and sleepless.

Fan-freaking-tastic.

He groaned as he rolled over in bed, trying to focus his thoughts away from Harper.

Yet the more he tried to *not* think of her, the more insistent his body became.

Her lips.

The way her green eyes squinted when she smiled.

That sexy round ass that always stole all his attention.

He tossed the covers off once more and stalked to the bathroom.

A cold shower wasn't exactly relaxing, but it would get his mind off, well, everything.

He sucked in a breath when the cold water hit him and realized that his leg had stopped throbbing.

But he suspected he'd simply traded one sleepless reason for another.

One he couldn't exactly medicate away.

Because the issue wasn't with his leg. It was with his heart.

Hours later, Sterling blinked as his alarm clock sounded. His eyes were grainy from the lack of sleep, but at least he'd finally gotten a little bit of shuteye after his cold shower.

It wasn't enough, but it was better than nothing.

He and Laken had to be gone by eight a.m. if they were to make it to Harbor View Medical Center before one. Traffic was always questionable in Seattle, and you never wanted to cut it close.

Damn, he hated the big city.

"You awake?" Laken knocked on his door, speaking from the other side. "Yup."

"Good. Coffee's on." He heard her walk away and down the hall.

Coffee, and lots of it, would be necessary today. His leg only protested slightly as he got up from bed. The pain medication still working, he was thankful for how it kept the edge off.

Sterling decided to forego a shower since he had taken a late one in the middle of the night. He threw on a gray T-shirt and carefully slid on some dark denim jeans.

As he went down the hall, the aroma of eggs and bacon greeted him.

He entered the kitchen with a smirk. "Cyler cooking again?"

His sister glared from her seat at the kitchen table. "Do you *want* me to cook breakfast?" She smiled sweetly. "I'll do it...." She spoke the words as a threat.

And a threat they were.

"No, no I'm good." Sterling quickly backpedaled. He loved his sister, and she was talented at many things.

Cooking was *not* one of those things.

Cyler chuckled from where he stood next to the stove. "Wise choice, my man."

Sterling nodded, accepting a plate from him piled with several rashers of bacon and a few fried eggs. "You coming with, Cyler?" Sterling asked as he sat down across from his sister.

"Nope. I gotta head to Yakima to check on a few housing developments. We're in the excavating phase, and I want to confirm a few details with the city."

Cyler was the contractor of CC Homes in Yakima. He usually spent four days a week traveling back and forth, but Fridays were always a toss-up.

"So, I'm just stuck with you," Sterling teased his sister.

"Yup. Rather, I'm just stuck with you. And you better be nice. I'm driving." She pointed her fork at him.

"I'll be on my best behavior."

Laken snorted. "Sure."

"So, since I did breakfast, you're in charge of dishes." Cyler rubbed his hands together as he addressed Sterling.

"Happily. Anything so that I don't have to eat—"

"Watch yourself," Laken interrupted.

"Happy to, man." Sterling smirked as he answered Cyler.

"That's what I thought," Laken muttered under her breath.

"Yeah, well, you two have fun. I'll see you when you get home tonight." Cyler walked over to Laken and kissed her head, lingering against her hair and then kissing her again.

Laken's eyes closed, and a small smile crept across her lips. "Now kiss me for real," she remarked as he pulled away.

Cyler chuckled and leaned down, covering her lips with his.

Sterling purposefully studied his eggs, waiting for the two lovebirds to finish. "Bedroom activities stay in the bedroom," he remarked as he studiously avoided looking at them.

"That's what you think," Cyler taunted as he pulled away from Laken.

"And we're done. Remember, dude. She's my sister. Let's not cross those lines. Don't make it weird. For the love of all that's holy, don't make it weird," Sterling pleaded, chuckling.

"Not making it weird." Cyler arched his eyebrow at Laken and left the kitchen.

"Finish up. We gotta go." Laken lifted her coffee mug and took a sip.

"Demanding much? Make yourself useful and get me some of that." Sterling gestured to her coffee mug.

"There's something missing from that question...." Laken relaxed purposefully in the chair, implying she wasn't about to move.

Sterling sighed. "Please?" he asked, giving her the puppy-dog eyes.

"Eh, sure." Laken grinned and went to pour him a mug.

"Thank you," Sterling was quick to say.

"Ah, look who is learning," Laken said to him.

Sterling finished his breakfast, and it didn't take long for him to stack all the dishes into the dishwasher and then meet Laken at the front door.

"Traffic looks pretty good so far. At least they aren't blasting on Snoqualmie. Gah, that was miserable," Laken said as she took her gaze from her smart phone and started toward her Honda.

"Yeah, but they need to make that pass wider. Damn thing has too much traffic, and it's not enough lanes."

"Yeah, but dynamiting through granite isn't exactly easy and takes forever! They're still not done. It's been what, three years?" Laken complained as they got into the car.

"Not sure. I haven't been around for most of it," Sterling answered. As he moved to get into the car, he had to make a few quick adjustments for the lower situation of the vehicle. It was much easier getting into Harper's or Cyler's trucks than this little Honda, and Sterling almost wished he'd suggested taking Cyler's vehicle.

But he made it in and slid the seat as far back as possible, stretching out his legs.

"You make this car seem so small." Laken glanced at him. "You and your super-long legs. Seriously, why didn't I get those genetics?"

Sterling grinned. "I'm sure Cyler thinks your short little legs are cute."

Laken grinned mischievously. "He sure as hell does. Especially when they're wrapped—"

"Okay! Done now, I totally walked into that one," Sterling groused.

Laken laughed as they drove away from the ranch house. "Yeah, you did."

They continued in silence for a few miles, Sterling's attention drawn to the passing landscape and the changing colors of the trees.

"So, this might be a random question, but it's been on my mind since Kessed and I had a girls' night and went over wedding stuff." Laken cast a furtive glance at Sterling, waiting for him to respond.

Sterling nodded once. "Okay, what's up?"

"So...are you okay with going to the wedding?" Laken asked in a rush. "It's just coming up here soon, and Kessed didn't want to put you in a weird position by inviting or not inviting you...so I said I'd ask."

"As usual, she has you doing her dirty work," Sterling pestered, watching as his sister's tense expression started to relax.

"Yeah well...some things never change."

"Damn straight," Sterling retorted. "And of course I want to be there. A week or so ago, I might not have been as okay as I am now, but..." He shrugged. "...seeing her and Jasper together, it makes sense. I get that. I honestly wish them the best." His lips twitched as he had an errant thought.

"What are you thinking?" Laken narrowed her eyes at him then turned her attention back to the road as they merged onto the freeway toward Seattle.

Sterling shook his head. "It's just that I was thinking...well, Kessed doesn't have a big brother to put the fear of God into Jasper like I did with Cyler. It might be awkward, but I kinda want to do the same thing for her. Have that man-to-man talk with Jasper, threaten him a bit. You know?" Sterling chuckled. "After all, turnabout's fair play." He shook his head, amused.

That would certainly turn the tables. Not that Jasper had been out of line to talk to Sterling yesterday. No. He was doing exactly what he should do as a protective older brother. He was looking out for Harper.

But with Kessed, all she had were her aging grandparents in Seattle. It would be a fun twist of things for Sterling to step up and give Jasper the same talk.

"You wouldn't," Laken said, but her lips twitched in amusement.

"Maybe, maybe not. We'll see."

Laken regarded him. "What do you mean when you said turnabout's fair play? Did Jasper talk with you?"

Sterling studied his sister.

Her lips weren't relaxed, and her cheeks were tense.

"You know exactly what I'm talking about. Kessed can't keep a secret to save her life, and you guys talk about everything. What do you know, Laken?"

Laken gave him a sheepish expression. "Not much, just that Jasper suspected that maybe you and Harper..." She let the words linger with implication.

"Me and Harper, what?" Sterling wasn't giving anything away.

Laken glanced from him to the road, her lips twisting. "You know... might be interested in more than friendship."

"Okay, and?"

"And..." She glared at him. "...and you're the worst person in the world to talk to regarding this stuff! Gah! Tell me already! It's killing me! Do you like her?"

"I've never understood that expression." Sterling rolled his eyes.

"You know what I mean!" Laken smacked his leg.

"Hey, no need to resort to abuse."

"Deal. Now..." She glanced to him, imploring him with her eyes.

Sterling sobered. "Maybe."

"Way to commit." Laken sighed. "That's all you're going to give me? 'Maybe.'" She mimicked his lower tone on the last part.

"It's complicated."

"No. It's simple," Laken argued.

"For you maybe, but—"

"Shhh. Nope. You get to just listen for a second." His sister lifted a finger and waited for Sterling.

Sterling motioned with his hand for her to continue.

"Pay attention." She speared him with a glance. "Love is simple. People are complicated. Okay? It's not love. It's never love. It's us. We are the ones that make it difficult."

Sterling nodded once. "I get that. It makes sense, but that doesn't make anything easier."

"Nope. And if you listened, I never once said it was easy. I said it was simple."

He tilted his head, thinking about what she had said.

Laken continued. "Easy and simple are not the same thing. Sometimes the simplest things are the most difficult for us to get our heads around." She shook her head. "But that's part of the beauty of it. So, all this to say, if you like Harper, don't let fear get in the way of going for something good. Love is simple, it's worth it, and you have a chance at finding it, why in the hell would you not take it?"

Sterling considered her point. Why wouldn't he take it? He'd be crazy not to jump at the chance, yet what if it didn't work?

What if he got hurt, or worse, hurt her?

"You're overthinking it. Don't," Laken asserted.

Sterling studied his sister. "You always were a smart one."

"I know. You got the legs. I got the brains." Laken glanced to his stretched-out legs and grinned, turning her eyes back to the road.

"Maybe I'll talk with Harper when we get back," he said, mostly to himself.

"Communication is pretty paramount," Laken agreed. "Seriously. Don't leave the poor girl guessing. We hate that." She gave a sharp glare.

"I thought girls like the whole mysterious-man thing."

"You think wrong. We like a little mystery, not obscurity. Be direct. If you like her, tell her. Be up front. Tell her she's worth the risk and remind her to guard her own heart too." She grinned. "Seriously though, this is gold. What I'm telling you here is gold. You should take notes." She gave him a pointed stare then turned back to the road.

"Mental notes."

"Sure, sure."

"So be direct, straightforward, and go for it."

"Basically, yes."

Sterling frowned. "But, how much of Harper's history do you know?"

Laken cast him a wary glance. "Enough."

"Me too, and you still think that this is solid advice?" Sterling asked.

His sister bit her lip. She turned on her blinker and passed a semitruck.

"That's a valid question, and yes, I do. Because you're being up front with her. Harper needs honesty. She needs to know where you stand." Laken's expression grew pensive. "You...you've always had this protector alpha thing going for you, and I have the feeling that you make her feel safe." She frowned slightly. "Does that make sense? And if I were to guess, I'd think that safe is exactly what Harper needs, craves even. And honestly, Sterling, you need someone to protect." She speared him with a glance that saw right through him.

"What?" he asked, startled by her insight.

Laken sighed thoughtfully as she studied the road ahead. "You've always been that guy, the one who stands up for the underdog on the playground, the one who looks out for everyone, the one who was willing to risk his life to make the world a better place. And since you don't have that, you're kinda aimless. Now"—she flickered her gaze to him, as if making sure she had his full attention—"that's not to say you need to use Harper's needing you as a crutch or a way to fill some misdirected need you have since you're not in the Marine Corps. What I *am* saying is that what she needs and who you are is a compatible match that, when in a healthy relationship, meets both your requirements in a way that could be beautiful. But you should make sure you're not looking for a crutch. She deserves more than that, and so do you. Am I making sense?"

Sterling nodded, slowly sifting over her words, evaluating himself. "Yeah, I agree. And I see that. But how"—his brows pinched—"how do you know I'm ready? That I won't screw it up—"

"You don't, but this is the best way to gauge things. Are you listening?"

Sterling nodded.

"When you stop thinking of her, and you're thinking of you, then that's when it's wrong. Love is always putting the other person first. If you don't do that, then you're screwing up."

Sterling nodded.

"Cyler and I, it's not perfect because we are not perfect. But every day, every time, I'm always thinking of him first. It's a habit as much as it's a choice. But he does the same for me, and pretty soon, it's a way of life. You can't go wrong when you love each other that way." Laken hitched a shoulder.

Sterling turned his gaze to the densely wooded Cascade Forest as they passed by Cle Elum. "Thanks." He turned to Laken.

"Anytime."

The rest of the trip passed quickly enough, with the exception of the Bellevue bypass—which was always a nightmare as far as traffic was concerned. Laken dropped Sterling off at the front of the therapy wing of Harbor View and went to park the car in the large concrete parking garage.

The pain medication was wearing off, just as he'd anticipated, but that didn't mean it wasn't a good thing. He wanted to have his body register the real pain during therapy so he could give the doctor an honest account.

He checked in at the front desk, and before Laken made it to the waiting room, the nurse called him back.

The cream-colored halls and the scent of disinfectant added to the sterile feel of the therapy wing. The nurse led him to a patient room and directed him to sit. The older Asian woman took his vitals and then left him alone in the room, promising the therapist would soon be in.

Sterling pulled out his phone and scanned through his email account. Seeing nothing of interest, he searched for the solitaire app.

The door clicked open, and he glanced up and saw Laken. "Hey, what took you so long?" he teased.

"Concrete jungle has a whole new meaning. Seriously, it's like a rat maze, and I couldn't find a parking spot." She rolled her eyes and took a seat in one of the red chairs beside the doctor's swivel stool.

The door opened again, and Sterling gave a tight smile to his therapist, Dr. Hanson.

"Hey there, Captain Garlington. How are you?" The white-coated man held out his hand, and Sterling shook it.

"Fine," Sterling answered simply.

"Nurse Myer." The doctor extended the same greeting to Laken.

"Doctor." Laken shook his hand.

"Well, Sterling, let's get started."

Over an hour later, Sterling was wiping the sweat from his forehead, his leg screaming at him in pain as he finished the last set of tests to benchmark his progress.

"Good, good. Go ahead and sit down." Dr. Hanson motioned to the bench in the therapy room they were in.

Laken was standing beside the doctor as they spoke in lower tones.

"Guys, please?" Sterling gave his sister an irritated glare.

"Sorry, just asking a few questions," Laken admitted.

"Your sister has some great insights. It's an asset that she's there to assist you," Dr. Hanson started. "From what I can see, your leg is progressing exactly as predicted, and I see no reason for you to not make a marked improvement over the next month. I'm signing off that you're safe to operate a vehicle as well. I agree that the horse therapy is helping with your agility and coordination, so continue that and..." He shrugged. "...I'll see you two in a month. Do you have any other questions?"

A smile tipped his lips at the news that he'd be able to drive. Sterling paused. He had one question, but it wasn't one he wanted to ask. It felt wrong; rather, it had a certain amount of shame attached to it. But he also needed to know. "I've been taking my pain medication, so is that something I need to refill or that I should start to wean myself from?"

Dr. Hanson took a deep breath, crossing his arms as he thought. He glanced at his notes. "I don't like prescribing refills unless it's absolutely necessary. You're progressing well, and I don't want you to become dependent on the medication, so at this point, no." He studied Sterling, as if trying to deduce his reaction.

"Sounds good." Sterling nodded, both terrified and relieved all at once. Terrified, because of the pain; relieved, because he didn't want to have the temptation of more medication available.

He didn't know what was the right course of action, so thankfully, the doctor had taken away the options.

He'd best start to learn to deal with the pain.

His leg throbbed in protest.

"Did you happen to bring your medication with you?" Dr. Hanson asked.

Laken studied Sterling.

"No, I took it last night but didn't take it this morning. I wanted to be aware of my body's pain levels during our appointment today."

"Good. I'll give you a small dose to take before you leave. Your leg has been through a lot, and I'm sure it is protesting." He gave a small smile and then nodded to Laken. "I'll have the nurse bring it into the patient room when she gives you the checkout form." He extended his hand to Laken, shook it, then turned back to Sterling. "Keep up the good work."

Sterling shook his hand and watched him signal back to the patient room. "Thanks."

The doctor gave a quick wave and disappeared down the hall.

Laken sat in the same seat as before, and Sterling took the one beside her.

As promised, the nurse came in with two small pills and a Dixie cup of water, along with the checkout form.

Soon they were on their way.

"Was that as bad as it looked?" Laken asked as they accelerated onto the freeway away from the skyscrapers of Seattle and back toward the sagebrush hills of Ellensburg.

Sterling sighed. "Yeah." He hated admitting it.

"I'm sorry," she answered softly.

"It's okay. I'm doing better, according to the doctor."

"Yeah, you really are, Sterling. Are..." She paused. "...are you being responsible with your pain meds?"

She speared him with a direct gaze.

"Yeah, I am," he answered, but there was a lingering feeling of uneasiness that settled over him.

"Good. Hey, do me a favor?" Laken asked.

Sterling waited, wary.

"Call Cyler. I think we all need pizza tonight," she added with a warm smile.

Sterling relaxed.

Sometimes the best thing after a hard day was good people.

Good beer.

And good pizza.

CHAPTER 12

Harper woke up early Saturday morning, needing to get a move on. The barrel race in Naches started that afternoon, and she wanted to get there early so that she and Spartan could have a moment to relax. As with most barrel races, the more experienced riders went first, then the lower divisions as the night progressed. So hopefully, it wouldn't be a late night, and she could duck out of there soon after she raced. All she wanted was a quiet evening of Netflix and a beer.

Life might be boring but at least it was predictable and secure.

She started the coffeepot and headed outside. Last night, she and Jasper had hooked up the trailer to her pickup, so all she needed to do was double-check her tack and load up Spartan once she was ready.

As she went into the barn, Spartan nickered, pawing the ground. He had spotted the trailer and was itching to go. He loved to race almost as much as she did.

The wind in her face, the speed, the way she had control...

It spoke deep to her soul.

She gave her horse a quick pat on his neck and headed back to the house, Spartan's impatient whinny following her.

A smile teased her lips as she heard him whinny again. The screen door slammed shut, and she winced, hoping she hadn't awakened Jasper or Kessed.

When she didn't hear any grumblings from their room, she headed to the coffeepot and pulled down a travel mug. She filled it to the brim and opened the fridge door, grabbing the sack lunch she'd made the night before. As she passed the pantry, she balanced the mug and sack lunch in one hand, and grabbed a granola bar for breakfast. This time, she was much more careful to let the screen door shut slowly and made her way to the pickup. The sun was well over the horizon, but it wasn't past eight a.m. Naches wasn't too far away, but registration started early, and the racing started at noon. So, she tucked her food and coffee into the truck and tossed her keys onto the driver's seat. She ran back to the house and quietly ducked inside to grab her purse then closed the door and screen door. After tossing her purse in the truck, she headed to the barn. Spartan nickered a greeting and bobbed his head impatiently, ready to go.

"All right, all right," Harper groused good-naturedly. "Let's get going."

She led the horse out of the stall and toward the trailer. It was an old, faded white one-horse trailer, but it did the job. Spartan waited while she swung the trailer gate open. As she led him forward, he took a funny little step then led with his right hoof into the trailer. Like most horses, Spartan had a foot he liked to lead with. The quick shuffle-step assured that he could do just that.

Harper tied off his halter to the trailer's hook at the end and patted along his body as she stepped down. She made sure everything was set up correctly then swung the gate closed, double-checking it was secure.

"You ready?" she called to Spartan.

He met her gaze through the bars of the trailer.

"Good. You didn't really have a choice," she told him and headed to her pickup. The motor started right up, and she slowly eased out of the drive. Her truck's engine roared with a little more emphasis with the added weight of the trailer, but that was to be expected. Spartan wasn't a small horse.

She turned on the radio and sipped her coffee as she took the freeway toward Yakima. The fall air was crisp and clean, energizing her as the canyon was bathed in the sun's rich glow. Fall was probably her favorite time of year.

As usual, she kept an eye on the trailer behind her. About an hour later, she took the cutoff toward White Pass and away from Yakima to the Featherland Ranch where the Fall Frenzy was held. She noted the other trucks with horse trailers that were heading the same direction, all probably competing. Her blood pumped with excitement at the anticipation of the race.

As she pulled into the Featherland Ranch about a half hour later, she was grinning with full excitement, impatient to get racing. Slowly, she took the gravel road to the arena and parked in the pasture set aside for the competitors and their trailers. After killing the engine, she stepped into the freshly mowed grass and inhaled deeply. The scent of horses, grass, and dirt sang to her, and she walked back to check on Spartan. He whinnied as soon as he saw her, and pawed the trailer floor and making a racket.

"Knock it off," Harper scolded kindly. "I'll be right back. I gotta make sure I'm all set and registered."

She blew a kiss to her horse and headed toward the barn. A long line of people were checking in, and she recognized several faces. The Frenzy was a fun event, and usually pretty family friendly. They encouraged kids to compete and even had a potluck on Sunday night after the last race. Harper had never stayed for it but had heard it was a fun time.

A few other people arrived and filed into line behind her, some of them familiar, one in particular. Harper steeled herself with a deep breath. Cassie Markston was one hell of a barrel racer.

And she damn well knew it.

Cassie had the current time to beat in their division this year, and that wouldn't have been so bad, if she hadn't crowed about it incessantly. It didn't help that Cassie also had a tendency to ask about Jasper.

Every. Freaking. Race.

And every time, Harper was more than honest about his almost-married status.

It pissed her off.

Harper tamped down her more aggressive nature and focused on the line ahead, hoping maybe Cassie wouldn't notice her.

Her luck lasted long enough for her to check in and get a race time, but she knew it had ended when she turned to head back to the truck and Cassie's big brown eyes zeroed in.

"Hey, Harp." Cassie gave a small wave, her gaze immediately flickering around Harper as if searching for someone else.

I wonder who? Harper groaned inwardly. She was thrilled Jasper wasn't planning on attending. With his and Kessed's wedding coming up in two weeks, they had plenty to do and had asked if she'd be okay with them sitting this race out.

"Hi, Cassie." Harper forced a kind smile, not halting her pace as she moved toward the pickup.

"Wait, is your brother going to be here?" Cassie asked, predictably.

Harper glanced behind her and didn't stop. "Nope, wedding's coming up. He's busy with his almost-wife. Bye!" She hurried on, knowing she was simply dodging the bullet temporarily.

She heaved a sigh of relief when the girl didn't follow her. She headed to the pickup and soon was tying off Spartan to the trailer while she got him all saddled. She loved to deck out her gear for races. The flashy silver and turquoise detail work on her saddle always added that extra splash of sparkle that she loved so much. She wore her blinged-out jeans and larger belt buckle, as cliché as it was. Her boots had turquoise stitching that matched the embellishments on her saddle and also on Spartan's bridle. The bright color stood out perfectly against his dark coat, making it flash when they raced.

Soon she was applying the finishing touches and glanced at her phone.

She had one hour before the racing started. She'd be one of the first to compete, so she needed to warm Spartan up before they were actually timed. She unhooked the lead rope and grabbed the reins. After grasping the saddle horn, she slung herself onto Spartan's back, murmuring softly to him as she led him away from the trailer.

Pickups with trailers made a steady stream into the pasture as people continued to arrive, and Harper paused as she waited to cross over toward the arena. Several others were heading the same direction, and she nodded a greeting. The arena gate was wide open, and Spartan filed in, his dark ears perked up, alert. He pawed the ground restlessly when she pulled back on the reins, eager to get around the barrels.

"You'll get going soon enough. Wait for a second," Harper whispered softly as she petted his neck. But she understood his anticipation. Her heart pounded an excited rhythm as she took in the layout of the arena. It was the usual setup, with the barrels rolled away to give more room for the riders to warm up their horses, but soon those barrels would be rolled back out, and the timing would begin. Each second counting. Each turn making or breaking your chances.

Some people jumped out of airplanes.

Harper rode like the devil chased her heels.

And loved every moment.

When she finished taking in the arena, she urged Spartan into a walk around the perimeter. On the second pass, she warmed him up into a trot, her grin widening as she relaxed into the familiar rhythm. The fall air blew across her face, cooling her in contrast to the intensity of the Indian summer sun. Others joined in around the arena, and Harper urged Spartan into a lope, keeping him from going too fast, yet warming up his muscles so that he'd be ready to go when their number was called.

Shit.

Harper glanced down and realized she hadn't put on the number given to her from registration. Sighing, she pulled up the horse, and he impatiently slowed down, tossing his head.

"Easy," Harper scolded gently.

Spartan settled but chewed his bit in a frustrated manner as she turned him toward the arena exit. Heading toward the trailer, she caught sight of a familiar truck.

Her brows pinched as the vehicle pulled into the pasture. The familiar electric blue wasn't an uncommon color for a Ford, but it wasn't common either. She almost followed it but turned toward her trailer instead, her priority being to find her number and get ready to race. Once she reached her trailer, she slid off the saddle and picked up the packet from the passenger side of her pickup. Sure enough, the number was safety pinned in the middle. The black numbers stood out against the white cardstock as she pinned it to her shirt just over her tummy and slammed the door closed.

"Okay, we're officially ready now." She arched a brow as she walked to Spartan and caressed his nose.

He exhaled his warm breath across her hand.

"Let's try this again." Harper sighed then mounted back on the saddle. Turning the horse back toward the arena, her gaze focused on a petite blonde and a tall, broad man beside her. As they crossed in front of another approaching pickup and headed toward the arena, she could have sworn it was Laken and Sterling.

But why would they come to her race?

She hadn't invited them.

Not that she didn't want them there; it had just never crossed her mind.

Her heart picked up speed as she guided Spartan back toward the arena. Each time she tried to get a clear view, something or someone would block her line of sight.

When she crossed the dirt road and had a clear path to the arena gate, she scanned the crowd. It was mostly people waiting to race, but a few spectators were scattered throughout in lawn chairs and leaning against the iron fence. She scanned through the people and a grin spread across her face when she recognized Laken.

And Sterling.

Spartan sidestepped when she tugged his head away from the arena gate, but he settled down and followed her direction, carefully moving past several others waiting near the fence.

"Hey!" Harper called out, flickering her gaze between Sterling and Laken, trying to keep the focus equal when she was tempted to keep her eyes on Sterling.

He was wearing a blue flannel button-down shirt, his skin a golden tan and his gray eyes hidden behind aviator sunglasses.

"Hi!" Laken waved enthusiastically. "There you are! We were looking for you!" She jumped from her place on the fence and strode toward Harper.

"I wasn't expecting anyone to be here! This is a nice surprise." Harper grinned in appreciation.

"Well, someone wanted to test his newfound freedom." Laken arched a brow then glanced over her shoulder to where Sterling was following.

His lips spread into a wide grin as he reached into his pocket and then dangled a set of keys.

"Ah, so you're saying the roads are no longer a safe place." Harper winked.

"With you driving, they never were to begin with," he shot back, taking off his sunglasses and giving her an amused grin.

"Eh, that's your opinion."

Laken shook her head. "So, you're racing soon? Kessed said you're usually one of the first, so we had to hurry if we wanted to see you."

"Yeah, I usually am."

Spartan stomped impatiently.

"Easy," Harper murmured softly. "I thought you were doing wedding stuff with Kessed today."

Harper flickered a glance to Sterling, quickly gauging his reaction. It was almost habit, but she was relieved to see that his expression hadn't been affected by her question.

Maybe he was really over it. Her heart did a little leap at the prospect.

She glanced back to Laken, pushing back her emotional response.

"We got most of it done this past week. Right now, it's more of the hurry-up-and-wait game. Which sucks, but at least we're not scrambling," Laken answered.

"Yeah, better to be prepared."

"Plus, with this one's new clearance to drive, I figured it might be smart if he had a traveling buddy," Laken teased as she grinned at her big brother.

"Wow, thanks. You really know how to make a man feel small." Sterling bumped his sister's shoulder jokingly. "But it is probably a good idea. As much as I really hate to admit it in front of you—and you." Sterling arched a brow as he met Harper's gaze.

"You might not live it down."

"Pretty sure I was never going to anyway," Sterling replied, beleaguered. "So, when do we get to see you do your thing?"

The announcer came over the PA system and gave a fifteen-minute warning.

"Soon." Harper smiled.

"I'll finally get to see you in action, see if you have moves to back up all that hot air you give off," Sterling goaded. His head tilted, showing off the cut of his jawline as he issued the challenge.

Damn, he looked good, and Harper glanced away to keep her thoughts together. Taking a deep breath, she met his gaze with a challenging one of her own.

"I'll remember that hot air comment next time we go around with Margaret. Your therapy just got an upgrade."

"Ouch." Laken grinned.

"Challenge accepted."

"Ten minutes," the announcer started. "Will the first participants please get ready?"

"That's my cue." Harper glanced to the opening gate and back. "I'll see you guys in a bit."

"I'll be waiting to be impressed," Sterling told her.

"Yeah, that won't take much. Trust me." Laken smacked her brother on the shoulder.

"I know." Harper arched a brow and grinned at Sterling, who was enduring the ribbing good-naturedly. She gave a tiny wave and directed Spartan back toward the arena entrance. Several others were already lined up, and she took her place toward the back where her number correlated with the others.

Soon the announcer welcomed everyone to the race and went through several details.

Spartan blew out a frustrated breath and chomped his bit.

"I know. I'm impatient too. Hold up. We'll get our turn." Harper glanced around, noticing several familiar faces. Cassie was toward the front of the line, one of the first to race. Harper exhaled a breath. It would be nice to know the time to beat.

It could also be a little intimidating if Cassie had a particularly good run.

Her thoughts then flickered to Sterling. For once, she hoped Cassie's fixation stayed on Jasper.

Sterling was an even more enticing prospect.

Damn it all.

Just thinking about it made her frustrated; a heat burned in her chest. She tried to think of what it was....

It wasn't jealousy.

She was being possessive.

Immediately, she wished that Sterling and Laken hadn't come. Not only was she all bent out of shape from this new reaction, but if Cassie caught wind of Sterling, Harper would never hear the end of it.

She blew out a frustrated breath just as the announcer called out the first rider's name.

The crowd cheered on the racer, and soon the time was called, signaling the race over.

17.89

Not bad.

But easy to beat.

She forced her head back into the game. Focus.

Leaning down, she breathed in the scent of leather, horse, and fresh air. She listened to Spartan's breathing, the sound of horses all around her. Finding her center, she exhaled a slow breath, running the race around the barrels through her mind, again and again. Slowly the line moved up, and with each race that started, she mentally ran through the barrels with Spartan, leaning, breathing, making mental notes on what to remember.

Cassie's name was called, and Harper listened, hearing the thunder of her horse's hooves as they wound around the barrels and then through the gate.

17.44

Harper exhaled a tense breath.

That was a good time.

Really good.

Spartan could beat it, but it would have to be a damn near perfect run.

In barrel racing, the tenth and one hundredths of a second counted, and usually made the determination of winner and loser.

All Harper needed was to beat Cassie's time by a hundredth of a second. But that was much easier said than done.

Cassie exited the arena and passed by the line, meeting Harper's gaze.

"Good run, Cassie," Harper congratulated her. There was nothing gained by being petty.

"Thanks." Cassie smiled, her expression skeptical. "Good luck."

Harper grinned but didn't reply.

She focused back on Spartan.

On the line ahead.

The race halted for a minute while they raked the dirt around the barrels, keeping the surface fresh for the next set of horses.

And as the minutes ticked by, she found herself at the beginning of the line.

So far, Cassie's time was the one to beat, and she tuned out everything around her as she focused on the arena. The dirt was kicked up around the barrels, the dark earth in contrast to the dry dust covering the rest of the arena, making a clear path of attack. Not too smooth, not too rugged.

Perfect.

Spartan's ears were perked, listening intently for Harper's command. As the rider ahead finished, she sucked in a deep breath, concentrating intently on her horse, on the timing line, on the arena.

When they called her name, she tightened her grip on the reins, the rope taut under the pressure. She adjusted her heel in the stirrups and blew out a breath.

"Hi-ya!" She kicked Spartan's flanks, and the horse leapt forward, anticipating the command. She crossed the threshold into the arena, signaling the start of the time. Spartan's hooves drove into the dirt, and as they approached the first barrel, she cut him just wide enough to circle to the left, leaning as his hooves slid and he turned sharply. Lifting her boot slightly, she just skimmed the edge of the metal barrel, thankfully not even moving it.

"Go, go!" Harper shouted, leaning over Spartan's strong neck as they crossed the arena to their next target, the second barrel. As they drew near, Harper pulled the reins sharply to the right, and Spartan responded with a damn near perfect turn that circled the barrel with no more than an inch of clearance between the metal and her boot. She leaned as they finished the turn; kicking him swiftly she urged him to the last barrel. Spartan's hooves continued to pound the dirt, his attention riveted on the barrel as it grew closer and closer. Harper didn't dare glance at the clock; all her focus needed to be on Spartan.

The barrel.

The turn.

She leaned to the right as she tugged the reins the same direction. Spartan's hooves kicked up dirt as he circled the last barrel, his body tense beneath her as he finished the tight turn. "Hi-ya, go, go, go!" Harper gave a final swift kick to Spartan's flanks, leaning forward to encourage him, her gaze fixated on the time line as they flew over it.

She slowly pulled up the reins, giving Spartan a chance to slow down carefully from his breakneck pace.

Harper held her breath as the announcer came over the PA system.

"Harper Matthews, 17.39. We have a new leader, folks!"

The crowed gave a rousing applause, and Harper's face flushed with heat as she grinned widely. "Good work, boy." She leaned down and smoothed Spartan's neck, crooning to him. "You were magnificent."

Spartan shook his head, his bridle jingling.

"I'm so proud of you." She kissed the horse's neck, inhaling the familiar scent. "So proud."

She straightened and headed back toward the trailer. With her run done, she didn't need to keep Spartan all saddled up. If anything, she'd be heading home after her division ended, which would be soon.

As she slid off Spartan's back, her legs protested the movement. They were tense from her rigid control during the race, and she hadn't realized she'd failed to relax once the race was over.

She'd pay for that tomorrow.

"Hey!" Laken's voice cut into Harper's attention.

"Hi! Sorry, I was going to take care of Spartan and then find you guys." Harper lifted a hand in greeting, noticing that Sterling's stride was strong, the limp completely gone.

"Sure you were. I see how it is, horses then people." Sterling eyed Spartan and gave him a wide berth as he came to close to Harper.

"Still scared of horses?" Harper teased.

"Shitless," Sterling answered boldly.

"At least you're honest." Harper rolled her eyes.

"That was a great run. I'm glad we got to see it! Is that a record for you guys? It seemed pretty near perfect," Laken asked, coming around and patting Spartan's nose.

"It wasn't bad. That's for sure. There's always room for improvement, but I'm pretty pleased." She grinned at Laken and stepped forward to tie off the lead rope to Spartan's neck so that she could take off the bridle.

"I wish you could have seen Sterling's face, Harper. Don't let him tell you anything other than he was duly impressed." Laken gave a challenging grin to her brother.

"Seriously though, there was dirt flying, and you were riding so freaking fast. How do you not fall? Really, inquiring minds want to know," Sterling asked, his gray eyes sparkling with interest.

"Practice." Harper slid the bridle off and hung it on the side of the trailer.

"And brass balls, apparently," Sterling added, earning a smack on the shoulder from Laken.

"Really?" She gave him an annoyed glare.

"I can honestly say I'd rather be shot at than do what Harper just did. I'm man enough to admit it." Sterling held up in hands.

"Some of us are braver than others," Harper taunted. "But to set the record straight, I think you're bat shit crazy for not minding the whole war idea. Freaks the hell out of me."

"Then we're even. You ride horses. I'll shoot guns."

"Deal."

Laken gave an exasperated sigh. "So what now?"

Harper started to work on the cinch of the saddle. "Now I finish with Spartan, comb him down, and make sure he has plenty of water. Then I head up to the arena as they announce the finalists, and when they are done, so am I." Harper met Laken's gaze for a moment then moved to take off the saddle.

"Hey, I got that." Sterling moved around Spartan's head and to the left side of the horse. "I've been told it's good for me to balance, you know, muscle development and such."

Harper took a step back, but couldn't go far with the trailer behind her, and Spartan in front of her. "By all means." She waved to the saddle. "Clearly, your therapist knows what she is doing."

"Sometimes." Sterling gave her a sidelong glance as he lifted the saddle from Spartan's back. "Where do you want it?"

Harper motioned to the front of the trailer where there was a small door to the tack storage. As Sterling turned, Harper's gaze slid from his dusty blond hair down to his broad shoulders. The tension caused by carrying the saddle made his musculature sharper, cutting a definite shape through his tight shirt. She flickered her gaze to his leg, taking a moment to appreciate the perfect shape of his ass before studying the way he walked. His limp wasn't present, but he was favoring the leg with a slightly uneven stride. "Walk even," she called out, unable to help herself.

"Don't peacock, you mean?" He glanced over his shoulder as he set the saddle in the storage area.

"You're walking like you're afraid to trust your leg." Harper met his gaze, keeping hers open so he wouldn't think she was teasing about something that could be taken as hurtful.

"She's right," Laken chimed in, reminding Harper of her presence.

Had she seen Harper's intent study of her brother?

Sterling twisted his lips as he turned back toward Harper. "You can't cut a guy any slack, can you?"

"Nope. Not when I know you can do better." Harper hitched a shoulder.

"And here I thought we were here to watch you and keep the focus off me for once," Sterling grumbled, but Harper noted that as he walked back, his weight was far more evenly distributed. "Better?"

"Yup," Laken answered.

Harper finished combing Spartan and made sure he was tied off securely to the trailer before she indicated to the arena. "You guys ready?"

"Waiting on you," Sterling answered.

Laken smacked his shoulder again.

"Aw, it's nice to have a change of pace. Usually, I'm waiting on you," Harper replied sweetly as she started toward the arena.

Laken unsuccessfully tried to hold back a snicker.

Sterling shot her a mock glare.

"What?" Laken asked, still laughing.

"You enjoy this too much," Sterling accused his sister.

"Yeah, I really do. It's nice to see someone set you on your ass."

"My pleasure." Harper gave a wink to Laken.

Sterling shook his head and ignored Harper's comment. As they approached the gate, the final rider was going through the barrels.

"17.67."

"How do they know when to start or stop time?" Sterling asked as they leaned against the iron fence.

"See that line in the dirt?" Harper pointed to the painted line that was all but obliterated.

"Yeah."

"Once you cross it, they start time, and then they stop time when you cross it again when you're finished," Harper explained.

"And you can't touch the barrels?" Laken asked.

"Yeah, you can, actually. You can't knock them over. If you do, they add five seconds to your time and basically eliminate you from the running. If you're lucky, you might be able to stabilize it if you know you're about to knock it over, and that's allowed, but usually your time suffers from it regardless. The idea is to not really touch them, just cut the circle around them."

"Makes sense. What do you get when you win?" Sterling asked.

Harper noticed the way he'd phrased the question.

When.

Not if.

A warm sensation filled her chest. It was nice to have someone believe in her.

She bit back a wry grin. "*When*," she emphasized, "I win, I'll get some prize money, bragging rights, etcetera."

"Cool," Laken answered.

The announcer came over the PA system once more, this time giving the rundown of the final times.

Harper listened intently as they started from the third place and went up. "In third, we have...Amanda Wilson from Yakima, Washington, with the time of 17.60!"

The crowd clapped and waited as he continued. "In second place, we have Cassie Markston from Toppenish, Washington, with the time of 17.44!"

Harper clapped, her heart pounding fiercely. She didn't watch the rest of the race, but she was still quite certain no one had beaten her time.

But there was always a chance.

She held her breath as the announcer came over the system again. "And in first place, taking home the grade prize of one thousand dollars cash, with a time of 17.39, we have Harper Matthews from Ellensburg, Washington!"

Laken squealed and pulled Harper into a hug.

Harper froze for a moment at the quick contact then returned the hug, welcoming the friendly action.

"Good work, Harper!" Laken congratulated her as she released her from their quick embrace.

"Not bad." Sterling regarded her with a wide smile, his gaze meeting hers, his expression approving and warm. "Come here." He opened up his arms and pulled her into a tight hug.

His chest was warm against her ear as she leaned in, prepared to immediately let go and take a step back.

But apparently, Sterling had other plans. His arms banded around her tightly, securely, as he gently kissed the top of her head. Her senses were overwhelmed with the scent of spicy aftershave and clean laundry all wrapped around a sexy man. It was sensory overload in the best way possible, and she didn't want to let go.

"Good work. You were amazing out there. It's well deserved." He released her then, and she reluctantly stepped back, instantly missing the contact.

"Thanks," she offered, forcing a calm she didn't feel.

"Hey, good work out there." A familiar voice shattered her warm fuzzies like a five-gallon bucket of ice water.

"Thanks, Cassie. You too." Harper flickered her gaze to where Cassie waited, her expression expectant as she focused on Sterling then back to Harper.

Harper bit her tongue to keep from saying something she'd regret. After taking a deep breath, she forced a smile. "Let me introduce you to Laken and Sterling."

Harper's shoulders were rigid with tension as Cassie gushed an enthusiastic greeting to Laken and then to Sterling. Cassie's gaze assessed him quickly, and Harper hoped Sterling hadn't missed the predatory glint in her expression.

"So, you're friends of Harper?" she asked in a friendly manner, as if she and Harper were close friends.

Harper barely resisted the urge to roll her eyes.

Or gag.

Maybe both.

"Yeah." Laken's expression flickered between Cassie and Harper, as if piecing together the real story. "We're actually just heading out. It was great to meet you." Laken gave her nurse-smile, the one that Harper had started to recognize she used when she was being kind and clinical all at once.

Harper's gaze flickered to Sterling. He was watching her, amusement clear in his eyes as he dared to glance at Cassie then back to Harper, raising a brow in question.

Harper felt a hint of pity for Cassie, since it was clear everyone had seen through her pretense, but it faded quickly when she offered to show Sterling around for the party later.

"Surely you don't want to leave just yet?"

"Actually, I'm leaving now, and Sterling here is taking Harper home. It really was nice to meet you. I'm sure we'll see you later." Laken shook Cassie's hand and walked away.

"Yeah, see ya." Sterling gave a curt nod to Cassie and followed his sister.

Cassie turned to Harper. "You sure are surrounded by some eye candy, aren't you?"

Harper bit back a groan. One of the eye candies she was referring to was her brother.

Ew.

"I gotta go catch up." Harper pointed behind her. "But good job and congrats on a great run." She backed up, gave a quick wave, then turned and jogged toward the trailer.

As she approached, she saw Laken give her a teasing grin. "Friend of yours?"

"Not really. More like one of those irritating horseflies that bites you in the ass when you're not looking," Harper answered with a little too much honesty.

"I actually do need to head back." Laken tucked her hands in her jean pockets.

"And I really don't want to go yet, because I'll be stuck at the ranch, and it's more fun to irritate you than her." Sterling ruffled his sister's hair.

"Joy." Harper gave a wry grin. "How can I refuse when you put it that way?"

"Eh, you didn't want to anyway." Sterling gave her a devastatingly seductive grin.

Her eyes widened, and she glanced away, cursing the way her body enthusiastically responded to his expression.

"Okay, and yeah...I'm going now." Laken gave an awkward wave and turned on her heel, leaving.

"Way to make that totally inappropriate." Harper rolled her eyes, pretending she didn't have her own inappropriate response.

"You love it." Sterling hitched a shoulder, drawing her attention to the rounded and sculpted form.

"Eyes up here." He wagged his eyebrows. "This is what girls feel like when guys study their rack." He shook his head. "Show some respect, Harper."

Harper's eyes widened in shock then narrowed in anger. But she couldn't figure out a decent response.

Because well, he was right.

She was distracted by his body. In her defense, it was rather amazing. Heaven help her if he ever took his shirt off.

"Still no response? Wow. I don't know how to take this," he teased, arching a light brown eyebrow.

Harper twisted her lips then grinned. "Why don't you make yourself useful and give Laken the keys in your pocket, and I'll get Spartan loaded up?"

"Staring at my pockets, Harper?" Sterling goaded, implying so much more.

"Why? Is there something to see? I must have missed that." She gave him the best setdown she could think of.

"Ouch." Sterling grinned then walked toward Laken. "I'll be right back."

Harper smiled to herself as she untied Spartan. She led him around. He stepped into the trailer and heaved a sigh, his body relaxing. "You did well today, handsome. I'm proud of you."

Harper left the trailer and closed the gate, making sure it was secure before double-checking the dirt around it for anything that might have fallen.

"Laken's all set, and I can see that Spartan is too. What else do we need to do?" Sterling asked, the afternoon sun illuminating the golden hue of his skin.

"Well, I need to go and check out at the registration table. You can come if you want, but I won't be very long."

Sterling nodded. "I'll walk with you. It's good for me."

"You're not limping as much. Does that mean it doesn't hurt, or is that your medication?" She tucked a strand of hair behind her ear, studying his expression before he answered.

"Both, but the medication keeps the pain at bay. It's just easier to think, to be normal when I don't have that hazy edge of pain always around my head, you know?" Sterling met her gaze, his expression tight.

"Yeah. I do." *More than you know*, Harper added mentally as they passed the arena and headed toward the registration table.

She waved hello to the senior gentleman at the table. After giving her name, she was congratulated again and handed the packet that would include her winnings.

"Thank you," Harper replied again as she and Sterling headed out into the parking lot.

"The day is still kinda young. What do you want to do?" Sterling asked.

Harper bit her lip. "Not ready to go home yet?" she asked, testing the waters.

Sterling shook his head. "Not yet. But we do have a horse in the back that might be less patient than us."

Harper met his gaze with a warm one. "Aw, look who's thinking of others...." she singsonged. "Spartan does need to get home, but I"—Harper glanced away, taking the risk but not brave enough to actually make eye contact—"but I don't have anything else planned today."

"Good," Sterling answered before she'd even finished.

Harper's gaze flickered to him then back to the pasture as they approached her pickup. "What did you have in mind?"

His grin widened, his gray eyes dancing with something she couldn't quite name.

"You'll see."

"But what if I want to know now?" Harper challenged, regarding him as she unlocked the pickup.

"Then you'll be disappointed. Sometimes it's more fun to be surprised. And Harper, you need a few surprises in your life. The good ones. So, you game?" he asked as he held the passenger door half open, waiting for her answer.

Harper took a deep breath. It was odd, but she was slightly worried.

Giving someone else control, even over something small, was a big step. Could she do that?

She met his expectant gaze. "Okay."

Sterling's answering smile filled her with all the warmth from earlier, and she relaxed into her answer.

Maybe it would be all right to give control to someone.

Every once in a while.

If it was the right person.

If.

And deep in her heart, she knew that she could trust Sterling.

Which in turn made her terrified.

Because when you trust someone, that means they can hurt you far worse than everyone else.

CHAPTER 13

Sterling could feel the tension radiating from Harper as they drove away from her home. The horse needed some time to relax after racing, so they'd headed to Harper's place first, easing Spartan from the trailer. The horse barely gave a backward glance as Harper left the barn. Then they took a moment to disconnect the trailer, and all the while, Sterling could feel the tension crackling in the air around Harper.

She was questioning herself.

He didn't blame her; he was questioning himself too.

Could he do this?

Not hurt her?

What was it that Laken had said? *Communicate. Be up-front.*

He could do that.

But damn, it was going to be hard to lay himself all out there.

Harper bit her lip as she drove down the gravel driveway and toward the main road.

"Okay, cowboy, where to?" she asked, regarding him.

Sterling shook his head. "Yeah, not a cowboy."

"Fine, well, what rank were you?" she asked, curious.

"Captain," he answered, the word creating a swirl of memories, many good, some painful, all of them nostalgic in a way that made him miss the Marine Corps so damn much.

"So, Captain," she corrected, a grin teasing her full lips.

The sound of his rank on her lips was erotic as hell, and immediately sent fire through his blood. It was an involuntary reaction that had him quickly finding a way to control it.

"Retired, remember?" he answered, thankful for the out that would alleviate the pressing problem.

"You're impossible. Fine. *Dude*, where to?" She rolled her eyes.

"*That* I can work with," Sterling teased, thankful to have navigated the sudden minefield. "Let's get something to eat, and then you can show me around Ellensburg."

"Yay. I always wanted to be a tour guide."

"Hey, you love it here, and it's always better to hear about it from someone who loves whatever they're describing," Sterling replied.

"You're right." Harper sighed.

"Say that again?" Sterling goaded.

"I'm right," Harper corrected, giving him a taunting glare.

"Sure, sure. Where do you recommend eating?" Sterling asked, scanning the terrain. His eyes cataloged the rough landscape, studying for exit routes and possible areas to take cover.

"Do you realize you're always on alert?"

Harper's voice startled him, and he glanced at her, slightly confused.

"You know, hyperaware of your surroundings, like Jason-Bourne-type stuff," Harper commented, her gaze flickering to him for a moment before darting back to the road.

Sterling's posture froze then he relaxed slowly. "It's a habit, and yeah, I do it constantly. It doesn't really have an off button."

"It's in your blood. I get that." Harper glanced at him.

"I don't know if I'll ever be able to step away from that part of myself," Sterling replied, feeling the weight of his decision to leave the marines heavy on his shoulders.

"Why would you want to?" Harper asked, her tone curious. Her green eyes were piercing in their intensity as she studied him before flickering her gaze back to the road.

Sterling folded his hands, feeling the truth of his words before he even spoke them. "Because it's not necessary. That's not my life anymore."

"So, that negates the fact that it's a part of who you once were?" Harper challenged. Her green eyes flashed.

"No." Sterling shook his head once decisively. "But I think the goal is to move forward, and not always be stuck in what I was...."

"I can understand that." Harper seemed to realize the truth of his words. "But at the same time, don't let your training be sidelined just because you don't need it right now. It's valuable, a part of you. And that's a good thing."

Sterling replayed her words, letting the validity of their truth sink deep. It was soothing—welcome. "Thank you."

She shrugged her shoulders, as if trying to downplay the charged atmosphere they were creating. But Sterling wasn't about to let the moment fade.

"What about you? What do you find is the hardest thing to move on from? If you don't mind me asking."

Harper blew out a deep breath. "There's a lot." She met his gaze then focused on the road, pinching her brows as if deep in thought. "I think for me it's more of what my reactions are versus what I'm holding on to. You know? Like...feeling in control. It's a response because I felt so out of control. Or feeling safe, because I never felt safe...things like that."

Sterling nodded; that made sense. He had seen different aspects of that play out in her personality, in the way she dealt with situations. It made sense after what she had endured. "I'd think that's only natural."

"Yeah...but that doesn't make it right, or easy. I think the thing to remember is that it's all a process, you know? One step at a time."

Sterling gave a dry chuckle. "Boy, that phrase has never meant so much to me as it has in the past few months. Damn, one step is sometimes so freaking hard." He thought back to his first days after surgery. The small things that he'd taken for granted for so long had become huge, monumental issues in his life. He realized just how far he had come.

But he also saw just how much farther he had to climb.

"Right?" Harper answered back, grinning.

The comradery was soothing. It was so freeing to talk to someone who wasn't just trying to understand the pain or the process, but was walking through it. He appreciated her all the more for it.

But it also kept him on his guard. Because they were both slaying their dragons, and neither one was whole yet.

"You're pensive all of a sudden," Harper commented.

Sterling gave her a sidelong glance. "Can't I be reflective and deep?" he harassed, earning an eye roll from Harper.

"Yeah, but it would be the first time."

"Damn, that hurt." Sterling winced then returned her grin. "So you never answered me. Where are we going to eat?"

"So, those were your deep and reflective thoughts?" Harper joked, her green eyes flickering to him.

"You'll never know."

Harper shook her head and giggled. "Let's go have pizza. We can stop in to Brooklyn's. As long as the delivery guys aren't all out, they are superfast."

"Delivery guys?" Sterling questioned.

"It's a small place in a small town. If everyone's out making deliveries, the poor kid at the counter, or the owner, has to take the orders and make the pizza. It takes longer, but it's worth the wait," Harper finished, turning down University Way.

"Really, I'm not picky. You had me at pizza," Sterling answered. "I missed it so much when I was out on deployment. You can ask Laken. I'd come home on leave, and I swear all I did was eat everything I'd missed. Pizza being the top of the list. You can't make that in an MRE."

"Ew." Harper's nostrils flared. "A friend of mine ordered a few of those for a camping trip when we were in high school. Never again."

"They aren't so bad once you get used to them. Some are...better than others."

"I'll take your word for that." Harper pulled into a horseshoe-shaped brick strip mall and parked in front of a Coca-Cola sign that read *Brooklyn's Pizza*.

As she put the truck in park, Sterling unbuckled his seatbelt and carefully stepped out onto the asphalt. His leg was stiff, but thankfully not hurting. He figured he had a few hours before the pain medication wore off. He flexed his toes before starting toward the glass entrance. The Central Washington University campus was directly across from the restaurant, its redbrick buildings complementing the same redbrick of the strip mall, almost making them appear like they belonged with the rest of the campus.

He tried to make it to the door before Harper, but she was quicker and held it open for him.

His lips quirked in a grin, and he grabbed the door too. "After you."

Harper gave him a wry grin but walked inside, the scent of parmesan, bread, and basil floating in the air. Sterling's stomach rumbled in appreciation.

"So, what's your favorite?" Harper asked as they walked toward the counter to order.

"I'm not picky. And I'm not just saying that. Aside from anchovies, I'm honestly happy with whatever. Do we order individual pizzas or one big pie?"

Harper studied the menu above then turned to Sterling. "That depends. Do you want to eat here, or do you want your tour right away?"

Sterling felt a grin tug at his lips. "What will take longer?"

Harper narrowed her gaze for a moment before glancing away as if uncertain. "Eating here and then driving around."

"Then I pick Plan B," Sterling replied, watching as her gaze met his. Again, she was studying him, as if trying to read his intentions.

Be honest. Be up front. Laken's words echoed again.

Not yet...but today. Today he'd at least start that conversation; only heaven knew where it would lead.

"All right." Harper nodded slowly.

"So, you want to share, or are you the kind of girl who doesn't share well? You know, these are important things I need to find out." Sterling cast her a wary glance.

"Ask Jasper." Harper gave a wicked grin.

"That's a no. You do not share. Okay, I want my own pizza." Sterling chuckled then rubbed his hands together as he walked forward to order.

He picked The Kitchen Sink pizza and motioned to Harper.

"First, we need to start with the jalapeño bread. And then, I'll have the chicken bacon ranch." She started to open her purse, but Sterling was quicker and handed over his card. When Harper noticed, she met his gaze, a question in her expression.

"Date night." He shrugged and signed his name on the receipt.

He could feel Harper's gaze on his back as he handed over the scrap of paper and stepped out of the way for the next customers. He scanned the room for an empty table and picked one in the corner, giving them the semblance of privacy. When he pulled out her chair, he finally met her gaze.

Amusement, awareness, and curiosity all flashed across her expression before she lowered her gaze and took a seat.

"So, date night?" Harper regarded him once he took a seat across from her.

Sterling shrugged a shoulder and rested his arms on the wood table. "I figured ambush tactics were in my favor. You can't run if you're already here."

"One flaw." Harper smirked.

"Oh?" Sterling grinned in response.

"Yeah, I drove. Totally could leave your ass here if I wanted to," she threatened teasingly.

"I guess it's a good thing you're not ditching me, then."

"Yet," Harper challenged.

"Hey, I'll take what I can get. Call me overconfident but I'll take my chances."

Harper rolled her eyes and leaned back.

"So, do you have any more races coming up?" Sterling directed the conversation back to where Harper was most comfortable: horses. He thought back to her race earlier that day. It was easy to see that she lived for each race. The world around her had utterly faded away, and she was focused intently on the circuit. Her purple and blond hair blew from under her Stetson hat, adding a fiercely colorful layer to her ferocious determination.

Sterling had never seen anything as magnificent as Harper racing. And even as she spoke about upcoming races, he could see that barrel racing was in her blood.

Not long into their conversation, the jalapeño bites arrived.

"You ever tried these?"

"Not these specifically. But I'm a fan of anything spicy. We used to have hot sauce we'd put in our MREs to give them a little bit of a kick." In truth, they just used the spicy sauce to cover up the bland flavors that seemed to run together day after day.

"These are amazing. Not too hot, but just enough to make them utterly addictive." Harper picked up a puffy round piece of dough and tugged on the trail of cheese it left behind. Several green jalapeños dotted the top of the bread piece, and she took a bite, her eyes closing in appreciation.

Sterling couldn't tear his gaze away. Harper moaned softly then popped the rest of the bite in her mouth, the sight both amusing and sensual as she did a little happy dance in her chair.

"That good, huh?" Sterling asked, watching as she took another one.

"Yes. That good. Even better than your grilled cheese." She arched a rebellious brow.

"We'll see about that," Sterling challenged, picking up one. His focus stayed on Harper, watching as she enjoyed another bite, this time licking a trail of cheese from her finger.

The simple act was sexy as hell, and his body reacted instantly.

As his jeans became tighter, he scooted his chair farther in, not needing to give the family across the way a show.

"You try," Harper encouraged.

Sterling took a bite, the hot flavor invading his senses and washing over him. It wasn't overly spicy, and mixed with the cheese and the soft dough, it was the perfect combination.

"Okay, so yeah, this wins. But in my defense, if I had added jalapeños to my grilled cheese, it would have kicked ass," Sterling said after he swallowed.

Harper opened her mouth to comment, but the pizza arrived, and she apparently thought better of whatever she was going to say.

After they finished their pizza, Sterling helped Harper package up the leftovers, and he stood from the table.

"You ready?" Harper asked as she lifted the pizza box containing their remaining pizza.

"When you are."

Harper started for the door, and soon they were pulling out from the parking lot. "So, a tour." Harper glanced at him as she turned onto University Way.

"If you don't mind," Sterling answered, his tone daring.

"Why do I feel like you're issuing some sort of challenge? Do you really think that putting up with you is that difficult?" she asked.

"No more difficult than dealing with you," he teased back.

Harper bit her lip to keep from grinning too widely. "I'm a ray of sunshine."

"I'm going to refrain from comment."

"Probably wise."

"I wasn't born yesterday."

"Nope, you were born a lot of yesterdays ago," Harper jibed.

"Was that an insult? Are you calling me old?" Sterling narrowed his gaze. "Just because I walk like I'm eighty—"

"You don't walk like you're eighty," Harper interrupted then added softly, almost to herself, "Believe me."

"Want to explain that?" Sterling asked.

"Nope." She didn't elaborate.

"Fine. But I'm not old. I'm twenty-eight."

"Old man." Harper gave him a sidelong glance.

"Whatever."

"Bet you can't guess how old I am," Harper dared. "Oh, and up here, we're going to pass by the place we have the Ellensburg Rodeo each year."

"I'll keep my eyes open. And I feel like we need to make a wager here."

"Regarding?" Harper asked too innocently.

"If I can guess your age." He played it cool even as his mind spun with different wagers, different ways to win.

"Deal. If you guess right, I'll—" Her gaze flickered to the road and back.

"An IOU. Collectable whenever the winner wants," Sterling interrupted.

"Deal." Harper nodded then held out her hand.

"I get twenty questions to figure it out." Sterling shook her hand.

"Ten, and they can't use numbers," Harper corrected and then nodded to the Ellensburg rodeo arena.

"Cool, do you race there too?" Sterling asked as they slowed down to survey the arenas.

"Yeah, but mostly it's bull riding and such. Not my thing."

"Funny, but I'd think it was totally up your alley." Sterling regarded Harper.

"I like to watch it, but it's not the same as watching barrel racing. I like horses more than cows," she answered.

"I think I like cows more than horses," Sterling replied. "I'll take a steak any day over having to ride a horse."

"That's not exactly what I mean, but fine." She gave a chuckle. "So, what are your questions? You have a few minutes till we get to the Yakima Canyon."

"Is that our next stop?"

"Yup." Harper swung the truck around and headed back on the road.

"Favorite song?" he asked.

"Johnny Cash, 'I Walk the Line.'"

Sterling frowned. That didn't exactly give anything away.

"One down. Nine to go," Harper replied in a tone that implied she was assured of her winning the bet.

"What was your first phone?" Sterling asked, a smile creeping across his face at his insightful question.

"Damn. That's a good question." Harper gave him a wary glance. "LG Cosmos."

Sterling nodded. "What did you use to talk with your friends online?"

Harper frowned again. "I just texted."

"Facebook account?"

"Yes."

"Twitter?"

"No."

"Paris Hilton or Kim Kardashian."

"Neither?" Harper gave him an annoyed expression.

"What I mean is, who was more of a hit when you were in high school?"

"Oh, Paris."

"And you already talked about Jason Bourne. Okay, how about this one. What did you have for your first drink on your twenty-first birthday?" Sterling asked, watching as her lips twitched slightly.

"Nothing."

Sterling gave her a sidelong glance, watching as her pink lips twitched in amusement. "How many selfies do you take a month?"

Harper grimaced. "Maybe one...usually with Spartan. So, it's not really a selfie."

"Sure, sure."

"Pain in the ass."

"Yup. What kind of dress did you wear to prom?"

Harper glanced to him, her lips twisting. "A red one."

"Nope, not good enough. Was it strappy, or sparkly...."

"Why do I feel like this is a trap?"

"Because I have a little sister. And I'm comparing all your answers to her...." He gave a wicked grin.

"Damn, I forgot about that," Harper grumbled.

"So, dress?" Sterling encouraged.

"Gah, okay. It was bright red with a halter neckline and mermaid fit. Not sparkly."

"Damn, I bet you looked amazing." Sterling whistled low, giving her a grin.

"I did, thank you very much." Harper flicked her hair behind her shoulder and gave him a flirtatious grin.

Sterling chuckled then considered her dress, narrowing the gap by a few years. "Finally, are you a spring, fall, summer, or winter baby?"

"Fall."

"You're twenty-five," Sterling answered then relaxed back in the truck's seat, watching Harper's expression freeze then thaw into an irritated grin.

"Damn."

"I'm good, I know." He stretched slightly, quite self-satisfied.

"No, I mean, damn, you're so close." She cast him a smug smile.

"No." He sat forward and ran his fingers through his hair. "I'm wrong?"

"Yeah, I'm twenty-four. I'll be twenty-five next month." Her lips pinched as she tried to restrain her laughter.

"That is freakishly close. I think it still counts." He crossed his arms over his chest.

"Nope. Not counting. You're still off. I'm not twenty-five yet. No dice."

"So freaking close." Sterling sighed. "Can I at least get some credit for being as close as possible?"

"Credit given."

"Thank you." He nodded. "So...your birthday is next month?"

"Yup." Harper nodded. "Check out over there." She nodded ahead. "We're going to start winding around the canyon. It's gentle right now, but as we get farther along, the cliffs drop off, and it's pretty spectacular."

"Yeah, I think Laken said something about this. But every time she mentions it, she and Cyler do this secret smile thing and I, yeah, I leave the room."

"I know, I get that. It's like with my brother and—" Harper stopped her words and bit her lip, casting a worried glance to her passenger.

It is now or never, Sterling thought.

"Kessed and Jasper are just as bad, huh? That's good. They better be. All I can say is that as awkward as it is for Cyler to be constantly checking out my little sister's ass, I'd be doubly pissed if he didn't love her like that. I'm glad that it's the same way with Jasper and Kessed. She deserves that."

Harper glanced from the road to him then back. "Is it hard for you still? Kessed and Jasper, I mean."

Sterling shook his head. "At first, yes. It sucks being rejected. Who likes that? Plus, Kessed and I go way back. But I think..." He frowned slightly then continued. "...I think I was holding on to the idea of Kessed being something safe and familiar, rather than pursuing her because I loved her like that. Does that make sense? It makes me sound like the biggest ass ever, but hindsight is always twenty-twenty. But it was never meant to be, I see that now. She's with who she belongs, and Jasper needs her too." He smirked. "I get the feeling she's the spice in his life, and he kinda needs that."

Harper's lips twitched. "Yeah, he'd be boring without her. And she'd be aimless without him. It just works." She smiled broadly. "I'm glad you're doing better with that. I know that Laken was worried about you."

"Laken worries about everything," Sterling replied.

"She loves you, like a sister. Trust me. As a little sister, it's our job to worry about our overprotective and overbearing brothers." She gave a little shake to her head. She froze for a moment then glanced to Sterling. "Did Jasper say something to you?"

"About?" he asked, trying to lure the answer out of her.

"Did he... He didn't threaten you or...assume..." She didn't finish, just kept glancing from him to the road.

"Is there a place we can pull over up here?" Sterling asked, growing slightly uneasy with how she was winding around the canyon cliffs and kept glancing back to him.

"Getting nervous?"

"Yes," Sterling answered honestly. Plus, it would be much easier to have that conversation without her focus divided between him and the road.

It was as good a time as any to lay it all out there. Unknowingly, she'd given him the perfect opportunity.

And this was one chance he didn't want to screw up.

It was a good thing he knew how to work well under pressure. Laying one's heart on the line seemed even more dangerous than enemy fire.

And way more threatening.

He was proof that your body could heal.

Something told him it wasn't as easy to heal a heart.

CHAPTER 14

Harper bit her lip as she crested the top of the canyon and started down the winding road, keeping her eyes open for the campsite on the other side. As the sign for Big Pines came into view, she pulled in.

"Can you take out my Discovery Pass? That way we won't have to pay to get in," Harper asked Sterling as she pointed to her glove compartment.

Sterling sorted through the papers within and lifted the pass with a questioning expression.

"Yup, that's the one."

Harper took it from Sterling's outstretched hand and hung it on her rearview mirror. There wasn't a person stationed at the check-in, but that didn't mean they wouldn't be back to make sure all the visitors abided by the honor system.

And it was far cheaper to pay for the annual or day pass than to be given a ticket for trying to sneak in.

Sterling hadn't engaged any further in their conversation, and Harper wondered what that meant. Was it good? Bad? Instinctively, she built up the walls around herself. If she closed off, then nothing could hurt.

And she had dealt with enough hurt for a lifetime. She didn't need any more.

But what had Jasper said to him?

As she put the pickup in park, she turned to Sterling, keeping the engine running to let the A/C cool the cab.

"So?" she asked, her curiosity fighting against her will to remain uninvested.

Protected.

"So, you asked a good question, and Harper, you deserve a straight answer."

Harper's shoulders tensed, her hands flexing slightly as she waited for whatever Sterling was going to say.

Fleetingly, she thought how pathetic it was that she was expecting something bad, something that would hurt.

That was always her first instinct.

It wasn't an expectation for good.

But for pain, for something that would hurt. And this was no different. Did she have any reason to think that Sterling was going to say something to hurt her? No, but that didn't change the fact that it was a real reaction.

Not because of anything he'd ever done.

But because of her.

The issue was within, and that was what made it so damn difficult to conquer.

"You all right?" Sterling asked, his gray eyes narrowing as he studied her in the close confines of the cab.

Harper took a shallow breath.

It was too close—everything was just too close.

"I need some air," she replied as she opened the door. After slamming the pickup door shut, she absentmindedly wrapped her arms around her middle and strode to the river, keeping her eyes on how it rippled across the canyon, lapping at the shore.

She heard his footsteps behind her then the jingle of her keys.

Hanging her head in irritation at herself for forgetting to turn off the truck, she hazarded a glance at Sterling, who was holding the dancing keys out to her. She gave him a tight smile and took them. "Thanks."

"No problem. I'm assuming you didn't want to keep the engine running?" he asked, but without sarcasm, just a gentle tone.

Harper relaxed slightly and shook her head. "No."

As she waited for Sterling to ask about why she'd bolted again, she grew tense with the anticipation.

Nothing good came from silence.

Did it?

Just when she was about to speak up, break through the silent barrier, Sterling bent down, sifted through some stones and picked up a few.

"You ever skip rocks?" he asked, glancing up at her, squinting in the bright sunlight.

Harper felt her body relax in posture, and a smile cracked her lips. "Once or twice."

"You any good?" Sterling asked, his grin widening.

Harper looked away, his expression causing butterflies to dance in her tummy. Damn, she both hated and loved the sensation. It had been a long time since she'd had that reaction.

It was innocent yet...not. That tingling sensation could lead to stupid choices.

And Sterling was a constant temptation to acting on those crazy impulses.

She took a deep breath of pine-scented air and cleared her head. "Good enough," she finally answered.

"I won't issue any challenges then. I've lost enough for one day," Sterling replied as he stood back up, taking aim.

"Where's your sense of adventure?" Harper asked, feeling more at ease. Teasing, sarcasm, even a little bit of flirting—those she could handle. Those didn't freak her out.

They were just surface interaction.

But things got real when she felt the pressure build in her chest, constricting her lungs and stealing her breath.

Skipping rocks? Baiting the bear? Now *that* she could do.

She bent down and picked up a flat river rock. After taking aim, she let it sail over the river just as Sterling hurled his as well. Both skipped several times before disappearing under the rippling water.

"How many?" Sterling asked.

"I think it was a tie."

"That sucks."

Harper giggled. "I know, right? The most anticlimactic ending."

"Round two?" Sterling offered her a flat rock.

Harper grinned, plucking the rock from his hand and flicking her wrist in anticipation.

"Ladies first."

Harper flung the stone over the river, watching as it skipped once, twice, then disappeared under the clear water.

"That was not my best throw." She winced.

Sterling winked. "I think it's safe to say I'll win this round."

Harper rolled her eyes but watched as he skipped the stone four times before it sunk to the bottom.

"Winner!" Sterling fist-pumped the air.

"All hail the champion." Harper sighed, giving a small clap.

"So, why did I freak you out earlier? I mean, I know kissing you can have that reaction—and I haven't figured out if that's a good or bad thing." He gave her a side grin. "But I guess the thing is..." He faced her, his gaze magnetic and stealing all her ability to run. "...I want you to run to me, not away. And I don't know how to do that, but...a wise woman once told me that I need to lay it all out there. So, this is me, probably making an ass of myself." He rubbed the back of his neck. "I want to be the one you run to, not from. And I can't promise that I won't screw up, or that I won't hurt you, but I want you to know that I think you're worth the risk. Because all the things you're scared of, I'm scared of too. And I know that this is a bigger step for you, so I'm putting the ball in your court, so to say. No guessing, no wondering. Here it is. You're in control. Just tell me what you want...if anything. And I'll do my best to be what you need."

Sterling took a deep breath and stepped back, giving Harper some space.

She thought over his words, her body simultaneously trying to run both away and to him, and in the confusion, she was rooted to the ground. His words were everything she needed, yet everything that freaked the hell out of her.

Control.

He had said the magic word.

Did she want this? Want him?

Hell yes! But could she do this? Really?

If she had control...

If it was on her terms, her pace...

Would that be enough to combat the fear?

I want you to run to me, not away.

She breathed in, breathed out, repeating the words over and over in her head, thankful for the space, but also knowing that she needed to give him an answer.

He deserved one.

Could she be as brave as he? Lay it all out there, damn the consequences? Even if it hurt.

If it failed?

Even if it gave her a broken heart?

Control.

She lifted her gaze and studied Sterling. His broad shoulders were tense, even as he was trying to appear relaxed, accepting of her choice.

It took a brave man to risk his heart with someone as messed up as she. She didn't just have baggage, she had a luggage factory. But it was also something that Sterling understood.

He was broken too.

Not in the same way, but broken was still broken.

And maybe, just maybe, two broken people didn't make a mess.

Maybe they made a whole.

"Okay." Harper breathed. Releasing the word into the air was both liberating and also terrifying—but didn't give her the oppressive pressure she'd expected.

It set her free.

"Okay..." Sterling took a tentative step toward her.

Harper took a breath. "I don't want to run away from you either. I'm scared as hell"—she shook her head—"but if you can be brave, so can I."

Sterling's face softened. "Can't be outdone, can you?"

"You're learning." She gave a gentle laugh.

"Starting to. I think I have a long way to go, though." Sterling took another step toward her.

"Eh, you'll get there." She shrugged, the familiar territory of teasing releasing some of the tension.

"I'm a quick learner."

"Unless it's on horseback."

"Mean." Sterling shook his head.

"At least you know what you're getting into," Harper challenged.

Sterling glanced to the rocky ground, a grin widening his full lips. He met her gaze again, his gray eyes dancing with amusement and... something else.

Hope.

"I'm pretty sure I'm at least marginally aware."

"You still think it's worth the risk?" Harper asked as he came toe to toe with her. Heart pounding, she couldn't tear away from his gaze. She not only needed to hear his answer, she needed to see it reflected in his eyes.

Wow, she was an insecure mess.

"Absolutely," Sterling replied immediately, his gaze warm, smoldering, as he lifted a hand and trailed a fingertip down her arm then laced her fingers within his own.

"I'm going to kiss you now. Is that okay?" he asked, murmuring the words, not breaking eye contact.

"Yeah." Harper's heart seized as she answered, fear and anticipation freezing her. She fluttered her lids closed when Sterling lowered his head, brushing his lips ever so softly against hers, then retreating.

She waited in anticipation, but when he didn't kiss her again, she opened her eyes and furrowed her brow. "Is that all?"

Sterling chuckled. "Apparently not." This time, he tugged her forward by their interlaced fingers, wrapped his other arm around her waist, and seared his lips across hers.

This wasn't a gentle kiss. It was a possessive needful kiss, one that made Harper's body temperature rise high enough to melt the freezing sensation of fear and awaken the long dormant desire she'd denied for so long. He took her lower lip in his mouth, caressing it with his tongue as his hand slid up her back, tangling in her hair gently, scattering her thoughts.

His lips were smooth and urgent as his tongue caressed hers, engaging in the dance of give and take, nip and slide, advance and retreat. Her other hand slid up his arm, discovering the geography of his biceps and how they sloped into his shoulder. He felt hard, like a warm stone under her palm, and she reached up to touch his dusty blond hair, tousled by the wind. Its soft texture was thick through her fingers as she tugged on it with a little more force than was necessary, but she was losing herself in the kiss, in the sensations of his body pressed against hers.

Sterling simply groaned against her mouth before sliding a hand up her back, under her shirt.

"Ah-hem."

Harper broke from the kiss and blinked in the bright sunlight. An old Indian fisherman walked past, his gaze flickering between the two of them, a grin on his wrinkled face. "Maybe not in public." He winked and strode on.

Harper's face heated till she was sure she resembled a tomato in color.

Sterling nodded to the old man then turned to Harper, bursting into laughter.

She covered her mouth as she started to giggle, then that amusement simply grew till she was doubled over. "So, that just happened."

"We may have gotten a little carried away," he replied as he tried to regain his composure.

"A little." Harper lifted her fingers, making a small space between them.

Sterling grinned, holding out his hand to her, waiting.

With only a slight twinge of trepidation, Harper laced her fingers through his again.

"So, I kinda jumped the gun, but you asked a question in the car about your brother. Do you want to talk about it?" he asked, tugging her close.

"Yes and no. Am I going to be angry at Jasper?"

Sterling chuckled. "No. He was just doing his job."

"So, that means yes."

"It means he loves you. And he had some valid concerns...about me." Harper nodded.

He tugged on her hand and led them along the rocky beach.

"So? What did he say?"

Sterling gave her the rundown, mostly information she would have expected from her overbearing, overprotective bear of a big brother. But rather than be upset, she was again reminded of how much Jasper loved her.

And how much he knew.

Even when he didn't ask her about it all the time, he knew.

The fear.

The insecurity.

The demons of her past that haunted her.

And he was just making sure that she moved forward, rather than backward.

She couldn't be upset at him for doing that.

But it was a little out of character. She wondered what exactly had initiated it?

"Why do you think he even brought it up?" Harper asked as she kicked a few rocks into the shallow river.

Sterling shrugged; she could feel the movement through their connected hands. "I was with you, and honestly, I had no reason to be unless it was because I had a good reason. As a guy, he saw right through that."

Harper glanced at him, giving a knowing grin. "So, you're saying you've had the hots for me for a while."

"Let's just say that it's been a constant struggle from the beginning," Sterling replied unabashedly. "Is that such a bad thing?"

"Nope. That's exactly how I'd prefer it." She swung their hands, then a thought filtered through her mind. "But what about Kessed? I mean, at first it was a real thing for you, the struggle." Doubt crept through her mind. If Sterling had been attracted to her from the beginning, how did that add up with Kessed? It didn't.

"Hold on." Sterling stopped walking and turned to face Harper. "I can see where you're going, and I need you to backtrack."

Harper nodded but kept her reservations as she waited for him to explain.

"It was authentic, the feelings I had for Kessed and the issue I had with the rejection. But it was also real, how I was fighting the attraction I had for you. One doesn't negate the other. And I hate how it sounds like I'm a damn player, but it's like this. While I was letting go of what happened with her, I was trying to fight my interest in you. Totally lost that battle, by the way." He bumped her shoulder playfully.

"Why fight it?" Harper asked, her reservations slowly slipping away.

"Because I'm messed up. I'm not whole yet. I don't know if I'm just being a selfish bastard, or if I'm just more stubborn than a mule, but I'm going to try and be what you need. And hope that I'm enough. That whatever it is that I am..." He released her hand and shrugged, his expression full of vulnerability. "...that it's enough."

Harper took a step toward him and cupped his cheek in her hand. "We're all a little broken...some more than others." She glanced down at her boots. "But sometimes that's okay. I need to believe that it's okay." She took a deep breath.

"Broken, but not beyond repair." Sterling wrapped his arms around her, pulling her in, hugging her in his strong embrace.

Closing her eyes, she melted into the secure feeling of being held. It had been so long, she'd almost forgotten what it felt like to have that safe, wanted, and cherished sensation saturate deep into the soul. It melted away the last of her reservations.

She knew that the battle wasn't over.

It wasn't won.

But maybe, just maybe, she'd won round one.

And that was enough for today.

CHAPTER 15

Harper had tossed the keys to Sterling as they left Big Pines Campground. He caught them in the air.

"You want to drive back?"

Harper didn't need to ask him twice. He was more than sick of his inability to drive and was thrilled to get behind the wheel again for the second time that day. Her old truck roared to life, and soon they were winding their way back home through the canyon.

It had been a surprising day, one that had filled him with more hope for the future than he had ever expected.

It was still a long road ahead, but it was thrilling to know that he wasn't traveling it alone. Harper's hand stayed laced in his all the way back to the ranch, and he marveled at each shift in her grin, or the way her green eyes would widen or narrow as she spoke. She had no poker face, and he found that endearing.

As they pulled up to the ranch, she squeezed his hand and released it as soon as he cut the engine.

The loss of contact was more noticeable than he would have expected and caught him off guard. It was alarming how much he had already fallen for this wild girl, and a slight wariness reminded him to be careful.

Because while he didn't want to break her heart.

He didn't want to get his broken either.

And it could happen, so easily.

And as much as he needed to believe he was growing stronger each day, he didn't think he could bounce back from that kind of injury again.

"Do you want to come in?" He pulled himself from his reflective thoughts and regarded Harper as he closed the cab door.

"I should probably head home. Jasper texted me earlier, so he knows where I am—"

"And who you're with?" Sterling asked, arching a brow.

"Yup. I'm pretty sure I'll get another 'talk' when I get there. But I don't mind."

"You're pretty patient with your brother."

"When someone's heart is in the right place, it's easy to overlook things." She shrugged.

Sterling didn't reply but was pretty certain that Harper was also more understanding than the average person. He hoped that understanding extended to him; he'd probably need it.

"Well then, I guess the question is, when can I see you again?" he asked, tucking his hands in his pockets.

"Tomorrow is Sunday. What do you have planned?"

"Nothing, absolutely nothing. Which makes me sound all sorts of lame, so let me change my answer," Sterling replied, earning a loud burst of laughter from Harper.

"You want to try that again?" she teased.

"Yes. I'm busy, but I think I can work in an afternoon date. Will that be okay for you?"

"Much smoother." She winked.

"I try."

"Hmm. Well, I guess I'll make that work, since you're so busy and all."

"Thanks for understanding my need for flexibility," he said with mock severity.

"Ass. So, when? One? Two?"

"One, I want you as long as I can get you."

"Wow, demanding much?"

"Yes. It's only fair that you know what you're getting into." He used her words from earlier at the canyon, watching as her expression softened.

"Good to know."

"But still worth it?" he asked, taking one step toward her then another till he could wrap his hand around her flannel-clad waist, her warm skin seeping into his palm.

"We'll see." She winked then lifted on her tiptoes and initiated a kiss.

Which was a miracle if he'd ever seen one.

Harper, not running away from him.

But *to* him, even if it was only a few inches.

He playfully nibbled her lower lip, keeping an imaginary boundary in place, knowing full well he needed no encouragement to go from zero to sixty. Even keeping the kiss light wasn't enough deterrent for his body. Wound tight with desire, he wanted to pull her close against him. He needed to feel the soft curves of her body against his—but he stopped the thought, forcing himself to gentle the kiss before slowly stepping back when what he wanted was to take her inside...map her body with his fingertips...make her forget her own name....

"So, tomorrow?" Harper asked, her expression hopeful and still slightly insecure.

"Can't get here soon enough." Sterling appreciated that her words brought him away from his thoughts.

Her face dimpled into a grin, releasing his hand as she backed away slowly.

Sterling gave a wave and turned toward the house, his leg starting to protest the movement. He frowned as the pain made itself known, especially as he took the stairs to the door. But he didn't want to limp if Harper watched him walk into the house, so he fought against the discomfort.

Because it was always easier to believe in safety with someone who was strong.

And if there was one thing Harper needed, it was to feel safe.

He could deal with that pain if that's what it took.

The pain medication was wearing off, but he didn't want to take another dose. That night before bed, he kept the medicine cabinet shut and limped to bed.

It'll be fine. He'd convinced himself.

That night at two a.m., Sterling's leg throbbed along with his head as his earlier determination started to burn to ashes. Knowing he needed to wean himself from the painkillers was different than actually doing it.

So close.

The medicine cabinet was only a few feet away in the bathroom; it would be so easy.

But he only had five pills left.

And no refills.

Not that he wanted one. No, he wouldn't be a statistic. He wouldn't fail. He would not get hooked into that addiction.

Never had he realized just how easy it would be to give in and how hard it was to resist.

The pain in his leg was a dull ache that simply wouldn't subside, but what was worse was the feeling that he wasn't in control. That emotional high from earlier was now the sensation of circling the drain, being pulled downward, and he wasn't sure how to stop it.

He refused to think about what he was doing as he rose from the bed. Gritting his teeth, he limped slightly to the bathroom and opened the medicine cabinet. He removed two pills and swallowed them greedily, eagerly anticipating when the world would right itself, and he'd no longer hurt.

Inside or out.

Twenty minutes later, he was lying in bed, his leg still throbbing as if he'd only taken a half dose of medication. Groaning, he pushed himself off the bed and made his way back to the bathroom. Flicking on the light, he studied the orange bottle, reading the dosage.

Two to three capsules by mouth.

He'd only taken two, so he twisted the top off and took another, then walked back to his bed, sinking down into the mattress and waiting, focusing on anything but the suffocating sensation of what if, ignoring the pain.

He woke up five hours later, his body protesting from the fact that he hadn't moved since shortly after two. Yawning, he rolled over and blinked at his phone.

Damn, that extra little pill had done its job.

It was alarming how he'd needed one extra dose last night, but he refused to dwell on it.

He'd been on his feet most of the day yesterday.

Today, he'd probably be wiser to take it easy.

A nagging thought flashed across his mind as he walked to the bathroom. *Should I talk to Laken?*

As much as he hated to admit it, last night bothered him.

Indecision warred in Sterling's mind as he studied himself in the mirror. As he took out his toothbrush and brushed his teeth, he decided to dismiss the idea.

It had just been too much yesterday.

For his leg—and for his heart.

One messed-up evening didn't mean he was building a tolerance...or that he was addicted.

It just meant he needed to back the hell off on his leg and give it time.

Time. When he considered the word, a smile tugged at his lips as he tried to keep them closed while he finished brushing. When he was done, he pulled on some clean jeans and pulled a clean T-shirt from his drawer. The light blue fabric was fitted, and he tugged it down over his abs. Flexing, he decided he needed to concentrate on the muscle groups that didn't need therapy.

Easing to the floor, he pounded out fifty push-ups, tucking his weaker leg behind his good leg. Feeling the blood pound through him, the world was brighter, the uncertainty that haunted him at night all but forgotten.

He swiped his phone from the nightstand and checked the time.

Seven thirty.

Was that too early to text Harper on a Sunday morning?

His finger hovered over the messaging app, then he clicked off his phone and tucked it back in his pocket. He could wait an hour.

The aroma of bacon and eggs floated down the hall as he opened his bedroom door, and his stomach rumbled in anticipation. "Good morning!" he called out as he walked into the kitchen.

Laken waved from her seat on the countertop, her face rosy with a blush as she cast a furtive glance at Cyler, who was whistling a happy tune not a foot away as he stirred something on the stove.

"I don't want to know." Sterling held up his hands, as was the usual response when he suspected his little sister was engaging with her all-too-willing husband.

"Nope, you don't. It will ruin your breakfast." Cyler turned and wagged his eyebrows over his shoulder.

"Dude. Seriously." Sterling gave a slight shiver of revulsion as he cast a questioning glance to the eggs Cyler stirred.

Laken burst into giggles. "Told you." She directed her comment to her husband.

"I didn't disagree!" He defended himself, casting an entertained smile at Sterling.

"What gives?" Sterling asked as he took a mug down from the overhead cabinet and poured himself a healthy serving of coffee.

Laken shrugged. "All we have to do is pretend that we're messing around, and you freak out. It's fun."

"Evil, both of you."

"Pretty much," Cyler replied, acting utterly pleased with himself.

"Speaking of fun..." Laken hopped down from the counter.

Sterling paused as the calculating glint entered his sister's expression. "What...?" he asked, instantly suspicious.

"Word is...you and Harper..." She arched her brows, grinning like an idiot.

"Whose *word*?" Sterling made air quotes to mock his sister.

Cyler answered. "Kessed, through Jasper, because apparently she didn't respond adequately to her texts and got the fifth degree—Kessed's words— when she got home. And it kills me that I know all this, but honestly, your sister hasn't shut up about it."

Laken smacked his arm. "Seriously?"

"I believe it. So, Jasper hounded her, huh?" Sterling asked, wincing.

"Well, Kessed said he asked a lot of questions, not hounding, per se," Laken hedged.

"Hounded." Cyler cast a wry grin to Sterling.

"I was afraid of that. Do you think...?" He turned his full attention to Cyler, needing a man's opinion. "...do you think I need to talk with Jasper? I mean, I get his angle, and I'd be pissed as hell if he didn't protect Harper this way...but he needs to know that I'm not going to intentionally hurt her."

"I knew it!" Laken started jumping up and down, clapping.

"Simmer, sis. Really." Sterling rolled his eyes then turned back to Cyler.

"Yes!" Laken fist-pumped. "I knew it!"

"Are you done yet?" Cyler asked with a gentle tone as he wrapped an arm around his wife's middle and hugged her close.

"Nope."

"Then at least be quiet so I can answer your brother's question." He kissed her mouth softly.

"Guys..." Sterling closed his eyes and drew out the word.

"Yes. You need to talk with Jasper," Cyler replied, and Sterling opened his eyes.

"Today?"

"Probably would be wise. You gotta realize Jasper is already going to have a few strikes against you for trying to steal Kessed, then you jump ship and go after Harper? Probably didn't settle well. You guys need to work it out, or else Harper won't be comfortable with the situation, and you're screwed before you even have a shot," Cyler explained.

"What he said." Laken kissed his cheek and walked out of the hug.

"Just lay it out, man to man, and you'll be fine. Jasper's a good guy, and if this works out with you and Harper, he'll be your brother. Think ahead, man, and do things the right way," Cyler added.

"Yes. I get that. I'll text him and see if maybe we can talk before I pick up Harper."

"When is that?" Laken asked, her grin back in full force.

"About one," Sterling answered.

"You've got plenty of time then." Laken pulled down several plates while Cyler put the eggs on the table along with a stack of buttered toast and a plate of bacon.

Sterling studied the food. "Guys, thank you. I really appreciate all that you've done for me. Not just the food and keeping me busy..." He directed the comment to Cyler, who nodded in response. He turned to Laken next. "...

but also for giving me a home. It's something I haven't had in a really long time, and I—I honestly forgot what it felt like. Thanks for reminding me."

Laken's eyes were shimmering as she looked down, biting her lip. After a breath, she turned back to Sterling. "Honey, we love you. This is your home. But thank you, it's...it's really great to hear that you're happy here. I was really worried you'd hate it." She shrugged, a tear trailing down her face.

Sterling was horrified. "Why in the devil would I hate it?"

"You've had a hard year, the most difficult part walking away from the marines. You loved being deployed, you loved traveling...this is pretty much the opposite." She shrugged a shoulder as Cyler reached across the table and grasped her hand.

"As a man, I get how you need purpose, something to aim for and strive to achieve. You had that, and then it was taken away. It's hard to find your footing, but you're getting there. And your sister and I...we care." As Cyler spoke, his baritone conveyed his sincerity.

Sterling was humbled, nodding to Cyler then offering his sister a small smile. "Thank you. I appreciate every moment. And don't worry about me, Lake. I might not be a cowboy, but I'm tough like one."

Laken chuckled. "You are." She wiped a tear away. "Gah, I'm so freaking emotional it's killing me." She sniffed delicately and wiped her eyes again.

"It's all good. Your tears don't freak me out." Sterling gave her a lopsided grin.

"Now that we've had our eggs properly salted..." Cyler winked at Laken, earning a glare in return.

Sterling chuckled but covered his mouth with his hand as Cyler continued. "...let's dig in."

Sterling took care of the dishes after breakfast, and as he was finishing up, his text alert went off.

He unlocked the screen and read the message from Laken with Jasper's contact information.

Now was as good a time as any.

He tapped in the number and frowned at his phone, trying to gather his thoughts.

Hey Jasper, would you be able to talk with me
later today?

After he sent it, he groaned in frustration, realizing Jasper wouldn't have a clue who had sent the text. He fired off another quick one.

This is Sterling.

The message bubble appeared, signaling a reply, and he waited impatiently.

Ten am?

Sterling expelled his pent-up breath and tapped a quick reply.

Sure. Where do you want to meet?

Jasper replied almost immediately.

I'll come to your place.

Sterling nodded, then tapped his agreement into the message box and sent it.

He had two hours, and that was a lot of time to think, damn it.

Opening up another message window, he started a message to Harper.

Still on for one?

When a bubble didn't pop up, he tucked the phone in his pocket and strode out to the barn. Cyler had mentioned that he'd welcome some help out there after breakfast, and Sterling wasn't one to dodge work.

If anything, today was the day for manual labor. Work out the stress and anticipation. Nothing sounded more welcome.

"Hey, can you give me a hand?" Cyler asked as Sterling walked into the barn.

"Sure thing." Sterling strode over to Cyler.

"Hold it right here. I got it level, but once I start hammering in the nail, it will probably try to move on you."

Sterling leaned against the pine two-by-four, holding it in place, keeping an eye on the bubble to make sure it stayed level. Cyler pounded in the galvanized nails with the practiced ease of a construction worker, and soon Sterling's job was rendered unnecessary as the nails held the board in place.

"Next one." Cyler nodded to a board leaning against the wall of the barn.

"Got it." Sterling picked it up and carefully swung it around so that it would fit beside the other beam.

Cyler set the level then tapped the board Sterling was holding with his hammer, making slight adjustments till the bubble hovered perfectly in the middle.

As Cyler was finishing up nailing the second board in place, he addressed Sterling. "So, your sister doesn't know, but I have something planned for the next two days. I'm going to need you to hold down the fort for me." He dusted off his hands and regarded Sterling. "Mostly, everything is taken care of, but you'll have to ride out and check on the herd, make sure none of the gates blow closed, and feed Margaret."

Sterling nodded. "Not a problem. So, where are you taking Laken?"

Cyler grinned. "We're going to Salish Lodge up by Snoqualmie Falls. They have wood-burning fireplaces in each room. She's going to love it."

Sterling chuckled. "Romantic."

"That's the plan," Cyler answered with a wink.

"Great, well, when do you leave?" Sterling picked up a pitchfork and headed toward Margaret's stall.

"We need to check in by four, but I'm hoping to be out of here by noon. It's not that far of a drive, but it would be fun to hike around the falls first," Cyler answered as Sterling tossed Margaret a flake of alfalfa. The green dust settled around her as the mare lowered her head to sniff at her breakfast.

Sterling opened the stall door and patted Margaret's large frame as he walked to the back of the enclosure to clean up the manure and lay down fresh hay.

"Here's the wagon." Cyler followed him in and set the wagon close.

"Thanks."

Cyler patted Margaret's rump as he left the stall. "I'm going to tell Laken. That way she has time to pack. Lord knows, that woman takes forever to accomplish that task."

"I had a childhood that was dictated by Laken's inability to pack clothes. Don't even start with me, man," Sterling teased as Cyler walked out of the barn.

Cyler gave Sterling a commiserating grin over his shoulder as he walked out into the sunlight.

"Well, looks like it's just you and me for a while, old girl." Sterling watched Margaret out of the corner of his eye as he completed his task. He'd come to a place where he wasn't totally scared shitless of the huge animal, but that didn't mean he trusted her.

Not by a long shot.

As he wheeled the wagon out of the stall, he patted Margaret's hindquarters, making sure she knew he was there so she wouldn't kick.

Not that he'd ever seen her kick.

But there was always a first time for everything, and he didn't want it to be him.

As Sterling slid the barn door closed, his phone buzzed. After pulling it out of his pocket, he saw that Harper had replied to his earlier message.

*One, it is. Of course, you have to brave my big
bad brother before that. You do realize he's
cleaning his gun right now...*

Sterling chuckled. As if that intimidated him. Guns were merely an extension of himself in combat. Hell, he half wanted to drive down to Harper's house and help Jasper do it correctly.
Grinning, he replied.

*Does he need help? Guns don't intimidate me...
Give me a horse and that's a different story.*

The bubble popped up.

*Damn, should have seen that one. Okay, he's not
cleaning his gun. He's planning on taking you for
a trail ride around a steep cliff.*

Just thinking about the confrontation had Sterling breaking into a cold sweat.

*Mission accomplished. I'm scared shitless. Happy
now?*

He could almost hear her laughter in his mind as the bubble popped up.

*Yes. But he actually is cleaning his gun, weird
coincidence. I'll tell him you want to help.*

Damn, Harper! Sterling wiped his hand down his face and closed his eyes. She wouldn't really, would she?
She continued the message.

*He says you should head over here if you want
to impress him with your...uh...'ability to handle
your weapon.' I don't even want to know...*

Sterling chuckled, recognizing the veiled threat and implication, respecting it as well.

Be there soon.

Good response. He's reading over my shoulder.
Ass.

Sterling rolled his eyes as he walked to the ranch house. Well, at least he was dealing on a level he was comfortable with: weapons.

As he opened the side door, he heard his sister's voice. "Check the weather for me, baby."

Sure enough, Laken was in full-on packing mode. Sterling gave an amused grin to Cyler who dutifully pulled out his phone to check the app.

"Warm enough."

"Meaning what exactly?" Laken asked from down the hall in the master bedroom.

"Meaning, if you pack a sweatshirt, it would be a smart idea, but not entirely necessary." Cyler bit back a grin, and Sterling saluted his efforts at torturing Laken.

"Gah, you know what I mean," Laken ground out.

"Actually, I—"

"Numbers, Cyler!"

Sterling chuckled, giving Cyler a high five as he passed and went into his bedroom to grab his wallet.

Frowning, he realized he was without transportation to Harper's home. That was something he'd have to fix, but he didn't have enough time today. Thankfully he'd always saved the majority of his income from the marines, not needing much of it since he'd been mostly overseas. Having a nest egg available was one of the only bright spots of the past year.

With a sigh, he walked back in the hall, watching as Cyler brought a suitcase out of her room.

"She's done?" Sterling asked, surprise in his tone.

"More or less."

"Cyler Myer, I can't believe you just grabbed a load of unfolded laundry and tossed it in—"

Cyler interrupted her tirade by letting go of the luggage handle and kissing his wife into silence.

Sterling glanced away but grinned at his brother-in-law's effective measures.

"Let's go. You don't really need clothes anyway," Cyler added when he released Laken from the kiss.

"Didn't need to hear that part." Sterling groaned. "Lake, can I borrow your car while you're gone?"

"Sure, the keys are hanging up. You feel comfortable driving?"

Sterling nodded. "Yeah, I won't be going far. Jasper wants to have a man to man."

Cyler slapped his back. "May God have mercy on your soul."

"Whatever. You're fine. Yes, take the car, have fun, and if you need anything, just text me."

"Laken, Sterling can take care of himself." Cyler tugged on her hand, leading her toward the door.

Sterling waved as they disappeared to the outside. As the sound of the pickup driving down the gravel road slowly dissipated, he soaked up the silence.

As much as he loved being with Laken and Cyler, it was pleasant to have a moment to himself.

He glanced to his phone.

Damn. He had to get a move on if he was to get to Harper and Jasper's home anytime soon.

He crossed to the front door, glorying in the fact that his leg didn't hurt at all, almost felt strong. It was an empowering feeling, one that made him almost seem whole.

Unbroken.

In control.

He snagged Laken's keys from the hook by the front door, made sure to lock up, then headed to her little sedan. As he drove to Harper's house, he tried to play out different scenarios in his mind of possible interactions with Jasper. Like he was preparing a raid, he imagined all the entrances and exits for the conversation, the danger zones, the difficult topics, and the areas that could prove problematic.

The trip passed quickly, and he soon was driving up the dirt road that led to Spartan's barn and Jasper's house.

He turned off the engine and tucked the keys in his pocket. As he strode to the house, he breathed in a calming breath.

The door swung open, and immediately all his tension melted like snow in the sunshine. "Hey, you." Harper leaned her shoulder against the door. Her hair was swept up into a high ponytail with the purple ends framing her face. Her open-neck sweatshirt slung low, exposing her sun-kissed shoulder.

"Hey." Sterling's gaze roamed her beautiful face. Her skin glowed, and he realized she wasn't wearing any makeup. "Damn, you look beautiful in the morning," he murmured softly as he stepped up onto the porch.

Her green eyes flashed with amusement before her cheeks colored slightly. "Thanks. I'm sporting the all-natural look today."

"I like it." Sterling's lips widened into a welcoming smile as he reached out and grasped her hand.

"Hey, you don't need to score any points with me. It's the guy inside. You ready for this?" Harper nodded her head once, motioning behind her, daring him with a sassy grin.

"I think you're more nervous than I," Sterling challenged.

Harper's answer rang in her amused laughter. "Whatever you need to tell yourself, Captain." She swung the door open wide for him.

"Oh, Jasper, you've got company!" she called out before Sterling could greet her brother himself. She led him to the kitchen.

"Hey." Jasper turned off the kitchen faucet and dried his hands on the nearby towel.

"Hey." Sterling waited for Jasper to make the first move, to direct the conversation. This was on his timeline, and Sterling was happy to let him lead.

"I'll, uh, just be back by about noon." Harper took a step toward the door, distracting Sterling.

He gave her a questioning glance.

She gave a quick smile to her brother before turning to Sterling. "I'm checking out a potential second racer. Her name is Audrey. She's a younger mare, but her bloodline is amazing. Fate's Fancy is her sire, and her dame is Calendar Girl's March—both award winners in the barrel-racing world. She's kind of a pill to ride, so she's been difficult to sell. I'm hoping that we hit it off." Harper winked at Sterling.

"Text when you get there and when you're done. Uncle Vince said it's legit, but that doesn't mean I blindly trust these people," Jasper warned.

"It's fine." Harper rolled her eyes. "But don't worry, I'll text. Okay? You actually have your phone with you?"

Sterling turned to Jasper and tried to get a read on his reaction. "Yup. Ever since you gave me that stupid little tile square, I can't lose the damn gadget."

"And that's bad?" Kessed asked as she walked into the room. She placed a kiss on Jasper's cheek and then gave a small wave to Sterling. "Aw, so you're not just brave on the front lines, huh? Way to show some balls today, Sterling." She poked Jasper's ribs. "Go easy on him."

"Why are you all picking on me?" Jasper growled. "Just let me know, okay?"

"Fine," Harper replied. Her gaze flickered between the men.

Sterling wondered what was going on behind those green eyes. She seemed indecisive about something.

She took a tentative step forward then straightened her shoulders, her resolve strengthening in her gaze as she focused on Sterling. It happened in just a moment, but she closed the distance between them and stretched to kiss his cheek, her scent of lemon lingering longer than she, as she spun on her heel and disappeared out the door.

Kessed's giggle had him turning to question her amusement.

"Have fun, Jas."

Jasper sighed but apparently wasn't about to let Kessed walk away yet. He snagged her around the waist and kissed her full on the mouth, creating an awkward silence in the room as Sterling diverted his eyes.

"See you later." Kessed's voice told him the coast was clear, and he glanced back to the parting couple. Kessed gave a small wave as she left through the front door.

Leaving them alone.

And there wasn't even a damn gun on the table to mess around with and clean up.

"So...why does this feel redundant?" Jasper asked as he strode around the table and pulled out a chair, motioning for Sterling to sit as well.

"Something does feel familiar." Sterling tested the waters by following Jasper's lead into the amusing aspect of their situation.

"I was led to believe you didn't have an interest in my little sister." Jasper drove his statement home as he speared Sterling with a hard gaze.

Sterling took a seat, pressing his forearms against the table and sitting forward. "I said she deserved better than me. Which is still the truth. And honestly, I was trying to talk myself out of any attraction I had because I know that she's been hurt, broken, and bruised in ways that no one should ever have to withstand. So, I laid it all out for her—no guessing, no playing around. She knows where I stand, understanding that I'm broken too. What do you need to know?"

Jasper tapped the table with his thumb, his gaze narrowing as he studied Sterling. "She comes home crying because you're an ass, or you break her heart..." He let the threat linger.

"You can take me out. I'll give you my own gun to do the job."

"I'm not going to prison over you. You'll be doing the honors yourself. Understood?" Jasper asked.

Sterling bit back an amused grin. Damn it all, Jasper was the kind of guy he could actually be friends with. "Deal."

Jasper reached across the table, offering his hand, and Sterling took it, firmly shaking once.

"Now that we have an understanding, let me tell you a little about my irritating little sister. If you're going to have a snowball's chance in hell, you need to listen up."

And Sterling listened as if his life depended on it.

Because he wasn't so sure he'd survive a broken heart.

CHAPTER 16

Harper pulled into the drive at just a quarter after noon, dusty, sweaty, and a mix of anxious and thrilled. Thrilled, because Audrey was going to be a fantastic addition to her barrel-racing team. And anxious, because Sterling's car was still there, and she had no clue in hell what her brother had said to him.

She walked up to the house tentatively then paused as laughter sounded from inside. Confused, she opened the screen door and saw Sterling at the stove with Kessed and Jasper at the table, eating what looked like grilled cheese sandwiches. *Figures.*

"What did I miss, because I'm thinking it was a lot," Harper said by way of a greeting.

"Your guy here can cook. Who knew?" Kessed lifted her sandwich in a salute to Sterling. "Seriously, though, I had no idea he could cook anything. Last I heard, Laken said he burned water."

"Hey, that was once." Sterling shook a spatula at Kessed while Jasper snickered.

"So, this is new. And I see no guns or blood, so I'm assuming we're all good?" Harper asked, tossing her purse to a nearby chair.

"Yup. Chill, and grab a sandwich," Sterling replied. "I kicked it up a notch with some hot sauce from the fridge. It's not the same as the jalapeño bread, but it's a definite improvement."

"Count me in." Harper took a seat at the table.

After Sterling served her, Harper tugged him aside while Kessed and Jasper fought teasingly over who was on dish duty. "So, what did my brother say?"

Sterling shrugged and popped the last bit of sandwich into his mouth. The definition in his face adjusted, highlighting his jawline. Her fingers itched to trace its line.

"It wasn't a big deal. I was honest with him, like I was with you yesterday, and that's pretty much all he wanted. No games. No breaking your heart. For the record, he didn't give a shit if you broke mine."

"Sounds about right." Harper released the tension in her shoulders as she laughed softly.

"Thanks." Sterling gave a wry grin. "Did you like the horse?"

"Yeah, I gave my verbal agreement to the deal. I'll have Jasper look over it later and compare her stats."

"Sounds good. Spartan is getting a girlfriend." Sterling wagged his brows.

"Spartan is a gelding. So, Spartan is getting a friend, platonically speaking."

"Ah, got it," Sterling answered. "You ready to go?"

Harper gave him a dubious glance. "Like this? I smell like horse and sweat."

Sterling leaned his head down, taking a deep breath along her ear.

The cool intake sent goose bumps prickling along her skin and caused a tickle up her spine. The world absolutely disappeared as Harper reveled in the sensation.

"You're perfect to me, but if you want to shower and change, I think I can wait a few minutes." Sterling patted her on the head, breaking the spell of sexual tension that he'd created.

Jasper cleared his throat.

Harper sent her brother a dirty look but turned back to Sterling. "Depends. What do you have planned today?"

"That's for me to know, you to find out and to be amazed." He flicked his fingers along her ribs.

Harper squealed as he tickled and swatted his hand away. "Five minutes." She held up her hand.

"Have at it."

Harper shrugged off her plaid shirt and tossed it into her room as she passed by then ducked into the bathroom. After taking what her brother called a "sea shower," she quickly brushed her teeth and wrapped a towel around her body as she darted from the bathroom to her room. She didn't miss the heated glance Sterling gave as she made the short walk, and with a wink, she closed her bedroom door.

She tossed the towel over a chair and quickly dressed, slipped her feet into some sneakers, and tightened her ponytail. Debating whether to add a swipe of mascara, she quickly grabbed her makeup bag and a few minutes later, decided she was ready.

Or not.

Mostly ready.

They'd been dancing around each other for more than a month. And in that time, she had learned a lot about Sterling's personality, his strengths, and his weaknesses. It gave her a sense of being prepared, which allayed some of her fears.

Some.

She breathed slowly through her nose, steeling herself before she opened her bedroom door.

"I'm ready when you are." She smiled at Sterling as she walked back into the kitchen.

His gaze swept over her, no doubt taking in all the details, probably ones even she would miss. His gray eyes were warm, heated, yet tempered with an appreciation that made her feel beautiful.

Damn, that felt good.

How long had it been since she had actually *felt* beautiful?

Hell, she would have been happy with feeling like she was *enough*. Feeling beautiful was almost too much. Like she had asked for one piece of chocolate and been given the whole factory.

"Jasper, thank you for your time this morning," Sterling addressed her brother, offering his hand.

Jasper accepted it and gave him a curt nod, his expression a firm reminder of everything they had discussed, if she'd read it correctly. She'd received a silent reminder from her brother herself a time or two...or hundred.

Biting back a snicker, she walked over to Jasper and gave him a hug. "See you later."

"You bet." Then in a low whisper, he continued. "You have your knife, Mace...something?"

Harper released her brother and smacked his arm. "You have to ask?" She wagged her head at him.

"That's my girl."

"Do I want to know?" Sterling asked.

"Just making sure I have *protection*." Harper shrugged, grinning widely at Sterling's surprised and slightly awkward expression.

He'd misinterpreted the play on words, just as she'd intended.

"Harper!" Jasper scolded, groaning.

"You know, a knife, pepper spray, stuff like that," she added, unable to hold back her laughter at making the situation utterly awkward for both her brother and Sterling.

"Thanks for clarifying, Harper," Sterling replied with a hint of sarcasm.

"I got your back."

"Yeah, sure."

Sterling opened the door for her, and they walked out into the afternoon sun. Even if it wasn't as warm as summer, the sun made up in intensity what it lacked in actual warmth.

"Driving, huh?" Harper asked as she followed him to the sedan.

"Yup. Afraid?"

"Slightly."

Sterling rolled his eyes but walked around to the passenger side door and opened it for Harper.

"Thanks."

As Sterling started the car, she asked again. "So, what's happening today?"

Sterling gave a slight shrug as he drove with one arm out the open window, his other hand relaxed on the steering wheel. "I have a plan, but first we need to pick up food. One little grilled cheese sandwich wasn't exactly enough."

"Pick up, as in take it somewhere else?" Harper asked.

"Yup. Do me a favor and call ahead to Yellow Church Café. I have the phone number in my notes section. I have it on good authority you love a sandwich called Holy Moley?" Sterling gave her a quick smile before turning his attention back to the road.

"How did you know that?" Harper asked, taking his phone from the dash.

"My code is my birthdate, 07-19-89."

Harper tapped the code into the screen. "Wow, I have your code... I feel like this is a huge step in our relationship."

Sterling chuckled, the deep sound welcoming and sexy as hell. "I bled my heart all over you yesterday. Pretty sure that my phone code isn't as large of step. But if information is important, my blood type is B positive, and I hate needles. My usual passwords are my first dog's name, which was—"

"Okay, I get it." Harper laughed. "Nothing to hide. I appreciate that. Now, what do you want to eat? They have a great burger."

"That's exactly what I want."

"Perfect."

Harper ordered their food, and when they pulled up to the bright yellow building, she waited in the car as Sterling promised to return shortly with their meal.

Sterling came back carrying two paper bags. Heavenly scents filled the air around them as he got into the car and handed the food to Harper. Soon they were driving away.

"So, where to now?"

"The petrified forest," Sterling replied as he pulled out toward the canyon that led to the Columbia River.

"Ginkgo Petrified Forest? Huh, I've actually never been there," Harper commented.

"Laken told me about it, and it sounded fun. You know, team building while you hold my hand to help me navigate the difficult trails. It's probably a stupid move, and I might not be able to hike too far, but I've heard the view is worth it." Sterling gave her a wolfish grin.

"Looking for excuses to hold my hand?"

"Yup."

"Smooth, because you're limping so badly these days." Harper rolled her eyes.

"I have a good therapist," Sterling added with a serious tone.

Harper shook her head. "Yeah, you do. The best."

"Hotter than hell too." Sterling gave a low whistle.

"I've heard she's a hardass."

"Just part of her charm," Sterling replied.

The rest of the afternoon played out with the same kind of give and take, push and pull. They'd eaten their lunch in the petrified forest parking lot beside the huge dinosaur statue. They'd navigated the trails and crested the hills, offering a fantastic panoramic view of the Columbia River Gorge, and they'd only run into one rattlesnake.

During that time, Harper's fears had melted away, and she realized that she often still struggled with being herself.

As if she wasn't enough and needed to play a role.

But not with Sterling. It was natural to actually be real, to make the smartass remarks, flirt, tease—just enjoy life.

It was beautiful.

But most of all, it was healing.

And as the afternoon wound into evening, she was reluctant for it all to end.

"I hope you don't mind, but I gotta check on a few things back at the ranch before I drop you off. If you're wanting me to take you home first, I understand, though."

Harper had her leg tucked under her knee as she lazily caressed Sterling's hand that she held as they drove back toward Ellensburg.

"That's fine. I'm in no hurry." She released a breath of silent relief.

"Laken and Cyler are out of town for the next day, so I'm holding down the fort. I should check on Margaret, and I have to ride out to make sure the gates are all open. We haven't had any more wind than usual."

"Welcome to Ellensburg, where the trees grow sideways." Harper cast him an amused glance.

"Yeah, learning that. It's been relatively calm today, but I need to check on them regardless."

"Cyler will make you a rancher yet."

Sterling chuckled. "Not exactly, but I'm learning different skills, and that's always a good thing. When he gets back, I think I'm going to see if he needs help on one of his construction crews. I don't have much experience, but the idea of working with my hands is appealing."

"I think that's a good plan," Harper replied as they turned onto the ranch's dirt driveway.

"Do you?" Sterling questioned.

She quickly studied his expression. Was he questioning her because he didn't believe her? Had she misspoken? Yet, as she regarded him, she realized he truly wanted her approval.

Huh.

It was empowering, and it softened her heart in a way she hadn't anticipated. While she understood, that in many ways, Sterling was broken like she was, it had never occurred to her that he might be insecure as well.

He was confident, powerful, and one of the few people who could probably take her brother in a fight. None of those traits lined up with insecurity.

Yet, there it was.

And she responded to it, as if it echoed in her own soul.

"Sterling, I think you're pretty much able to do whatever you put your mind to. But you need to find something that you love, that you can throw your energy into, that gives you purpose. You're more like me than I realized." She watched the scenery out the window as they pulled up to the house.

"Purpose is necessary," he added with a grin.

"Exactly. You're used to working with your hands, and you're simply trading the M27 for a nail gun. Seems logical." Harper shrugged, proud of her neat comparison.

"Nicely done."

"Thank you." She gave a little head bow as she opened the car door. She glanced to her phone on the dash and made the impulsive decision to leave it. "So, what's first?"

"Margaret, always Margaret, and then let's ride out along the pastures on the quads, sound good?"

"Lead away, Captain."

Sterling paused, his shoulders slightly tense as he turned to her. "Harper, when you call me that, it..."

Harper's heart seized. Damn, she hadn't even thought of it, but it had to hurt, being reminded that he wasn't enlisted any longer. "Sterling, I'm sorry—"

"No"—he held up a hand—"it's not that. It's just... Honey, it seriously undermines all the self-control I'm trying to have. Because all I can think of is how you'd sound calling me that when I have you in bed. And I don't need any help with my imagination, Harper. So, give a guy a break." He tucked a stray strand of hair behind her ear and walked away, his shoulders still tight, stretching the fabric of his T-shirt, offering her a tempting view of the years of hard work to build those muscles.

Damn. Harper blew out a stuttering breath, her heart pounding, her body reacting to his words.

Wanting them to happen so badly it ached.

Down, girl.

She took a calming breath and followed Sterling, purposefully filing away the information for later.

Heaven only knew she'd love to explore that idea...but along with the arousal came a shiver of fear.

Sex equaled pain.

Not at first, but Brock had made their physical relationship one that undermined everything that she had dreamed sex to be.

Pleasure was traded for punishment—and not the kind that was erotic.

The time she should have gloried in her body, she'd been shamed.

When she would have given anything for control, all her dignity had been shredded.

But it will be different with Sterling...right?

She had to believe that, but it didn't erase the fear.

Control. She had to be in control.

Maybe, if she initiated everything on her terms, her way...

She followed Sterling into the barn, her anxious mood fracturing into a million pieces as she watched Sterling's careful movements around Margaret.

A laugh escaped her lips. It was so weird that Sterling was still somewhat afraid of horses.

Horses. She trusted them more than most people she'd encountered, yet he couldn't even walk around one without keeping a wary eye on the poor thing.

"You know they can smell fear."

Sterling gave her a mock glare. "So I've been told." He disappeared below the fence and then popped back up holding a piece of blue twine from the alfalfa. "I didn't realize this was still attached when I pitched the damn thing in," he grumbled.

"You did the right thing, Sterling. I know Cyler appreciates your help."

He gave her an irritated glance as he slid by her to the stall gate. The poor mare didn't even seem to care that he was there. She was too interested in her dinner. But Sterling was acting like she was going to bolt and trample him.

She giggled.

He pulled the stall gate shut with a click and walked away, dusting his hands off. "Okay, fences?"

"Fences," Harper affirmed, still grinning from her residual amusement.

"I know you're laughing at me. I'm ignoring it," Sterling grumbled as they closed the barn door and walked around back to where the quads were parked.

"I didn't say a word." Harper lifted a hand.

"You didn't need to," Sterling replied as he started up his ATV.

Soon, they were passing through the pastures, and Sterling double-checked everything. His whole demeanor was more confident than even two weeks ago. He wasn't comfortable with horses, yet he got the job done. The guy didn't really even like cows, but he took care of them well and had learned what he needed to know to do the job right. It was rare to find someone with that kind of dogged determination. It would have been easy for him to wallow in pity, yet he'd risen above it.

Again and again.

"All finished!" he called out, pointing back to the barn.

Harper followed, enjoying the cool breeze against her face as they passed the scrub brush and Russian olive trees with their heavy resin scent.

They pulled behind the barn and parked, then Sterling extended his hand in invitation.

Harper accepted, savoring the warmth, the security his touch represented. As they walked hand in hand toward the drive, the underground sprinklers came on over the yard. She noticed a rushing sound of water, then frowned at the sight of one sprinkler shooting a geyser into the sky.

"Damn it," Sterling swore and released her hand. He jogged over to where the water shot upward.

Harper followed, pretty sure she knew what was happening. Damn sprinkler heads.

Just as Sterling was approaching the broken one, another one broke, shooting water into the air and raining down on him.

Harper bit back a laugh as Sterling startled then appeared to sigh as his shoulders rose and then fell.

"Where's the control box?" Harper called out.

Sterling turned and walked out of the spray, wiping down his face. "Barn."

"On it." Harper whipped around and ran toward the barn. Scanning the walls, she found the sprinkler box then opened it and flipped the switch from automatic to off.

The sound of water slowed and stopped.

Running back to the yard, she watched as Sterling bent down and picked up two sprinkler heads.

"Broken, huh?" she asked, walking up to him.

"Yeah, I didn't know they shot up like that." He gave a small grin to Harper.

She shrugged. "Happens. Since it's irrigation water, sometimes the filter misses something, and it jams in the sprinkler. Then the pressure builds up and...boom!" She made an explosive motion with her hands.

"Boom." He plucked at his soaked T-shirt.

The fabric bounced back and clung to Sterling's wet skin, giving her a perfect outline of his abs. Her mouth went dry.

"Up here, Harper." He snapped his fingers twice, a wicked glint in his eye.

Harper's cheeks heated, but she hitched a shoulder. "The view is better there."

Sterling grinned, but he looked away to the house. "Well, I probably should change before I take you home. Laken will kill me if I soak her car." He gave a half grin as he turned back to her.

Harper wondered at his quick shift in conversation topic, but assumed it was probably due to that self-control he was trying to maintain.

And the temptation to snap it was almost beyond her ability to withstand. "I'll help." She walked toward him holding out her hand, waiting.

Sterling studied her with his powerful gray stare, as if trying to read her intention. He squeezed her hand, and they walked toward the house. The air was electric while he dug the keys from his wet pocket with his other hand and unlocked the door.

Harper took a deep breath as they entered, questioning her sanity as she followed Sterling down the hall. "So, Laken and Cyler are gone?"

Sterling paused, watching her. "Till tomorrow." He regarded her cautiously, the same way she would approach skittish colt.

Only the skittish colt was her.

Her hand trembled as she released his grasp and slowly ran her palm up his wet shirt, the chill sending a shiver up her spine, her heart pounding adrenaline through her system. Fight or flight.

Only it was just love.

It was alarming how much they felt alike. Yet were so different.

At least they should be.

In a perfect world. Not the one where she existed.

"Harper." Sterling whispered her name, caressing it with his rough tone, sending her nerve endings to crackling with understanding.

Her fingers bumped over the ridges in his abs, and she slowly gripped the wet fabric, her nails biting into it as she tugged upward, exposing just a hint of tan skin.

She breathed out slowly, her breath hitching as she kept her gaze low, not able to bring herself to meet his eyes.

Not yet.

As she lifted the fabric higher, a low groan rumbled through his chest, and instinctively, her gaze flickered up, meeting his scorching gray eyes. Her hands paused, and she got the sense that he wanted her to move faster, but she was paralyzed.

So rather than move, she waited.

Breathing in, breathing out, and then Sterling closed his eyes, breaking the trance.

Free, she found her courage and lifted his shirt up over his head, while he raised his arms to assist. His dog tags clinked as they landed back on his chest. The wet garment hit the floor, and she zeroed in on the metallic necklace that represented Sterling's past life.

He sucked in a breath as her cold hands skipped across his skin, lifting the tags to study them. It was an intimate exchange to hold his past in one hand and his present in another as she laced her free hand through his. She studied the words.

Capt. Sterling Garlington

Her gaze froze as she read the first word again.

Captain.

She remembered his earlier words, his warning. *Don't call me that unless...*

Tugging gently on the metal chain, she watched as he slowly lowered his head. Her lips hovered just above his as she rallied her bravery.

"Well, then, *Captain...*" She closed the distance between their mouths, his heat immediately flowing through her lips and igniting her entire body, burning away her hesitation.

Sterling's hands snaked up her arms and pulled her in tightly against his body. His tongue teased her lower lip as his hand dipped under her shirt and trailed along her bare skin, leaving a fiery trail of need in his wake.

She tilted her head, the kiss spiraling out of control as Sterling's chest pushed against hers, backing her until she was pinned against the wall. His hands moved to her hips, spanning them, then tugging her in tight. His length pressed against her, large and thick.

Reaching down, she traced along the ridge, a grin teasing her lips. She watched his reaction as she touched him through the wet denim. He was beautiful. Masculine. A living, breathing fantasy. Lips, swollen and wet, parted as he panted. Need and steely control flashed through his eyes as he thrust into her touch, closing his lids with pleasure.

"Harper." Sterling groaned her name as his hands gripped her hips, before he released her abruptly.

A moment later, he grasped both of her hands in one of his and laced his fingers through hers above her head before gently pressing their foreheads together, his breathing erratic. He plastered his body to hers, meeting her lips with a hunger that left her breathless. He cupped her breast, and her hands jerked at the intense pleasure, but she couldn't move them.

Panic seized Harper, and at her jerk, Sterling released her and stepped back just enough to give her room. His chest rose and fell with desire, yet confusion and caution seemed to war within him.

"It's just..." she started, not quite knowing how to finish. Her head dropped forward as shame washed over her. "I needed to move...my hands."

When Sterling didn't answer, she gathered her courage and looked up. His stormy eyes had her trying to take a step back, but the wall prevented any further retreat.

"He hurt you." Sterling spoke the words as a realization, not a question.

Harper absently rubbed her wrists, remembering the rope burns, remembering the *pain*.

But no scars.

At least not ones that were visible.

Sterling took a slow breath then extended his hand.

Fight or flight.

Her heart pounded, all earlier fearlessness gone as she stood on the knife's edge of indecision.

Sterling made the choice for her. Closing the distance, he wrapped his arm around her waist, pulling her in tight as he placed the softest kiss across her lips. After drawing back, he spoke gently. "We're going to heal all those scars on your heart, honey. No pain here...not with me. Just pleasure. The kind that makes you forget every single memory of what sex was before. Because we're not just going to have sex. We're going to make love, Harper."

Her tension slowly eased when he kissed her again searchingly, as if pulling her consent from her soul before it ever was voiced.

"But I need one thing from you," Sterling murmured against her lips, pulling her gently away from the wall and reaching a hand up her back, lifting her shirt softly.

"Anything." Harper was lost, certain she'd agree to anything at this point.

She raised her hands and watched his eyes map her curves.

"Harper, I *need* control."

No, anything but that.

She took a deep breath, opened her mouth to speak, but Sterling shook his head. "You need to learn that sometimes you need to let go, and honey, you can't do that unless someone else leads you. Let me take you there, because I can't have control unless you *give* it." He paused, lips parted, his abs tight, his shoulders broad and tense as he waited for her answer.

"Permission. You're asking for permission?" Harper not only saw the difference, she felt the difference, deep inside her core.

Sometimes control wasn't giving up.

Control was letting go.

In that moment, she realized how much she desperately wanted to let go, to stop holding herself together with raw tenacity.

To be held together by someone else. Have someone else's arms around her, keeping the pieces in place, rather than constantly holding them herself.

Swallowing hard, she nodded, unable to speak. She felt the walls around her start to crumble, piece by piece.

Parts of her heart once again started to gain feeling after having been numb for so long.

Hope.

It was powerful.

It was dangerous.

And somehow, even though she'd been through hell and back—

It had survived.

Like her.

"Come with me." Sterling tugged on her hand, guiding her toward a bedroom. Eyes on him, she followed wordlessly, knowing everything was about to change.

And being willing to embrace that change for the first time.

While Sterling led her toward the bed, she scanned the room. She smiled as she realized that it fit so well with what she knew about this amazing man. Sunset-filtered light illuminated the tidy rows of boots against the wall beside the closet. The room was neatly ordered, mirroring his military background. No discarded clothes lying around, no random towels, just organization at its finest.

"Making judgments, Harper?" Sterling asked.

She turned her attention back to him, noting his arched brow and amused grin, even as she was distracted by his full lips and shirtless body. "Maybe," she replied with far too much breath in her tone to sound credible.

"I'll remember that." He nodded, yanking her hand and quickly moving her toward him.

"Oh?" she asked, making eye contact, trailing her fingers up his forearms and over the mountains of his biceps.

"Damn, your hands on my skin make me forget every thought in my mind, honey."

Grinning, Harper tiptoed her fingers across his chest, playing.

"Ah, you reminded me." Sterling gave a predatory grin and, with a quick shove, sent her gently flying onto the mattress. Before she could gasp or laugh at the playful gesture, Sterling was on top of her, pressing against her body, nipping at her neck, and sending shivers down to her toes.

"I'm going to teach you another thing, sweetheart," he murmured against her neck as his hands reached behind her and unhooked her lacy black bra.

The sudden release of the tension in the straps gave her a moment's pause, but Sterling's lips on her neck scattered the thought a fraction of a second later.

So. Good.

"This, right here..." He rubbed his nose along her neck, tickling her gently till she giggled softly. "...is also fun." He arched back, meeting her gaze with a wide grin.

Harper returned the smile, unable to help herself and not wanting to, desperately wanting to believe everything he'd said, needing it to be true.

Not just sex, making love and enjoying it!

"Fun, huh?" Harper asked then hitched her leg up above his waist and shoved at his shoulder.

Grinning, he gave in and rolled over onto his back.

"This is how cowgirls ride," she dared as she bent down and playfully bit his lip before kissing him fully. His tongue darted in to meet hers, dancing, playing, loving.

He cupped her breasts, weighing and toying with them, causing her body to hum, her heart to pound, and her hips to roll in anticipation. Sterling's mouth left hers, and he moved her a bit higher. He trailed kisses down her neck, traveling lower till he took her breast in his mouth.

She couldn't suppress the gasp of pleasure as she damn near saw stars explode in her vision.

"You're forgetting one thing," Sterling mumbled as his lips traveled from one side to the other, his warm tongue doing wicked things.

Harper heard his words but couldn't form a response.

"This is no rodeo, honey." With quick movements, he flipped her over on her back, immediately branding her neck with his hot mouth.

Harper was powerless to offer any argument but simply bowed her neck more fully to give him unhindered access as she reached up and tugged on his blue jeans. She found the belt and blindly unlatched it.

"Say please," Sterling whispered against her neck before returning to her lips. He bit her lip gently before pulling back and waiting.

Harper took a shallow breath. "Please," she whispered, a prayer on her lips.

"Please, what?" he asked, nibbling down to her breast.

Gasping, she arched her back as his dog tags tickled her shoulder, reminding her of the word.

"Please, *Captain*."

"Yes, ma'am." Sterling rose on his knees and slid from the bed.

Harper turned her head to watch, her heart still pounding a mad rhythm with her arousal.

Sterling stripped down to his plaid boxers, a small smile teasing his lips as he strained the stripes still covering him. Yet, as he kicked off his jeans, Harper's focus lowered to his leg.

Angry and red, the scars that hashed across his calf from his knee to his ankle were still shiny and looked painful in appearance. Though he walked without a limp anymore, it was clear his injury wasn't fully healed. In contrast to his other leg, he was missing a good portion of his calf muscle, and Harper's heart seized at the pain she knew it still caused him.

"It's not exactly pretty...." His hands were fisted as if he were waiting for her assessment of the damage.

"Sterling, people wear their scars differently. Some on the inside, some on the outside...but scars prove that we survived. And survival is beautiful, no matter how it ends up looking when we're done."

He took a deep breath, nodding once. "Scars outside." He pointed to himself. "Scars inside." He pointed to her heart, lingering there and placing his palm over the pounding. "Let's start fixing yours."

And with a soft kiss, he pressed into her, and Harper willingly stepped backward till her knees hit the bed then lay down, ready to let go.

Ready for her scars to show.

And for someone to finally find them beautiful.

CHAPTER 17

Sterling knew he had to move slowly, but more than anything, he wanted to simply own the woman on the bed, body and soul. He recognized that her trust was a fragile thing, and it wouldn't take much to break it.

When she'd kissed his scars, he'd almost come undone. It had been the most powerful, erotic, and meaningful gesture any human had ever given him. As long as he lived, if he forgot all other things, he'd remember that one moment.

Harper's eyes met his as he dispatched his boxers and slid his hands down his body, his blood heating as her gaze lowered. He took in her beautiful breasts, his fingers tingling to feel them once more, to lose himself in their soft spheres. His perusal traveled lower to where her cutoffs covered the rest of heaven.

Striding to the bed, he ignored the slight pain in his leg, cursing the fact that the drugs were starting to wear off. But as he slid a finger around Harper's waistband, the discomfort was forgotten. She curved her back, allowing him access to sliding her little bitty shorts off her tight ass. Damn, she had curves in all the right places.

He'd once heard that eternity could be seen in a woman's body. Damn, that had to be true, because he was seeing it right now in every inch of Harper. Her pink lacy panties left little to the imagination, and he enjoyed the slight tease they offered, so he didn't remove them, yet. Rather, he wanted to soak in the moment and heal her a little bit too.

On the nightstand, Sterling saw a bandanna that Cyler had given him the first day he'd come home. He reached over and grabbed the neatly folded blue square and shook it out. "Do you trust me?"

Holding his breath, he watched as Harper slowly nodded, swallowing hard.

It was a yes, a hesitant one, but he could work with that.

Gently, he knelt on the bed and grasped one of her hands. Placing a soft kiss on her wrist, he inhaled the sweet scent of her honey, tangy and sweet. As he raised the scarf toward the bedframe, he felt her stiffen.

"Trust me," he whispered, and she relaxed just enough for him to wrap the bandanna around the pedestal and then around her wrist, leaving enough length for her other hand.

Reading his intention, she offered her other wrist.

Offered.

Sterling met her gaze, trust echoing in her expression, and he lowered his lips to her palm, kissing that one as well. As he tied that hand to the frame, he brushed his lips on hers. "Does this hurt?"

She arched up to kiss him then answered, "No."

Sterling nodded, then darted his tongue in, meeting her warm mouth, wanting to lose himself in every part of her body, but restraining himself, building it up—for them both.

"What about this?" He bent down and flicked his tongue against her perfect breast then retreated, waiting to hear her words.

He could feel her heart pounding through her soft creamy skin, hear it echo in the stillness of the room.

"No."

"No what?" he demanded gently, nipping at her tenderly.

"No, Captain." She breathed, desire in her eyes, needing him like he needed her.

He kissed along the faint line that led to her navel then lower, nuzzling his nose against her thigh, just shy of where he wanted to be. "Does this hurt, baby?" he asked, tasting her soft skin.

"No...Captain." She was breathing heavily, and his body pounded with the same tension, the need for release nearly driving him mad.

"Can you touch me, Harper?" he asked, moving his nose gently and kissing up to her hipbone before nipping at it.

"I can't."

"But are you safe?" he asked, knowing he needed to walk her through this to set her free.

"Y-yes," she stammered, not from fear or indecision, but from passion denied as she focused on his face. A wildness gleamed from her eyes that reminded him of how she looked when she raced.

Running.

Racing.

But not away.

Rather than focusing on the horizon, her focus on was on him, and it was erotic as hell.

"Sterling..." She spoke with an almost demanding intensity.

He trailed kisses back up to her lips, trying to steal her words.

Wanting to steal her heart.

"Captain," she mumbled against his lips, and his body damn near ignited. "Not to be demanding...but since I'm on the pill..." She didn't finish.

Sterling knew what she needed, desired.

But he wanted her to say it.

To ask for it.

It was his way of giving control back...when she was otherwise powerless.

"Say it, Harper," he commanded, slowly removing the lacy pink panties that were torturing him. Moving to hover just above her lips, he aligned their bodies in every way, taunting.

"I want you."

"Want?" Sterling asked, caressing her with just the lightest touch.

"I need you." She raised her body against him, her arms still tied to the bedpost as she met his gaze.

Sterling slowly eased into her, his body pounding with anticipation, with too many months of denial, with the primal instinct to go deep. But she was tight, surrounding him with such a powerful pressure that his world damn near went black. It had clearly been a while for her as well.

Rather than follow his lead, Harper wrapped her legs around his backside, pulling him down. The second he was surrounded by her heat, the will to fight every instinct that was yelling at him from within to go slow was forgotten in the passion.

He lost himself in her over and over. Sweat beaded on his back, trailing down his spine as he fought to hold on, to wait till she was cresting with him. Yet as Harper's body wound up tighter, it was impossible to hold on. Just when he'd reached the edge of his control, she screamed his name, her body careening over the edge in her release. Sterling looked down at her body, heard her cries of pleasure he'd given her and joined her, his orgasm rushing through him like a tidal wave until there was nothing left but cool, calm waters and her.

Harper...beneath him, kissing every part of his neck and chest she could reach...

Bliss.

Heart pounding, he rested his head against hers, breathing in her air, exhaling his into her lungs, being one.

His leg started to tremble, and he reluctantly rolled to the side, his body both relaxed and tense as his other senses started to take account. Pulsating pain radiated from his calf, and he rolled his ankle around, trying to alleviate the cramp that had started.

Well, that's not exactly sexy.

But apparently, that was his life now. Damn, it sucked to have to deal with that after the most incredible orgasm of his life.

Harper rolled over to her side, and he turned to meet her green gaze.

"Sterling?" she asked, her eyes looking upward.

"Yeah?" he replied, his gaze rising to where her hands were tied.

"You can let me go now." She grinned shyly.

"Honey, who says we're done?" he asked, kissing her nose. Still, he reached up and untied the simple knot and released her hands.

"Are you all right?" Harper asked, glancing down at his leg then back, her brows pinched in concern.

"Yeah, I'm fine." Sterling sighed. "Well, half of me is blissed out, but the other is trying not to cramp. So..." He gave a chagrined smile.

"Let's wait on round two then."

"So, I made the cut, huh?" he asked, rolling out of bed and watching as Harper did the same. Unabashedly, he memorized her naked body. Damn, God had been in a good mood when He made her.

"You'll do." Harper grinned and walked into the bathroom. "Give me a minute."

She closed the door, and Sterling did several stretches to his leg while he waited. When she was finished, he traded places with her, taking a moment to open the medicine cabinet and pull out his prescription.

Two. He had enough for now...or tonight.

But no more.

His body cringed inwardly at the thought.

He opened the cap but misjudged the angle, and the two little pills rolled down the sink before he could catch them.

Damn it!

He could only imagine the pain he'd be in later, but maybe it wouldn't be as bad as last night. Lord only knew he needed to wean himself from the damn things anyway.

But that was easier said than done. All too clearly, he remembered the sweating, the pain, the ache. With a deep breath, he tossed the bottle into the trash.

No. He'd be fine.

After he finished cleaning up, he walked out to the bedroom to find Harper gone. He quickly changed into some basketball shorts and a T-shirt and walked, trying not to limp, out to the living room, but she wasn't there. He checked the kitchen next and found her over the kitchen sink, her hair a tangled mess from making love, filling a glass of water. Quick as a flash, it was as if everything fit. Something about her standing there made him wonder what it would be like to come home to her in their kitchen, in their home, to the life they'd build together.

And he wanted it, so damn badly, a trajectory, not just aimlessly moving through life. To have a purpose, just like Harper had said. But rather than a career, maybe it was a person.

Her.

And everything else revolved around it, like the moon orbited the earth. The give, the take, the perfect balance that brought out the best in both worlds.

Harper turned and, upon seeing him, gave a slightly shy grin. "I kinda feel like I ran a marathon."

Sterling chuckled. "You too, huh?" He grabbed a glass and filled it up as well. As he drank the water, Harper sighed.

He set down the glass and grasped her hand, tugging her till she was close enough to hold tightly. Chin resting on the top of her head, he asked her, "Why the big sigh, honey?"

She relaxed in his arms, mumbling the words against his chest. "I need to go home."

"And you don't want to?"

"No. Does that freak you out?" Harper leaned back, studying him.

"That you want to stay or that you have to leave?" he asked, trying to lighten the mood.

"Ass." She rolled her eyes, but he could see the answer was important.

"Freaked out," he answered honestly, keeping his expression sober.

She tensed.

"The thought of you leaving isn't something I'm prepared to deal with just now. Give me, oh, I don't know, a few years—decades, something like that."

She shook her head, but Sterling was dead serious.

"Harper, someday you're going to marry me. Not today, not tomorrow, and probably not next month, but I can honestly tell you that someday, you'll be mine. I hope that doesn't freak you out." He turned her words around, grinning slightly even as he was anxious about her reaction to his candid words.

"That sure of yourself, huh?" She tilted her head, studying him, probably evaluating if he was serious or not.

He decided to take it a step further. "Is that so wrong? To be that sure about someone?"

Harper shook her head slowly, her green eyes darkening. "No. It just doesn't happen that often."

Sterling refused to let her go, so he shrugged while he held her, the motion ruffling her long hair slightly. "Often doesn't mean never."

Harper gave a slight grin. "True."

"And you didn't answer the question. Does it freak you out?" he asked.

"No more than you usually do," she replied, grinning with more freedom.

"Good to know." He released her but reached out to hold her hand, wanting to have contact, never wanting to let go. "So, you need to leave? Are you sure?" he asked, though he knew the answer.

"Yeah, Jasper's probably blowing up my phone right now." She rolled her eyes.

"Where is your phone?" Sterling asked, realizing it hadn't made a sound.

Harper blushed. "In the car. I kinda left it there on purpose."

Surprise slowly registered through Sterling as a grin broke across his face.

Harper shrugged.

He groaned, wanting her all over again, and again after that, never being able to have enough. "Damn, how do Kessed and Jasper do it? Not run off to Vegas just so they don't have to be apart?"

She grinned. "So...Kessed pretty much lives at our house. But I won't lie. There's been talk. And if I wake up and they are gone, I'm checking Vegas first, because Kessed is not into this big wedding thing."

"I thought it was going to be a smaller wedding," Sterling commented as Harper started out into the hall. He followed her lead, still holding her hand.

"It is, but it's all big to Kessed, who is happy to have a justice of the peace. I think Jasper is the one who wants all the bells and whistles."

"I'd have never guessed," Sterling replied, surprised.

"Yeah. We'll see how it plays out. They have less than two weeks. C'mon... Captain. Let's get me home."

"Harper..." Sterling warned, his body all too ready to have a repeat performance.

With a giggle, Harper pulled her hand away and ran out the front door.

Sterling shook his head and followed slowly, knowing he'd been bested.

After all, sometimes when chasing what you loved, you didn't have to run. You just had to catch up, even if it was a walk.

CHAPTER 18

Harper couldn't stop the grin that kept creeping across her face. True to form, Jasper had inundated her phone with texts, but they'd ended up with one main goal.

Call me back.

It wasn't surprising, as much as he blew up her phone. He hated tapping out long messages. So, as Sterling drove her home, she'd called her brother to find out what he wanted.

Turned out, there had been an emergency on one of the ranches, and he was probably going to be out all night with Kessed. No big deal, but he was as caring as he was annoying, so he wanted her to know so she wouldn't go home to an unexpectedly empty house.

Harper sighed contentedly, soaking up the idea of belonging to someone. As Sterling made the drive back to her home, she thought back over his words.

Someday, you'll be mine.

His words echoed deep in her soul, feeding a need she didn't know she had vacant.

When they pulled into the house, Sterling turned off the car and reached for her hand as she walked to the front porch. "I had a great time today," he started conventionally.

Harper laughed, the anticlimactic statement the understatement of the year. "That's all you've got?"

"Need to up my game, huh?" He grinned, his eyes crinkling at the edges, his shadow of a beard giving him a rugged appearance in the semidarkness. She caressed his face with her gaze, trying to remember when she'd felt like this.

Never.

"You want to come in?" Harper asked as they paused in front of the door toe to toe. She stretched up and playfully nipped at his lips.

"Hell yes." Sterling emphasized his answer with a kiss that left her breathless and scrambling for the doorknob. She almost tripped over the threshold, but Sterling's arms corrected her, and they shared a laugh at their eagerness.

Tugging on his arm playfully, she led him to her room, fleetingly thinking about how she had left that afternoon a different person than she was now. Sterling's hands pulled at her clothes as his lips first nibbled at hers, then diving and devouring like his hands as they mapped her body while she stripped down.

Unlike last time, there was no tentative movements, no fear. Harper surrendered winningly, and in turn, Sterling found himself having to give up control when she took command.

And when she couldn't hold on, Sterling's name was on her lips; it was her litany, her prayer.

Sterling followed her in his own release, and she gloried in the sound of hearing her name.

The silence that followed was almost holy, and Harper closed her eyes, resting in the sensation of being thoroughly loved. She rolled from her position over him and snuggled into his embrace as he wrapped his arm around her shoulders. He held her close, her head over his heart. The mad rhythm was soothing, comforting, safe.

Safe.

"I think I'm going to fall asleep," Harper mumbled, not wanting to move and having the sensation of being a jellyfish.

Sterling chuckled, but the sound was strained slightly, and she glanced up at him. "You all right?"

A slight sheen of sweat dotted his forehead, and he nodded once. "Yeah, I just showed up to my A-game with the B-squad." He nodded toward his leg.

"Does it hurt?" Harper asked, concerned.

Sterling took a deep breath. "Not bad. It's part of life, at least now."

Harper nodded and relaxed when he kissed her forehead tenderly.

"I'm going to clean up."

She gave a wolf whistle when he stood from the bed and walked to the door, gorgeously naked.

"I'm...going to get dressed here. I know Jasper is gone and all, but..." Sterling gave a chagrined glance to Harper.

"Weak," she taunted.

"Pain in the ass," Sterling grumbled and picked up his clothes. With a narrowed glance, he accepted her challenge and walked into the hall toward the bathroom, albeit rather quickly.

She noted his limp and wondered if maybe he was in more pain than he let on.

But she didn't dwell on it; rather, she lay in her bed, languid, satisfied, and wanting to fall asleep.

But not alone.

Damn it.

Taking a deep breath, she stood and wrapped her bathrobe around her body just as Sterling walked into her room, his smile wide, welcoming.

Home.

Harper kissed him on the cheek.

"Harper I'm going to leave before I talk myself into staying, or rather let you talk me into staying."

She giggled at the statement; it wasn't far from the truth.

"But can I see you tomorrow? It's Monday, so I don't know what you have planned...."

"I work tomorrow. Mondays are usually busy with paperwork since Jasper will probably have had emergency calls over the weekend, but I'm free after five. Can I see you then?"

"I'll be here waiting." Sterling kissed her lips, lingering then growling as he pulled away. "You're addictive, Harper." He shook his head.

"I kinda like you too," she answered.

"Tomorrow." He whispered the word like a promise.

"I can't wait."

With one more kiss, he headed toward the door and disappeared into the night.

Grinning widely, Harper padded to the bathroom and started the shower. After time in the hot water, she toweled off and pulled the tube of toothpaste from the cabinet. Her gaze flickered around the familiar arrangement, landing on her prescription. In a bold move, she picked up the bottle to toss it in the trash.

But there wasn't the rattle of the few pills she'd left inside.

After twisting the cap off, she realized it was empty.

Had she taken them? She frowned as she thought. No, she hadn't.

She used the restroom and padded back to her bed, her brow pinched as she tried to solve the mystery. Tossing in bed, she came up with several different scenarios. Maybe Jasper had finally thrown them out, and if so, it was for the best. But usually he told her when he did stuff like that. He might be bossy, but he was always honest.

It was only a few pills anyway. Who would even know what they were? Her heart froze mid-beat then picked up double time.

Surely Sterling wouldn't...

No. He wouldn't.

Not after knowing how hard it was for her to trust him, to trust anyone.

Not after promising her brother that he wouldn't break her heart.

No.

Yet the smallest voice asked her... *What if?*

Her heart fractured a little at the thought, and she dismissed it, silencing the question.

It was too hard to even consider after everything they'd shared.

With a resolute mind, she tried to force herself to sleep and was successful for a few hours, but as the night wore on, she gave up and went to the barn.

As she patted down Spartan, she thought of a plan.

She'd just ask.

After all, Sterling promised he'd never lie, right?

Which sounded exactly like something a liar would say.

Which meant one thing.

She'd been screwed.

Again.

She wrapped her arms around Spartan's neck and wept.

CHAPTER 19

Sterling's hands shook as he lay in bed. Gripping the sheets with his fingers, he tried to control the tremors, to think outside of the mutinous response of his body. Hell, he'd gone through training to deal with torture if he were ever a POW. He could deal with this...whatever it was.

He knew what was going on, but admitting it out loud, even in his own mind, was like raising a white flag of defeat. It had only been a few weeks, a few pills.

He couldn't be addicted.

And it was impossible for him to be experiencing withdrawals. Wasn't it?

Shame washed over him as he thought back over his last minutes at Harper's house.

But his leg had hurt so damn bad that his body had broken out in a cold sweat after their second round. It had been all he could do to stand and walk to the bathroom. When he'd opened the medicine cabinet to at least find some Tylenol, he'd zeroed in on the orange bottle like a man wandering in the desert and finally finding water.

Sterling had known he should close the cabinet door, walk away, and forget about it, but instead he reached out and read the label.

The same exact prescription as what he had at home, the empty one. Before he could question his actions, he grabbed the bottle, swiped the medication, and tucked it in his pocket.

He felt like the biggest bastard in the world for what he'd done, but it was as if he'd had an out-of-body experience. He'd wanted those little pills, needed them like air. Clearly, since he had potentially sabotaged his entire relationship with Harper if she ever found out.

Even now, he wanted to tear apart his shorts to find the little pills, but something held him back.

Harper.

His head throbbing, he breathed in deeply through his nose. *Think around the pain. Think around the need.* He repeated the mantra, but it wasn't helping. If anything, it was reminding him that relief was only a few steps away.

Why didn't he just swallow the pills?

Why hadn't he taken them right away in Harper's bathroom?

Because deep down he knew he didn't want this.

A low growl escaped his lips as he fought against the hungry monster within. It was like fighting for inches in battle, rather than miles. Crawling along the dirt and mud, not knowing if he'd survive the next stretch. A violent tremor racked his body, making the headboard bump against the wall. Sterling stood from the bed then dropped to his knees, reaching for the shorts and feeling the small shapes in his pocket. He took out the pills and studied them in his hand.

He was about to lift them to his mouth, swallow with a hunger that was terrifying, when he had the sobering thought. *What about tomorrow?*

His hand fisted around the small spheres, squeezing them tightly as he re-asked the question.

What about tomorrow? And the day after that? What happened when he didn't come across the medication? What lengths would he take to get his next day of relief? Would he try to use Laken's connections as a nurse? Right now, as his body shook, he admitted that he'd consider it.

The realization was like ice water pouring over him, and before he could talk himself out of it, he practically crawled to the toilet and tossed the pills in. But one lingered, stuck to his hand, taunting him.

Only one.

He flicked it into the toilet and flushed, watching them disappear.

With a shuttering breath, he used the sink to stand and looked into the reflection of the mirror.

Addiction had many faces.

Never once had he thought that his would be one of them.

And as much as he hated to admit it, he needed help.

Again.

Pride be damned, he might be addicted, but he wasn't going to be a statistic where dependence won the war in his life.

So, with a decided limp and a sacrifice of the last of his dignity, he walked back to his room and pulled out his phone. Middle of the night or not, he was doing this now when he had the balls to do it.

He unlocked his screen, tapped the name, and listened to it ring.

Just when he thought he was going to have to lay it all out in voicemail, Laken answered sleepily, "Are you alive?"

He would have smiled if he hadn't been so damn depressed. "Laken..." He took a deep breath, forcing the words that didn't want to be spoken. "...I need your help."

The tension on the phone was palpable as he heard sheets rustling on the other end and Cyler's voice ask if there was an emergency.

There was...just not the kind that usually happened on a ranch in the middle of the night.

"Anything, you know that, Sterling. What's going on?" Laken's voice had the edge of professionalism that bled through when she was hyperaware.

"What are the symptoms of drug withdrawals?" he asked, sitting on the bed as his legs shook from the strain of holding him up. The question alone would put her on high alert; it would say everything he didn't know quite how to articulate.

"How long have you been on the medication?" Laken was in full nurse-mode now.

"A few months, on and off, but recently I've been on it regularly."

"What are your symptoms?"

Sterling ran a hand down his face, mopping the sweat. "Chills, sweating, shaking like a damn leaf and..." He took a breath, needing to steel himself for the rest of the truth.

The whole. Damn. Truth.

"Yes?" Laken encouraged.

Sterling closed his eyes and braced his hand with his forehead. "I stole Harper's prescription meds that were in her bathroom cabinet. I didn't take them, but damn if I didn't want to," he answered.

"Take or ingest?" Laken needed clarification.

"I didn't swallow them."

"Where are they now?"

Sterling glanced up toward the bathroom. "I flushed them."

"Good, that's good, Sterling." She released a small sigh. "People don't realize just how easy it is. I should have taken the pills and administered them to you dose by dose—"

"Laken," Sterling interrupted. "This is not your fault. This is me, all me. And I...I need help making it right. Lord knows, I have to tell Harper, and she's probably going to never forgive me, and I don't know if I can ever forgive myself for that. I just... How can you love someone but love the hit more, Laken? How does that happen?"

"It happens more often than you think," his sister answered, and he could hear the sheets rustle then silence on the other end. "But several bad choices don't determine your course, Sterling. You're ahead of the game in this. Sometimes people don't stop till they've destroyed everything good in their lives. You've screwed up with Harper, yes...but being honest will give you more of a chance to fix this than lying. That's for certain."

Sterling nodded. "I know."

Laken sighed into the phone. "We'll get through this, I promise you."

Shame mixed with gratitude washed over him. "Thank you. I'm sorry that—"

"Shh, nope. Stop now. I appreciate your apology. You're forgiven. We're moving on, but don't you dare let this turn into a pity thing. Hear me?" Laken's tone was firm, brokering no argument.

"Yes, ma'am." The faintest hint of a smile teased his lips.

"Listen, we're heading home now—"

"But—"

"Damn it, Sterling. Just be glad."

He released a sigh. "I am. Thank you. I really do appreciate it."

"You're welcome. Cyler says hi, and he'd be happy to hog-tie you if you think that's necessary. I said no, but he wanted me to offer. Ass."

Sterling chuckled in spite of himself. "Tell him I'll remember that, and if necessary, I'll let him."

"Fine. Now this is what you're going to do. Pay close attention, okay?"

A violent shake rattled his teeth, but he nodded, focusing on her words, picturing them through the haze of pain, the fog of need.

"Sterling, it's going to get worse for you in the next few hours. While I'm on the phone, I want you to find a few extra blankets, several water bottles from the fridge, and your cell phone charger. Next, I'm going to call Harper—"

"No, let me—"

"You're not going to be in any position to say shit. It's going to be the flu like you've never had before, with hopefully less vomiting. You haven't been on them long enough to deal with more than these types of symptoms, but, oh! One question. Do your joints ache?"

Sterling was still caught up in the idea that Laken would be calling Harper, but he tried to focus on her question. "Yeah, my whole body hurts, and my damn leg feels like it's been set on fire."

"Yeah, that's normal and probably won't get any worse as far as pain, so hold onto that."

"Praise God," Sterling offered in sincere gratitude.

"But everything else is going to get worse for the next day or so. And you need someone to be there till we can get to you. That's why I'm calling Harper."

Sterling shut his eyes in defeat, in utter failure, certain that Laken was not only asking for the impossible of Harper, but the impossible of him as well. He'd promised her that he was strong enough to hold her broken heart, and now...for her to see the truth...

That he was a failure...

It was too much, and as his body shook, his teeth chattered, jarring his face just enough to send a lone tear down his cheek. His soul touched the gravel found only at rock bottom.

"Sterling?" Laken asked gently.

He wiped the tear away, angry at the weakness it showed, the desperation it displayed. "Yeah."

"You're going to win."

Sterling repeated her words over and over in his head, soaking them up, gripping them like a lifeline in the middle of the ocean. He would survive this. It wouldn't win.

But damn if he didn't feel like he had no energy to fight it.

"You're not alone. I'm going to go now, but I need you to text me every half hour, okay? It will probably take us a few hours to get packed up, checked out, and down there, all right?"

"Got it, every half hour."

"Sterling? I love you," Laken added with a slight catch in her voice, thick with emotion.

"Love you too, sis."

He ended the call and leaned back onto the pillow, closing his eyes. After taking several deep breaths, he rose and stumbled down the hall, his leg burning, his joints protesting, and his teeth chattering like he'd taken a swim in a frozen lake. Sweat trickled down his temples, and he kept swiping it away, gritting his teeth with each step till he made it to the hall closet and pulled down several thick quilts. After laboriously placing them in his room, he repeated the same painstakingly slow process to the kitchen for the water bottles, but never once was Harper far from his mind.

And he cringed to think of what she'd find when she came face to face with his failure, his weakness.

Assuming she even showed up at all.

He wouldn't blame her if she refused.

Nope.

The only one he had to blame was himself.

His own damn self.

The thought of losing her was crushing him.

He'd promised he'd never break her heart.

Instead, he broken both hers and his own at the same time.

CHAPTER 20

Harper's wheels spun and kicked up gravel as she pulled out of the drive and headed toward Sterling's home. A million emotions all fought for dominance in her mind and body as she remembered Laken's phone call.

She had been out with Spartan, crying her stupid eyes out, and for good reason apparently, because Sterling was a rotten-bastard-pain-in-the-ass who she was either going to murder or nurse back to health.

She wasn't quite sure which one she'd act on.

Currently, it was a toss-up.

She was about to turn onto the main drive when headlights flashed over the hill. She waited, and as the truck's blinker lit up, she cursed.

Jasper and Kessed.

Of course they'd be coming home right now from their emergency call.

Not able to even formulate words, she pulled out before they could stop beside her truck in the drive and ask why she was leaving at such an odd hour.

Sure enough, as she crested the hill away from the house, her phone buzzed.

Blowing out a frustrated breath, she answered it on speaker. "I don't have time or energy to explain. Have Kess call Laken."

She figured that was the safest bet; that way she didn't say something she wasn't supposed to, not that she cared currently...but it was just easier.

And right now, she wanted easy.

Because the next fifteen minutes were going to be hell.

Scratch that, the foreseeable future.

Thanks, Sterling.

"Okay..." Jasper's tone reminded her she was still on the phone.

"Gotta go." She ended the call and focused on the road.

Alone with her thoughts, she attempted to digest all the information Laken had given her, but mostly, she just had to accept the fact that Sterling was addicted to his medication.

The same medication she was currently missing.

Laken hadn't said it outright, but all the dots connected, and betrayal stung deep. Chest tight, she struggled to take a deep breath, to right herself in the chaos, but found that her center was gone.

When she'd come home from the hospital, it had been Jasper that kept her strong.

And somehow, today, it had shifted to Sterling.

A tear slid down her cheek. Now who was left?

Alone.

Again.

Instinctively, she wrapped her free arm around her middle, breathing in, breathing out.

Lies.

What hurt even worse were the lies.

She could look past the addiction; she could even look past the fact that he'd stolen the medication.

He'd led her to believe he knew what he was doing, that he wouldn't intentionally break her heart.

But he'd done a stellar job of smashing it to pieces.

Why had he promised when he'd known, he'd *known* he couldn't keep it?

Damn him to hell.

I'll never lie to you.

She was right. It was exactly what a dirty, rotten, filthy liar would say.

Angry, hurt, and frustrated, she twisted her hands and her steering wheel leather squeaked in protest.

When she pulled into the ranch house drive, she took in a shuddering breath. The house was dark except one window that had a faint glow.

Sterling's.

Harper bounded out of the truck and stomped to where Laken had said the hide-a-key was located and angrily unlocked the door, damn near snapping the key off in the lock. She made her steps loud, hoping the sound hurt his head like hell as she strode down the hall, half wishing Cyler had a baseball bat somewhere close.

You think you're hurting now....

Tears of frustration flowed in succession down her cheek as she approached the bedroom where she had let her heart go, where she had given herself body and soul to that man...only to return less than a day later to find out what a piece of shit he was.

The door was cracked open, and she shoved it wide, crossing her arms, ready to give him a piece of her mind, since he'd decided to steal a piece of her soul.

All the air rushed out of her as she glanced around the room. Blankets were strewn, bottles tipped over, and water pooled on the floor below. Clothes were in small heaps, and the bed was nearly vibrating. The contrast to earlier was enough to pull her up short. Blinking, she walked toward the shaking bed, inch by inch growing closer to seeing his face.

His normally clear eyes were watery and bloodshot, his jaw rigid as his body shook violently. His gaze slid over to hers.

"S-s-sor-r-r-y," he bit out, his teeth chattering between each letter.

Her brow furrowed as she studied the man before her—broken, weak, and shaking. She tenderly traced his jawline, cupping his cheek, and measured the feverish temperature of his skin. Wordlessly, she removed her hand and grabbed the blankets from the floor and covered him.

Next, she went to the bathroom and grabbed some towels to mop up the spilled water. Sterling's teeth chattered, and his body fought the dependence he was trying to overcome.

And Harper saw herself—what she was, what she'd fought, and what she'd overcome.

Maybe she wasn't as broken as she thought.

Maybe she'd healed up a long time ago...and maybe she just wasn't strong enough to realize it.

Till now.

"H-h-h—" Sterling started, and Harper slowly walked over, keeping a careful distance.

Just because he was hurting didn't mean he was forgiven.

And just because he was sorry didn't mean jack shit.

He could be sorry for his actions, or he could be sorry he got caught.

She was tempted to assume the former, but she was reserving judgment.

Arching her brows, she waited.

"Ca-n, you t-t-t-ex-t La-k-k-k-ken?"

Nodding once, she picked up his phone from the side of the bed and unlocked the screen, remembering the code from earlier. She opened the message app and was about to ask what to say when she noticed the earlier text.

Checking in.

She read Laken's response.

> *Called Harper. She may or may not show up.*
> *Hold on till we get there, okay? You're stronger*
> *than what your body feels right now. Remember*
> *that.*

Her fingers hovered above the screen as she typed.

> *This is Harper, I'm checking in for Sterling. He's*
> *pretty much exactly like you described.*

The bubble popped up, and Harper waited.

> *Thank you for coming, Harper.*

Harper gave a mirthless snort.

> *Yeah well, Kessed might be calling you because I*
> *peeled out of the driveway...*

Harper waited.

> *Heard about that...I filled them in. No hiding*
> *things. We're family. Jasper and Kessed know,*
> *and you should probably take your phone off*
> *silent...this is from Kessed who just texted me*
> *while I was texting you.*

Harper grinned, unable to stop herself. *Leave it to Kessed.*

> *Forgot it was on silent. I'll grab it and text them*
> *back. Jasper's probably pissed as hell.*

She glanced around the room for her phone.
Damn, she'd left it in the pickup.
Sterling's phone buzzed, and she glanced down.

> *He's not as angry as you'd think. More*
> *concerned about you, according to Kess.*

Harper was pretty sure that after the concern wore off, Jasper would be pissed, but she'd deal with it later.
Or she'd encourage it.

Again with the toss-up.

I left my phone in the truck. I'll run and grab it.
I'll keep you posted on my end till you get here.

Laken responded immediately.

Thank you.

She locked the screen and tossed it onto the mattress next to Sterling. The bed was still shaking along with his body, and she glanced at his face, reading his expression. Fear, frustration, and failure echoed in his eyes, and her heart pinched at the sight. She reached down and cupped his forehead, watching as his eyes slid closed at the contact.

Damn, he was so easy to love.

So damn hard to hate.

Even when she wanted to, even when she had such a good reason.

An angry tear slid down her cheek. As she lifted her hand, his gray eyes opened and met her own.

"I'm pissed as hell at you, but right now, I'm here." She spoke softly, making no promises.

He nodded shakily. "Th-th-thank y-y-you."

The words were soft, their depth echoed in his tortured gaze, and Harper took a step back, needing the distance. "I'm going to get my phone, I left it in the truck. I'll be right back."

At his nod, she walked out into the hall to the front door. As she stepped outside, the night was shifting into dawn while the stars faded to the east as the sky grew lighter. The gravel crunched under her feet on her way to the truck. Sure enough, her phone was on the passenger seat, displaying yet another missed text.

Rather than read through everything, she unlocked it and called Jasper.

"Harper, for shit sakes, and you get pissed at me for not answering my phone," her brother said by way of greeting.

"Good morning to you, too," Harper replied with sarcasm, but her body relaxed hearing his familiar tone.

"How is he?" Jasper asked with far less anger than she had expected, even given Laken's assessment.

"Suffering."

"Good," Jasper replied.

"There's the brother I know and love." Harper sighed. "But really, he's in a bad way. Even though I want to beat him with an old metal bat, I'm glad I'm here."

Jasper sighed into the phone. "Yeah, Kessed's been texting with Laken back and forth. I guess it happens pretty easily, the getting hooked."

Harper glanced to the gravel. She hadn't become addicted per se, but she also hadn't been willing to let the meds go either. It would have been so easy for her and Sterling to switch places. The thought was sobering.

"Harper?"

"Yeah, sorry. I'm here."

"Did...I mean, did you ever struggle when you got home from the hospital...?" Jasper asked the question she really didn't want to answer right now.

"Yeah, I did." She spat out the words quickly, closing her eyes as she waited for his response.

"Is that..." Jasper paused. "Is that why you never threw out that prescription? I mean, I kept tabs on it. Not going to lie about that. I know you never took the pills, but you never threw them out either...."

Harper kicked a rock, sending it sailing across the drive. "Yeah, it's pretty much what you think it is."

"Whoa," Jasper answered, and Harper waited for the rest of the response. "I'm glad you stopped when you did, Harper."

"Me too." She glanced back to the ranch house. "I'm going to go. Sterling shouldn't be alone right now."

"I'm proud of you, sis."

"Eh, you're all right too, I guess." Harper gave a small laugh. "Love you. See you later."

"Later."

She ended the call and headed to the house. When she walked back in to Sterling's room, she noted that the shaking had subsided somewhat but hadn't stopped completely. His phone buzzed from the bed, and she lifted it.

Be there in thirty minutes.

Laken was in Cle Elum, and Harper couldn't decide if she was glad that she'd be relieved of watch duty, or if she wished she had longer.

"Sterling?"

His gaze focused on her, and his jaw clenched to keep his teeth from chattering.

"Laken's about thirty minutes out."

He nodded then took a deep breath through his nose. "Har-per," he whispered softly, the effort in speaking obvious in the way his jaw clenched.

"Yeah?" She steeled herself, waiting for whatever came next.

"I took your leftover medication." He spoke without stuttering, but as he finished, his teeth chattered violently.

She grimaced at the sound. "I know."

He nodded once then spoke again. "I flushed them, but I was still wrong. I'm s-s-s-s—"

Harper leaned forward and pressed a finger against his lips. "Thank you." It was all she could give.

While part of her was relieved that he hadn't swallowed the medication, and honestly, it should have been obvious since he was clearly going through withdrawal symptoms, that didn't negate the fact that he'd stolen them.

It might be something she could forgive.

It just wasn't something she could forget.

And their relationship might not survive that.

What she needed to figure out was if she wanted to even try.

Half of her said yes. The other half said no.

And all of her was petrified.

Fear was calling the shots, and that was the least trustworthy emotion of all.

What she needed was time. And when Laken arrived, that was exactly what she'd get.

If that was what she needed, what she wanted...

Then why did it feel like her heart was breaking all over again?

CHAPTER 21

It had been a week of sheer hell.

When Laken had come home, Harper had kissed his cheek, said goodbye, and asked for time.

And who the hell was he to deny her anything?

It had all been Sterling's fault, so he'd nodded, said a prayer, and watched the woman he loved walk out of his room, and possibly out of his life.

He'd wrestled with a broken heart, knowing he had no one to blame but himself, while also dealing with the withdrawal symptoms.

Laken had explained that it was opioid dependency and educated him on all the stages he'd encounter. As each day rolled into the next, one symptom would subside only to be replaced with a more powerful one. Yet after the first three days, he'd started to see a light at the end of the tunnel.

Or maybe that was just the fact that he hadn't slept in three days.

Another side effect—insomnia.

But throughout the whole process, Laken had been there, tag-teaming with Cyler, and Sterling's respect for his brother-in-law had increased.

As the week wound down, he found he had more than enough time to think, process, and torture himself with his foolish choices.

I should have known.

I should have asked for help sooner.

I should have never taken the pain medication.

A thousand *should haves* and no excuses.

When Friday rolled around, he finally asked Laken if Harper had contacted her at all.

Laken took a seat on the bed, and Sterling tried to prepare himself.

"She asked me to text, so I have."

He frowned, knowing he was missing something. "And?"

"And she hasn't replied." Laken reached out and touched his shoulder. "I'm sorry. That might not mean anything, or it could mean everything. Regardless, I think today you need to get out and get some fresh air. You've been cooped up in the house too long." Laken shifted the conversation effectively, though Sterling's thoughts still lingered on Harper.

As always.

And he vowed that if she'd give him even half a chance, he'd do everything in his power to earn her trust, no matter if it took him till his dying breath.

"C'mon. Let's go."

Laken offered her hand, and Sterling took it, using some of her strength to help him stand on his weakened legs. But thankfully, the joint pain had subsided and all that was left was a dull ache in his thigh that wasn't overly bad.

"How's the leg?" Laken asked when he was standing.

"Better than I expected."

"That's good. Can you manage from here?" Laken let go of his arm.

"Yeah." Sterling nodded.

His sister walked out of the room, and he was about to follow when he glanced at his phone and, on a whim, grabbed it and put it in his pocket.

Laken turned from her path toward the kitchen and gave him a soft pat on the shoulder.

He crossed to the front door. As Sterling stepped out into the morning sunshine, he breathed in deeply, feeling like a prisoner who had just been granted a pardon, experiencing freedom for the first precious moments.

A smile slowly moved across his cracked but healing lips as he soaked in the warmth of the sunshine, the crisp fall air, and the scent of dry earth. He walked along the gravel drive toward the barn in a familiar limp, but rather than feeling weak, he was thankful for the slight pain and the feebleness he felt.

Hell, even the scars.

Each dull ache reminded him that there were no drugs blocking his senses.

Every limp reminded him of what he'd overcome.

The scars reminded him that he was healing.

Maybe not whole.

But whole enough.

As he walked into the barn, his gaze fell on Margaret, and he walked toward her, memories of Harper flooding him like heavy rain. He owed that woman more of an apology than what he'd been able to stammer out earlier. She deserved to ask him questions, throw punches, even run him over with her damn horse.

He pulled out his phone, snapped a picture of Margaret, and sent it as a peace offering to his friend.

Sterling wandered out from the barn and toward the fire-scarred hillside, remembering how he'd kissed Harper, remembering how he was terrified he'd break her heart.

As if somehow, deep inside, he'd known the truth.

His phone buzzed, and he glanced to the screen.

Making friends?

He grinned, thankful to have any response from Harper, let alone one that was full of her sexy sass that he missed so much.

> *Trying. I've been told that horses are good listeners.*

He waited as Harper typed a response.

Cheaper than a therapist.

Sterling chuckled, then decided to take the risk.

> *I want to apologize. But if you can't accept that right now, I understand. Because it's not only about me. I'm learning that. Just because I need to apologize doesn't mean that it's more important than what you need. And if you still need time, it's yours.*

He wasn't sure if that made total sense, but it was a shot. And it gave Harper the choice.

Love is patient. Love is kind.

Is not self-seeking...thinks of others.

He remembered his grandma saying that often. He'd been so young when she passed and hadn't fully grasped the depth of the words.

Their truth.

He loved Harper with every fiber of his being.

But loving her meant that he'd think of her and what she needed first.

Not him.

Her.

Even if that meant letting go.

His phone buzzed, and he breathed in deeply and then read the message.

> *You damn well do owe me an apology. If you're
> in the barn, I'm assuming you're well enough to
> have at it. Be ready in ten minutes.*

Sterling re-read the message, a wide grin breaking across his face.

> *I'll be waiting.*

Sterling didn't expect a response and made his way back toward the barn, a frown puckering his brow as he considered just how to apologize for so much. He didn't even know where to begin.

He was still processing his thoughts when he heard a truck come up the drive.

Heart pounding, he leaned against a worn beam and waited.

Harper stomped into the barn, hands on hips and a pissed-off expression on her face.

He'd never seen anything more beautiful.

"Hey," he greeted, drinking in the sight of her, just in case it was one of the last times.

"Well?" she asked, hitching a shoulder and cocking her head. Her green eyes flashed with hurt and anger as she approached him, daring him to try to fix the mess he'd made.

Worst of all, he had nothing.

An apology wasn't enough.

It was the truth, so that's where he started. "Harper."

She paused about a yard from him, her blond hair pulled into a low ponytail that curled at the purple tips. Wide lips were set in a firm line as she waited, arching a brow in defiance.

Damn, he loved her.

He stood fully, not using the beam for support as he regarded her. "I hurt you, and I said I wouldn't."

She nodded.

"I said I wouldn't lie, but instead I stole. When you should have been able to trust me utterly, I went behind your back. And all the ways I promised to be strong, I had no right to lead you to believe I was anything other than weak. You've seen me at rock bottom, and right now, I'm only hovering an inch or two above it, and that's on me. All this..." He pounded his chest as he gave his head a slow shake. "...is on me. My fault. My weakness, my stupid, fucked-up mess. And you deserve more than an apology, but it is literally the only thing I have to offer you."

He held his hands up in surrender, breathing in the sight of her as emotions flickered across her expression more rapidly than he could catch.

The air was thick with tension as he waited, surrendered, fully expecting to watch her beautiful ass walk away.

Her lips parted. "Was it all a lie?"

Sterling frowned. Shock followed by despair knifed him in the heart as he understood her question. "No, never. Even when I took those damn pills from your bathroom, I came clean. Harper, the person I lied to wasn't you. It was me. I tricked myself into thinking I was strong enough, that I wasn't dependent on the drugs, that I wasn't dependent on you, on anyone, all the while promising you that I was able to be there for you, when I didn't have my own shit together. And I'm sorry. I'm so sorry, but Harper, none of this..." He flicked his finger between the two of them. "...was fake. It was as real as it gets, and I'm the reason that now it's broken. And I'd give anything to make that right again." He studied her face, the curve of her cheek, the perfect shape of her nose, wanting her so badly, yet loving her enough to want something better for her than what he had to offer.

"It's been a long week." Harper sighed, but it wasn't a relaxed sound. It was tense like her shoulders, and Sterling steeled himself for what was surely the setdown and breakup he deserved. She continued. "Did you ever wonder why my medication was still there? It had been almost two years since I was in the hospital, Sterling." Her blond brows furrowed.

The thought hadn't crossed his mind, yet as he pondered it, he started to wonder if Harper knew more about dependence than he'd thought.

Had maybe even experienced it.

The concept rocked him. "No, actually. I hadn't considered it."

Harper blew out a slow breath, causing her perfect lips to curve into an *O* shape. "I kept them on purpose. Because I liked how they made me feel, how the medication gave me a sense of stability, of knowing everything would work out in a time when I wasn't so sure. I wasn't dependent like you were, but I wasn't able to fully let go either."

He wanted to reach out and grasp her hand, to hold her tightly and smell her sun-kissed hair, to share that understanding with her, because he knew exactly what she meant. The drugs had made him feel powerful. They'd made him feel in control and...happy. And they had come at the time in his life when those very things had been in short supply.

Damn, he wished he'd known it before he'd even taken the pills home.

"So, what I'm saying is that I understand. That doesn't make what you did right." She lifted a hand. "But it means...it's not unforgiveable, Sterling."

He gave a slow nod, beyond grateful to have her forgiveness, but knowing it fell so short of what he truly wanted.

Her love.

"Thank you, Harper. That's more than I deserve," he answered openly.

"Maybe, but that's the best part about being forgiven. You don't have to deserve it," she answered.

"Regardless, thank you. And for what it's worth, I'm sorry again, and again." He ran his fingers through his hair.

"I learned something too this week." Harper tapped the wooden floor with the toe of her boot.

"Oh?"

"When I saw you in bed shaking like a leaf...it was sobering. I mean, that could have been me. So easily. Yet, here I am, years later on the other side and still running scared." She gave a frustrated snort. "Sterling, you taught me how to run *to* something, not away. And what I need to know is if you're done running too." She took a small step toward him, her green eyes darting down to the ground before meeting his once more. "I've never been more terrified than I have been in this past week, not for myself, but for you. Because you have some choices ahead of you, and each one affects your future, and as much as it freaks the hell out of me, it affects mine too. So, what is it going to be? What are you going to run *to*, Sterling? Because if it's anything other than me, I swear I'll—"

Sterling cut off her threat with a kiss, losing himself in her soft lips, the sweet and spicy scent of lemon and cinnamon clinging to her skin combining with the minty flavor of her mouth. Harper pressed into the kiss, her lips as eager as his as they danced together. Her tongue flicked against his, then retreated as she tugged on his lower lip playfully, eliciting a groan from deep within him.

If he didn't stop now, they were going to give Margaret a show.

Easing back, he pressed his forehead against hers, inhaling every breath she let go, wanting every part of her mixed with his. "I love you so damn much. I swear, if I have to live without you, it might kill me," he confessed. "But I'd let you go, Harper. I would, because I know you deserve someone so much better than—"

It was her turn to complete his words with a kiss, and after she seared her love over his mouth, she pulled away, confessing it with her voice. "I love you too. Don't you ever scare me again like you did this past week. We clear?"

Sterling tenderly kissed her nose. "Understood."

"Now, since that's all settled..." She backed up and looked him over. "...what's next?"

Sterling sucked in a calming breath, knowing they needed to talk. There was time for coming together later. Someone up above must have been looking out for him. "Cyler agreed to hire me, saying I needed to get my ass out of the house and do something so I didn't wallow, though I think Laken might have added a few words in here or there."

Harper giggled softly, the harsh edge to her expression long gone.

"And he has his crew members routinely drug tested. So, I'll be held accountable with that. I'm not going to expect that I won't be tempted, Harper. I'm going into this with eyes wide open." He traced the line down her cheek to her chin.

"Good."

"And I'm going to stay here for the next year or so, just to make sure I'm doing what I need to, and they're going to routinely test me here as well."

"So far the plan sounds solid." Harper reached down and grasped his hands.

He grinned. "The best part is that in about eight months I'm going to be an uncle too."

Harper's face broke out into a huge grin. "No way! Does Kessed know?"

"Yeah, but I think everyone's sworn to secrecy till she's a little further along."

"Is Cyler freaking out?"

Sterling chuckled. "He's—what did you call it?—peacocking?"

"Ha! I bet he is. He has a reason to!" Harper laughed, the sound the most relaxing thing Sterling had ever heard.

"I think that's all. It's mostly just one day at a time." He sobered, squeezing her hand.

"One day at a time. I think I can manage that." Harper rose on her toes and brushed a featherlight kiss across his lips, driving him mad with wanting her. "As long as each day means we do this together."

Sterling drew back, wanting her to read the sincerity in his gaze. "Together. That's a future worth living for."

Harper kissed him once again, and he reveled in the tenderness, thankful that this wasn't a kiss that meant goodbye.

It was a kiss that was in a long list of many to come.

EPILOGUE

"Damn."

The bridesmaid next to her swore as Harper gripped the bouquet with both hands; then with a triumphant squeal she fist-pumped it in the air, her eyes landing on Sterling.

He gave her a wink as his dove-gray suit highlighted the steel color of his irises, sending shivers up her back and making her want to leave the wedding reception early.

Except it was her brother's wedding. Someone would notice if she was gone.

Damn it.

Sterling sauntered over to her, his limp giving him a sexy swagger that he didn't even realize. "That's my girl." He studied the bouquet, offering his hand in a high five.

"Skills," Harper said.

"You know what this means, right?" Sterling asked, studying the flowers and then glancing up to meet her eyes.

"It means I win," she deliberately taunted, knowing what he was getting at, but wanting to play.

"It means that you're next," Sterling corrected, his hand slowly caressing her waist as he drew her in close.

"If you're lucky." She gave a daring grin.

It had been an amazing two weeks, a time of healing, growth, and a lot of hard realizations.

Sterling had started working on one of Cyler's construction crews, and had signed up with a local therapy group that helped people deal with opioid addiction.

It had been a difficult decision, but Harper had signed up as well.

As the music played over the speakers, Sterling tugged on her hand, drawing her attention back to the present. "Have I told you how stunning you look in that purple dress?" he crooned as he murmured the words in her ear.

Shivers of pleasure danced up her spine. "A few times. And technically, it's lavender."

"All I'm doing is imagining all the ways I can take it off."

Harper pulled back, meeting his scorching gaze. "It's one of those dresses that require nothing underneath."

Sterling groaned, pressing his head against hers as they swayed side to side with the music. "Killing me here."

"Good."

Sterling chuckled, the sound echoing of freedom. "I love you, Harper Matthews."

"I love you, Sterling Garlington," Harper echoed, the words resonating deep in her soul.

Sterling twirled her then glanced over her shoulder, grinning. "Follow me." He took her hand and led her outside of the white tent that held Jasper and Kessed's reception party.

The fall air was crisp, and the stars scattered across the night sky as Sterling led her just far enough away for the music to be softly playing in the background, the sounds of the party fading.

"So, I've been thinking." He frowned slightly, caressing her fingers with his while he spoke. "There's something that's just not quite right."

Old insecurities tickled her mind before she pushed them away. Finding her center, her strength, she studied Sterling, trusting his love.

He'd fought for it.

He'd fought for her.

He wasn't going to stop doing that.

So, she waited.

"Your name...it's missing something." His gray eyes were almost silver in the moonlight, the fierceness in his expression powerful, stealing her breath. "I just think it would sound so much better if your first name had my last name behind it."

Something cool pressed into her hand, and she glanced down, her gaze flickering over to Sterling as he knelt on one knee.

"There is nothing or no one in this world that I love more than you, Harper Matthews. You've seen me at my worst, and you've loved me when I didn't deserve even your pity. Every day I wake up thinking about you, and every night your name is a prayer on my lips. I don't deserve you, but I swear I'll love you, think of you first, give my life for you if that's what it takes, because I love you unconditionally, without reservation, and more than I could ever say. Please, marry me?"

Harper's heart pounded with each syllable from his lips. The sincerity in his eyes even more powerful than his words. This man, who had fought for every inch of his life, who was strong enough to admit when he was weak, who was willing to declare when he was wrong, who loved her more than she'd ever been loved, wanted her.

Needed her.

Just like she needed him.

Like air.

"Yes, Captain, my captain."

Sterling's response was immediate and enthusiastic as he rose and met her lips, kissing her deeply, joyfully, with utter abandon as the flavor of the passion was salted with her tears of joy.

He rested his head against hers. "Thank you."

Giggling softly, she sniffed and brushed a tear away from her jaw. "So wasn't expecting this tonight."

"I like to catch you off guard," Sterling teased then took the box from her hand and opened it, showing her the ring that would circle her finger.

An emerald-cut diamond was seated in white gold, and he plucked it gently from the velvet case and slid it on her finger.

At her questioning gaze, he shrugged. "Kessed measured for me."

"So that was why she wanted me to try on her ring!" Harper said, surprised.

Earlier that week Kessed had asked her to put on her engagement ring, saying she wanted to see what it would look like on stage. So she had her back up and wave her finger around. It had been utterly ridiculous, but Harper had played along, thinking it was some weird wedding quirk of Kessed's.

Now it made sense.

The sneak.

That meant that Jasper had known too!

"Jasper?" Harper asked.

Sterling gave her a wry expression. "Asked permission first. I figured he'd shoot first and ask questions later if I didn't."

"Wise move."

"I'm learning."

"Wow." Harper grinned, her face aching from the extent of her smile.

"We should probably go tell Kessed and Jasper. They're waiting." Sterling tugged on her hand, caressing the ringed finger softly and lingering over the beautiful stone.

"Kessed won't mind since it's her wedding?" Harper asked, concerned.

Sterling kissed her nose. "Honey, she was thrilled to have a front row seat."

Harper rose on her tiptoes, kissing him lightly on the lips, savoring the man that was hers, forever.

"I love you."

Sterling squeezed her hand tightly as they started back toward the reception tent.

"I love you more."

A stubborn cowboy has sworn never to forgive or forget—but one special woman may find a way to change his mind...

Hospice nurse Laken Garlington helps people face the end with peace and dignity, surrounded by their loved ones. But the son of her new patient didn't come home to reunite with his dad. So why *is* Cyler Myer back in horse country? It's clear the sexy, six-three hunk with the steely eyes has a score to settle, and Laken doesn't plan on being collateral damage...no matter how irresistible she finds the prodigal cowboy.

Dying is too good for the father Cyler will never forgive—not in this lifetime.

Showing up at his family's Washington State ranch is the first step in his plan. But revenge takes a back seat to desire when Cyler meets a bossy beauty who arouses feelings he isn't ready to face. As they work together to save an ailing mare, Cyler realizes he must decide where his true destiny lies. With darkness...or with the woman who offers the promise of redemption with every kiss.

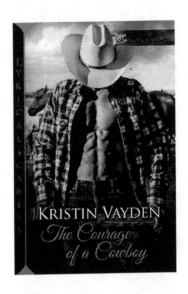

Nothing like a wedding to get a girl dreaming of happily-ever-after…

Kessed Ling's best friend's big day is finally here. It's especially exciting because it's Kessed's chance to show her childhood crush she's not just a young bridesmaid, she's a full-grown woman—with red hot desires. But when her long-awaited prey barely blinks an eye at her, Kessed retreats right back into her deeply guarded heart. Doesn't matter that chivalrous Jasper Matthews steps in and offers a shoulder to lean on. Kessed is no longer in the market for a man, despite how unsettled the strong, silent groomsman makes her feel…

As a veterinarian, Jasper better understands a skittish filly than he does willful Kessed Ling. But when fate finds him playing ranch hand alongside the raven-haired beauty, Jasper realizes she's a woman running scared—and he's just the man to tame her. So with soothing words and bold kisses, Jasper sets out to show Kessed how good it can be between a man and a woman. Especially when the man is falling hard and fast in love…

About the Author

Kristin Vayden is the author of twenty books and anthologies. She is an acquisitions editor for a boutique publishing house, and helps mentor new authors. Her passion for writing started young, but it was only after her sister encouraged her to write did she fully realize the joy and exhilaration of writing a book. Her books have been featured in many places, including the Hallmark Channel's *Home and Family* show.

You can find Kristin at her website, http://kristinvayden.weebly.com, on FB as www.facebook.com/kristinvaydenauthor or on Twitter: @ KristinVayden.

Printed in the United States
by Baker & Taylor Publisher Services